Because, Because, Because, Because, Because

Stories

William Marquess

Fomite

Burlington, Vermont

ISBN: 978-1-947917-53-8
Library of Congress Control Number: 2020936544
Fomite
58 Peru Street
Burlington, VT 05401
www.fomitepress.com

For my parents, again

Make it

so that I can say it plainly, if not simply,
let these things go down with me.
Keep me faithful to loss.

John Engels, "Adam Remembers Moving"

Foreword

I wrote these stories in fiction workshops at Saint Michael's College between 1998 and 2011. Every year, I did all the exercises with the students, heard what they thought about my drafts, and completed a story with the help of their suggestions. This process underscores an essential fact: I am more teacher than writer. I undertook the stories largely for pedagogical reasons—to present an example of a writer making his effort, living with deadlines, working with criticism. Probably the results demonstrate some of the limitations of "workshop stories," written with a particular audience in mind. But I can't regret the process, for without that audience I would not have written them. And more: I would have had less fun. It has been splendid, year after year, to go out in the fictional fields with those students.

Rereading the stories for this collection, I have found fingerprints recurring—characteristic rhythms, ideas, even actions. What does it suggest about me that protagonists in two different stories suddenly punch someone out? I'm not sure I want to know. But I have decided to leave such repetitions, making only small revisions. At some point, a parent must let children go into the world. I present them here in the order in which they were written.

My first and abiding debt of gratitude and love is inscribed in the dedication. Close behind, my dear friends: I think you know who you are. To Saint Michael's College I owe the opportunity that has been my life for twenty-five years. Finally, the students: it was all for them.

Contents

THE WEIGHT

The entire world is within Dewey's grasp. Already, he has taken Europe and fortified it against attack; soon he will sweep out across the steppes of Ukraine, march through the Middle East, overwhelm Asia and Africa. It's only a matter of time before his loyal troops cover the globe in their brilliant blue.

Of course, Lou will offer some resistance in Kamchatka, with its bridge to North America, where Stephen's brown armies have been squatting since the beginning of time. Stephen always goes for North America. Lou, who always takes black, has no power base; he just fortifies random countries and flares out in unpredictable directions. Angela isn't much of a threat; her green soldiers are barely clinging to Australia, and she's a pacifist, anyway. But Dirk has amassed impressive red squadrons in South America, and could strike either north or east according to his own inscrutable lights.

It's Dirk's move now. He lifts his glasses to check his country cards, contemplates his positions, shakes the dice in his fist. Dirk always takes forever to roll; he says he's consulting the war gods. He rattles the dice. "Roll!" shouts Lou. "Roll dice and die, you red bastard!"

Dewey takes a sip of cold coffee. He knows that impatience is just what Dirk wants: he is tempting the rest of them to go for too much too soon; then he will wipe someone out, and take their precious cards. Dirk is a poli sci major.

It's after midnight on a Thursday in late October, and the six residents of Wesley House are all wide awake. In addition to the five at the table, Melanie is stretched out on the sofa, reading. God knows how she can concentrate on her bio textbook during this global crisis. Lou dips an absent-minded hand into the big punch bowl of Cheez-Doodles, official snack food of World Conquest. Finding it empty, he calls out, "Wench! More grub! An army marches on its stomach!" Melanie doesn't look up from her book. Stephen sips from a peanut butter jar full of Sucker Punch — Rebel Yell and Pepsi, with maraschino cherries — and sings along with The Band.

Pulled into Nazareth,
I was feeling 'bout half past dead . . .

Lou joins in on the chorus, then turns to Dirk. "Come on, Dreck! My troops are falling asleep in their trenches." Still pondering his options, Dirk starts to peel a banana. Then, finally, he makes a move: from Venezuela, he attacks Lou in Central America, captures it in a single roll, and takes his card.

"That's it?" says Lou. "One measly banana republic? You pathetic pinko wusscake." Lou trades in his cards for a fistful of black armies and piles them all on North Africa, intent on its bridge to Brazil. He never fails to attack his attacker right back, even if it doesn't suit any geopolitical strategy.

He licks a finger and holds it up in the air. "All right," he says, "the wind is at my back." He scoops up the three red dice. "Say your prayers, Bananaman. Louie the Incorruptible is about to bust some chops."

Dewey sometimes marvels at how well this group gets along. This time last year, most of them hadn't met, and none of them had heard of Wesley House. They were all failing, in their own ways, to fit into the neo-Gothic quadrangles of the university. Dirk and Angela were transfers who met in a Durham apartment complex, where they became laundry-room friends while talking about how they missed campus life. Lou and Melanie were a couple who had given up their campus housing in order to live together, and then, after breaking up on friendly terms, had gone looking for housemates. Stephen was a religion major who said he had too much fun as a freshman, carousing on Animal Quad; he thought there had to be more to life than keggers and busloads of sorority girls from Raleigh. And Dewey — well, Dewey just hated his all-male freshman dorm: the chatter about sports, the sexual posing, the business majors in polo shirts sitting on their triple-decker frat benches. He practically lived in the library that year. Then he saw the ad in the student paper. It described this house, a ten-minute walk from campus, and it called for "an experiment in Christian community." The six of them are the experiment.

Not that it's a house, really. It's just the former headquarters of the Methodist campus ministry, jerry-rigged into a home. The living room where they sit waging war is actually a lobby, with an interior wall of glass that opens onto a chapel, complete with two pulpits, an organ loft, and pews to seat two hundred. There's a small but functional kitchen, and downstairs in the space beneath the chapel is a cavernous Fellowship Hall. The building was intended for churchly office work and Sunday services, potluck suppers and youth groups. When the Methodists built a new campus center and couldn't sell this place, the lefties on their board decided to let students use it as a communal house. Offices and storage space were converted into bedrooms. It's a strange place, but for these six orphans of the university, Wesley House is almost heaven.

They first met in this room, late last spring, to make plans for the coming year. They all seemed nice, Dewey thought—nervous like him, homeless and eager to please. Dirk, who had arranged the meeting, said, "Stephen's not here, but we should get started." He suggested a "chore wheel" to be taped to the refrigerator. They agreed that Melanie and Angela would take the two rooms in the kitchen wing, with its self-contained bathroom. Lou wanted to be sure that overnight guests would be cool. They talked about meals, and rent, and sharing the bills. Dewey looked out the front window towards the green woods across Jane Street, and thought, This is going to be fine.

Then Stephen arrived. His reddish blond hair flowed out of his Ohio State cap down to his shoulders, framing wire-rim glasses. He said he wouldn't mind the dark basement room that no one had taken, and then he started talking about their "mission." Wesley House should be more than just a place to sleep and eat; they were here to create an "intentional community." It wasn't that they needed friends, he said. "Friends are easy. But friends aren't the same as community. Community is like family—people you didn't choose, but you have to love them anyway."

Dewey thought, Put a sock in it. But maybe Stephen was just fond of grand pronouncements. Maybe it was part of being a religion major. Anyway, they would all have their own rooms.

Their first big project in the fall was a party to show off their new home. They bought food and drink for dozens, set up a stereo for dancing in the Fellowship Hall, and put out candles in other rooms, where guests might choose quiet conversation. Dewey took part in the preparations, but when the evening came, he was desperate to get a paper done. He stayed on campus until ten o'clock, thinking he could still make an acceptable appearance. He wasn't a dancer. Maybe everyone would have kicked back by then. When he got to the Fellowship Hall, the Allman Brothers were blasting—but no one was there. Upstairs, the living room was dark. But a glow came from the chapel: candles of various sizes and shapes were burning all around the sanctuary. That's where he found his housemates, with one friend of Angela's, reclining on sofa cushions. Stephen jumped up.

"Dewey! What if they gave a party and nobody came?" He was as high as a chipmunk. For some reason there was a stepladder standing next to one of the pulpits. Stephen climbed it and spread his arms wide like a priest. "Bless us, Father, for we have no friends." Everyone laughed. "Heaven help us," he said. "We're all we've got."

Louie the Incorruptible flames out in one turn. After several excruciating consultations with the war gods, Dirk wipes him off the map.

"Live fast, die young, leave a beautiful corpse," says Lou.

Stephen, who has had a few refills of Sucker Punch, neglects to cash in his cards, thereby stranding his men in the Eastern US. "Look out, Cleveland!" he hollers, as the red horde sweeps north from Central America.

"How can you want to defend the US?" says Lou, who flits around the shoulders of the remaining players, checking their cards and making faces. In Wesley House, faith in America is not high. The Vice-President is being investigated for shady business deals. The President is under fire for a break-in at some hotel. The Nobel Peace Prize has just been awarded to the man who orchestrated the bombing of Hanoi. The Comet Kahoutek is coming. Newsmagazines buzz about the end of the world.

On campus, nobody seems to care. A few aging radicals, reduced to writing long letters to the student newspaper, fondly remember the Vigil of '69, when they took over the Administration building. This year, the biggest event on campus has been The Streak, in which four hundred students set a national record that stood until two nights later, when five hundred streaked at Penn State. Lou, a renegade English major, is writing a jeremiad for the yearbook about the politics of onanism, arguing that for several years the student body has just been playing with itself.

"What else have we got?" says Stephen. "My country, wrong or wrong."

"Sieg heil!" says Lou, and then hums "Taps" as Dirk swallows the Western US.

By two a.m., Dewey has discovered once again that you can't win from a base in Europe: there are too many ways to lose it. His legions have been reduced to a blue splotch on Iceland, which he calls his Fortress of Solitude. Angela is still hanging onto Australia, talking about *satyagraha*, deploring the bloodlust of the men. Lou says, "What are you gonna do, start a hunger strike? You'll never win that way."

"Depends on what you mean by winning," she says.

Dirk laughs his world-conquering laugh.

And the room goes quiet. The Band stopped wailing a

while ago. Melanie has fallen asleep face-first in her book, long brown hair shading her eyes. Stephen sinks into a mattress on the floor, beneath the open window. Outside, the last crickets are singing. "So," Stephen says. "What are we going to do about John 3-16?"

They have all been waiting for this question. Drunk or sober, Stephen is the conversation-starter, and he is full of theories. He says "Music from Big Pink" is a concept album, all about a character he calls The Worried Man. He says that in Van Gogh's self-portraits, the left eye always flares with anger while the right eye is lanced with weary compassion. He says love is the ability to accommodate the Other without diminishing her otherness. It was Stephen's proposal that they take in people like John 3-16.

The deal with the Methodists is simple. In exchange for nominal rent, they have agreed to a rudimentary civic vision. Each of them does some volunteer work, like being a Big Brother or tutoring at a local school. In addition, they offer their spare basement room, a big empty storage space, to homeless people sent over by the YMCA for three-night stays. They have furnished it with a queen-size mattress, and they call it The Crash Pad.

For the first month or so, there was no problem. Dewey was hardly even aware of their "guests." He seldom goes downstairs, and doesn't worry about security; he thinks it's cool that they don't bother with keys for the house. Of course, he's in the library most of the time. He's double-majoring in English and French, taking a really tough Shakespeare survey and a graduate course on Proust, and he can still hear his father's voice asking what went wrong that time he got a B+ in high school.

At dinner, which is more or less required, he has listened with amusement to stories about Dora Dora Dora, the stuttering dervish of a baglady; Cindy and Ron, the sweet hippie couple with the baby girl named Patchouli; Esmerelda, the Queen of the Roller Derby. Because they are doing such good work by taking these people in, Dewey has started slacking in his own volunteer duty, which was to tutor an eight-year-old at the Francis Marion School. Midterms are coming up soon.

Then John 3-16 came along. That was the name he offered when the Y sent him over, three weeks ago. A tall, spindly man with knotted brown hair that obscures his face, he seems to be stranded somewhere in his late twenties. He wears faded hospital scrubs. He doesn't talk to house members. Most of the time, according to Stephen, he just sits down there on the floor of the Fellowship Hall in cross-legged silence. But Lou says he has heard the man talking to himself—"chanting, actually, stuff like 'The People, united, will never be divided.' He's like a one-man liberation army."

John 3-16 didn't even ask about staying beyond three nights; he just stayed. Stephen went to talk to him about it, and came back saying the guy could really use an extension. Just until he got his feet on the ground. He didn't have anywhere to go. They called the Y to say that the spare room was booked for now.

Then things started disappearing from the refrigerator in their living quarters, where guests from the Y are asked not to go. When Dirk asked Lou about a vanished gallon of milk, Lou said, "Bite me, Dirk! I didn't take the damn milk." Late one night, when Melanie went to the kitchen for a cup of tea, she found John 3-16 at their breakfast table, eating a bowl of Cap'n Crunch and reading the cereal box.

He looked up with a spacy blue gaze, but he didn't say anything. Melanie managed not to scream; she just went quickly back to her room.

Tonight, she wants to talk about it. She raises her head from her textbook and parts the hair from her eyes. "Tell him his time is up."

Lou, who is a wiry little guy, is bouncing around the room on the balls of his feet, tossing a plum from one hand to the other. "We can't just kick the man out," he says.

"Yes, we can," says Dirk, still shaking the dice in his fist. He and Dewey and Angela are the only ones left at the table. "It's our house. We pay the rent."

"The guy creeps me out," says Melanie. "He was just sitting there like he owned the place. I'm sure he was high on something."

"Oh, and you've never touched a controlled substance," says Lou. Melanie cuts her eyes at him. Everyone knows that Lou still carries a torch for her. "John 3-16 is a man of peace," he says. "He's like—Woody Guthrie or somebody."

"Woody Guthrie wasn't a dopehead who stole people's food," says Melanie.

Stephen clears his throat. "I thought we agreed to help him."

Dirk says, "The man could be sick, Steve. We can't go trying to save the world. We're not qualified."

"What qualifications does it take to let someone use a spare room? I can talk to him about the food thing." Stephen looks around the group. "I thought this was part of our mission. If we can't help someone in such obvious need, how are we different from any off-campus apartment?"

No one answers. Stephen says, "What do you think, Dewey?"

Dewey thinks this is a stupid nickname. He got it back

in September, as a counterpoint to Louie. Stephen was supposed to be Huey, but it didn't stick. Right now, Stephen is looking at him intently.

"My father says the more people you try to love, the shallower the love."

Angela gives him a look. "I thought you always disagreed with your father."

"That doesn't mean he's always wrong."

Stephen sighs. Angela gets up from the table and settles on the mattress next to him. "We need to have a house meeting," she says.

"We need to tell the Y that three nights is the limit," says Dirk.

"We need to stop taking in psychopaths," says Melanie.

Lou snorts. "John 3-16 is not a psychopath. He just understands how fucked-up this country is."

Dirk rattles the dice. At 2:30 a.m., his five o'clock shadow is approaching werewolf proportions. "Lou, this guy could be dangerous. He could do something terrible."

"The *world* is dangerous. How do you know *I* won't do something terrible?"

"I don't. But I know you, so I can make that leap of faith."

"You didn't know me two months ago. You just trusted me because I had been screened by the Admissions Office."

Dirk doesn't try to answer this. He says it's just a matter of policy: they agreed on three nights. He suggests that they put it to a vote. He must figure that Dewey will side with him and Melanie, maybe Angela, too.

"Wait," says Stephen. "A vote? Is that how we do things?"

"It's a democratic society," says Dirk.

"Yeah, but is Wesley House a democracy? Do we live by the majority? I thought we worked by consensus."

"But we'll never reach consensus. We'll be here all night."

Stephen nods, and sinks back into the mattress, taking Angela's bare feet into his lap. "OK by me."

Dewey checks his watch. He still has a hundred pages of Proust to read for a nine o'clock class. "Can we vote on whether or not to vote?" he asks.

Lou laughs. "Listen to Major Major," he says.

Stephen sighs again, as if he's carrying the weight of the world. Dewey can't stand all this melodrama. They're just a house full of students, for God's sake. When Angela takes her teacup back to the kitchen, he gets up, too.

"Hey!" says Dirk. "We didn't finish the game."

"Don't worry," says Dewey. "We'll leave the board just as it is, so you can conquer the world tomorrow. OK? But I'm warning you: my general in Iceland is brilliant. You know where he keeps his armies?"

"Where?"

"In his sleevies!"

Everyone groans, and Dewey heads for his room. They can settle this John 3-16 thing however they like. He has work to do.

But he's too tired to focus on Proust. His French-English dictionary seems to have been printed in Tasmania: every translation needs a translation. What the hell is a plinth, and who cares what color it is? Before nodding off over his book, he sets the alarm for 5:30, so he can do the reading before class.

Dewey's room is a converted hallway at the back of the chapel, leading from the sanctuary around to the rear of the building. It's a small, narrow space, but there's room for a desk and some shelves, and they've built in a snug sleeping loft. When you turn the hallway corner underneath the loft, you pass through a hanging bedsheet and head downstairs to a door that communicates with the Fellowship Hall. It's the strangest of strange rooms in the house, but Dewey likes the privacy. The chapel is his buffer zone from the world.

When he walks through it at 5:35 to get a cup of instant coffee, he can smell the dope that Stephen and Lou must have smoked after everyone else crapped out. In the living room, in the moonlight that filters through the front windows, he can dimly see that Stephen is still there, sprawled on the mattress, his baseball cap crooked, glasses askew, snoring away. Dewey tiptoes through to the kitchen and gets his coffee, taking the kettle off the burner before it whistles. On his way back through the chapel, cup in hand, he sees a dark shape on the floor of the sanctuary, just below the altar.

Has he been here all evening? Or did he come up the back way just now, through Dewey's room? Perhaps he's asleep. Dewey is hoping to walk on by, to get on with his reading. But then the dark shape speaks.

"You can't kick me out."

Dewey can see now, his eyes readjusting after the bright kitchen light, that John 3-16 is sitting crosslegged right at the foot of the cross, his hair curtaining off most of his face. Only his mouth is visible as it moves.

"I can save you," it says.

Dewey knows this is stoned-out mumbo-jumbo, but he can't help wondering, Does he mean save *me*, or save *us*?

"From what?" he asks. He didn't mean to say anything.

"If you can't see that," says the mouth, "You're really lost, brother."

Dewey doesn't have time to stand here and be insulted by a burnt-out hippie. He walks on to his room, shuts the door, and settles in at his desk.

Forty-five minutes later, when the window above his desklamp is starting to go pale, he realizes that he has just been doodling in the margins of his Proust. He gets up to look out into the sanctuary. There's nobody there.

That night, John 3-16 is gone. At dinner, Stephen reports that the two of them had a talk, in which he told John 3-16 that some of the residents weren't happy about his staying so long. He says John just looked sad, and left. Lou is furious, sputtering about the hypocrisy of the house—how they profess a belief in community as long as community means people like them. Dirk says it's just the arrangement they made with the Y. Melanie says it's a question of safety. Angela remains silent. Dewey says that this way, at least, other transients will have their chance to use the Crash Pad.

Later, when he walks through the living room on his way to brush his teeth, he sees the game sitting unfinished on the card table. In the bathroom, above Stephen's room, he hears "Music from Big Pink" coming through the floor.

A few days later, at the breakfast table, Dirk and Lou and Dewey are having a silent breakfast, reading their own sections of the newspaper before rushing off to class, when Dirk almost chokes on his Raisin Bran. Lou and Dewey look up at him, but his mouth is full, and all he can do for a moment is point with a spoon at the regional news.

"Listen to this," he says finally. Angela, who is making tea in the adjacent kitchen, pokes her head in at the door. "'Yesterday in Warrenton police apprehended a twenty-eight year-old Durham man on charges of burglary and assault with a deadly weapon. Winston Small, who gave the name 'John 3-16,' is alleged to have broken into the Rock City Diner and to have struck the owner, Kostas Constantine, when Mr. Constantine refused to give him food. Small will be arraigned in district court next week.'"

There is a moment's silence. Milk curdles in Dewey's mouth. Then Dirk looks at Lou and says, "That could have been one of us."

"That's *because* of us," says Lou. "The man was *hungry*, for Christ's sake."

The semester steams towards its end. Dirk insists that no one touch the unfinished game, but there is no time for it now. The living room is littered with books and notes and coffee cups. Dinners grow shorter. There are no new guests in the Crash Pad. Did Stephen call off the arrangement with the Y? Dewey is too preoccupied with a paper on *Macbeth* to inquire.

He does notice, though, that Stephen hasn't been around much. A couple of times, he isn't even there for dinner. In the evenings, when Dewey comes in from the library, he no longer hears The Band ringing out from Stephen's stereo. Of course, Stephen has papers due, too. Maybe he's working on one of those theories of his.

The Vice-President resigns in a cloud of scandal, and the President proclaims, "I am not a crook." The Comet Kahoutek turns out to be a dud. Thousands of true believers gather on a beach in Mexico, expecting the end of the world in a flash of dissolving clarity; instead, it's a twinkle so dim that most of the comet-watchers focus on Venus by mistake.

The rainy chill of early winter settles in. No longer able

to hang their laundry out in the side yard, the residents of Wesley House have to rig up lines across the empty Fellowship Hall. The basement grows dank and detergenty, and their clothes never really get dry. One evening in late November, Dewey is taking down his whites when Angela walks in with a full laundry basket.

"What's the buzz, Angie?"

She nods, and starts hanging things up.

He points to his laundry. "I'm ready for Wet T-Shirt Night at Sudie's."

She smiles wanly. She is pinning up sheets; she seems to be staring right through them. Finally, she speaks.

"Have you talked with Stephen lately?"

"No. I mean, he seems to have been awfully busy."

"Busy getting bombed."

"What?"

"Last night I couldn't sleep, so I was reading in the living room when he came in. Three-thirty. He stumbled in and passed out on the mattress."

"He wasn't there when I came out this morning."

"I put him to bed."

"Oh." Dewey takes down his last few items. He doesn't have a basket; he just tries to carry everything in his arms. "I guess he was blowing off steam."

Angela drops her hands to her hips. "He wasn't blowing off steam. He's heartbroken, Granger."

After all these weeks, his real name sounds odd. He feels stupid standing here with a pile of jumbled clothes under his chin, two socks dangling as if they were trying to make a run for it.

Angela goes on. "He had such big hopes. You know the way he thinks about things." She lets a little silence go. "I guess he was wrong about us."

"We're all busy people, Angie. Maybe it's just not realistic to have such hopes."

She nods, and he says he really should do something with these clothes. He hauls his stuff out the door at the rear of the room, up his back stairs.

But as he stands at his beat-up old dresser, folding shorts and t-shirts, he finds that he's missing a sock. He heads back downstairs to look for it.

By the time he gets down there, the lights are off. Angela must have finished hanging up her things. There's no switch at this end of the hall. He starts walking through in the dark.

He's barefoot, and the linoleum floor is cool and grainy. Whoever was supposed to clean down here hasn't done the sweeping lately. Maybe that was his chore this week. He stumbles into one of Angela's sheets, and has to fend it off with his elbows around his head. He stands still for a moment, trying to get his bearings. The basement is silent. He wishes he had left a trail of black-eyed peas behind him.

After a few seconds, he hears the distant heartbeat bass of somebody's stereo. He smells the clean dampness of the laundry, and white forms start to take shape in the dark, floating like weightless spirits. He feels the air parting and recombining around his face.

He sits down on the floor. Everything is more confusing than ever. Armies outgrow sleevies. Houses can't be saved. But he is going to sit here for a while. There's a whole world down here.

MONDEGREENS

It was Wednesday night at the Road House, and the Queen City Sheiks were cooking. Mike played lead, Tom was on rhythm and vocals, Pete hit the drums, and I tried to keep up on bass. My name is Austin. Everyone called me Ozzie then, a name I couldn't stand—but the Sheiks could have called me Moss-Butt, as long as they let me play.

Tom swung his guitar to his side and clutched the microphone stand. "I shouldered my cross," he sang, "I looked east and west. I didn't have no steeple, no, no, in my defense."

We had debated this lyric, out in Mike's garage, listening to the scratchy old Stony Jones LP over and over. It sounded to me like "I didn't have no seagull."

"What sense would that make?" asked Tom. He said the song was about salvation. Stony Jones, who made a legendary pact with the devil, knew that God had abandoned him; that's why he used the Christ image. Yeah, yeah, I thought, I took AP English, too. Pete, who was Tom's little brother, sat at the drum kit reading *Spiderman* while he waited for us to settle the issue.

"Why does it have to make sense?" said Mike. "It's only words."

"Easy for you to say," Tom said. "You don't have to sing them." Mike liked to make up the words that we couldn't figure out. In his versions, songs were full of things like "pizmotality" and "wonsitude." He said Stony Jones didn't have no seewomma. Tom rolled his eyes. As usual, since he did the vocals, he got to make the call. Now, on stage at the Road House, "steeple" definitely sounded wrong.

There wasn't a stage, actually: we just set up in the front window of the long, low-ceilinged room, twenty paces from the bar at the other end. In between, there were four wobbly formica tables with folding metal chairs, and along the walls on each side were three wooden booths. I surveyed the audience, such as it was on a humid weeknight in July—two couples in booths and an old guy on a barstool. So I had a clear view of the sleek blond girl when she walked in alone, ordered a beer, hitched her pale blue dress up to sit on a stool, and turned her attention on us.

It was the kind of flimsy summer dress that only a skinny girl who knows she looks good would look good in. Her long straight hair caught a glint of red from the Budweiser sign above the bar. She was too well-groomed, too sure of herself, for the Road House. Maybe she was looking for a story to tell the girls at school.

If so, she had come to the wrong place. The Road House just wasn't story material. It had been Cap'n Bligh's Fish 'n' Chips until earlier that year, when the owner, an enormous goateed man who told us to call him Uncle John, decided that the real money was not in HMS Bountiful Fishwiches but in good old American alcohol. He thought it would flow more freely if he called the place a jook joint and taped up photos of Leadbelly and Blind Lemon Jefferson. He can't have been aiming at a black clientele: they mostly steered clear of Robinsonville, this treeless commercial strip between the leafier suburbs and the parkway into Cincinnati. Besides, at the time, most of the black kids were listening to K. C. and the Sunshine Band, not Muddy Waters. It seemed to me that no matter what kind of joint you put behind that plain glass façade, squeezed in between Bi-Lo Pharmacy and Carolyn's House of Style, some people would never stop there and others would stop because they always had stopped. But Uncle John said, "You got to be able to change when the time comes."

That was where we came in. We were the Queen City Sheiks, baddest blues band in the Eastern Hills of Cincinnati. Of course, "baddest" could cut in more than one direction, but any way you sliced it it was true, because we were also the onliest blues band around. This was before blues was cool, when most garage bands were still covering Question Mark and the Mysterians. So you could say Uncle John was ahead of his time. Or you could say—as Mike said—that he just had his head up his outsized butt.

Still, as Tom pointed out, Stony Jones used to play at cathouses and barbecues. What mattered, he said, was not the room but the show. And although Tom wasn't much of a singer, he did put on a show. At school, he had always been a golden boy—athletic, tall and thin, with royal blue eyes and a crown of dark curls. He said that the heart of the blues was sincerity: you got to feel it, he said, and if your voice cracks on the high notes, well, you're just being sincere. This made him about the sincerest singer in town. His father had bought him a beautiful Les Paul, which he knew how to cradle and swing so the lights flashed in its enamel. He couldn't play a lick—Mike carried all the guitar parts—but he looked good up there, air-strumming as if he had touched the hem of Gospel Truth. Just now he was throwing himself into the lyrics—literally: where the original went "Save poor Stone if you please," now the protagonist was "poor Tom."

I looked over at Mike. During practices, he balked when Tom got too deep into his Mister Blues act; Mike had more music in one of his eyebrows than Tom would ever learn. But he knew Tom was the front man, The Sheiks' public face. Uncle John treated him like the second coming of Elvis. Without him, we wouldn't have this regular gig, Wednesday through Saturday all summer long; we'd just be banging around in Mike's garage. I saw that Mike wasn't making faces at Tom's sincerity. He was gazing at the girl in the come-hither dress.

Tom croaked the final chorus, and I fingered a G, ready to tear into the riff that opened "Meatpacker Blues," which was next on the playlist we all had taped to the backs of our instruments. But before Tom could give us the usual "One, two, onetwothree**fa**," which he shouted as if he was teaching schoolkids to count, from the bar there came the loud and lonely sound of one person clapping. The girl.

Tom did his grateful poorboy bit—"Thankya, thankyavermuch"—and declared that it was time for a break. He placed his guitar on its stand and headed for the bar with a purposeful stride.

The rest of us followed. Pete wasn't old enough to drink legally, and Tom never gave him a second thought, but Uncle John did not inquire closely if I ordered two beers.

When we got there, the girl was saying to Tom, "I love that song. But you've got the words wrong."

"I *told* you," I said to Tom.

She glanced at me, then turned back to Tom. "You said, 'I didn't have no steeple.' It's 'I didn't have no sweet woman.'"

Tom said, "Of *course*. That makes perfect sense." Nodding

at me, he added, "Austin thought it was 'I didn't have no seagull.'"

She laughed, and looked at me again. "Seagull? 'I didn't have no seagull'? What kind of defense is that?"

Just then, Mike tapped Tom on the shoulder and said, "It's not time for our break yet." His Stratocaster was still strapped over his shoulder.

"Well," said Tom, smiling at the girl, "I was getting parched."

"We've got three more songs before the break."

"Take it easy, Mikey. It's not like our fans are going to riot." The two couples in the booths had settled into their beer and pretzels.

Mike's shaggy brown mustache bristled. He was a good four inches shorter than Tom, and his dark droopy eyes and shoulder-length hair gave him the look of a hippy gnome.

Uncle John leaned over the bar. "Relax, cowboy. Have a beer." He had seen Mike get his back up before. Besides, when there was nobody in the place, he encouraged us to take long and frequent breaks: we had to pay for our own drinks. He cranked up the radio, so that when Tom turned his back to us, we couldn't hear a word of his conversation with the girl. Mike cadged a cigarette from John and sat at a table with me and Pete. He took two puffs, then set the butt down in a tray and watched it become an ashen snake.

After the break, he tore the place up. I mean, I always knew he was too good to be bumping along with our earnest impersonations of Delta misery, but I'd never heard him burn like that. Instead of the usual sharp little scripted licks, now he leaned into solos that arched over our thudding accompaniment like darkening rainbows. After each song, Tom gave him a little nod, as if to say Nice, but knock it off, that's not the way we practiced it. The girl applauded each number. During the next break, Tom went right over to the bar; she stood to meet him. Mike and Pete and I sat silently at our table.

Mike said, "What do you think, Oz? She's not wearing a bra, is she?"

"Nope."

"Not that she needs one," he said. He took a pull on his beer. "Five bucks says she's not wearing panties, either."

Pete's eyes bugged. He was just a sophomore with a Dennis the Menace cowlick, but he was a good-natured little goober, and he kept a steady beat. "How are you going to find out?" he asked.

"Do I have a bet?"

My father had always warned me about gambling—but this was just a little wager among friends. "You're on," I said.

Mike went up to the bar. "Hey, John," he said, "It's ridiculously hot in here." He pointed at an electric fan above the bar. "You got that thing directed at the ceiling, man. Mind if I reposition it?"

Uncle John shrugged, not even turning his head from the Reds' game silently playing on the TV above the bar. Mike stood on a stool, turned off the fan, which was connected to a long extension cord, and pulled it down to the floor. He squatted over it, just to the side of the girl, who stood talking to Tom, holding a drink with both hands. Mike seemed to study the controls of the fan. Then he hit one of the buttons, and with a sudden whoosh it was on high. Her dress flew up around her waist, revealing a swatch of white cotton.

"Hey!"

"Whoops!" he said, fumbling to find another button, as

if he were too immersed in his ineptitude to think of turning the fan away from her. "Sorry! John! How do you work this thing?"

The girl tugged the dress down to her hips, glanced around the room, and glared at Mike. He finally got the fan turned away from her, and looked over at me and Pete with a shrug. She followed his glance. Then, looking at us, she grasped her hem on both sides, and, like a great bird flapping its cumbersome wings, she lifted and lowered her dress, giving us a flash of tan midriff before the skirts settled again. She cocked her head at Mike and curtsied with a smile. Then she turned back to Tom, who looked like a kid with too many Christmas presents to open.

Mike left the fan on the bar and walked back to us grinning. "I owe you five bucks," he said.

Before we finished our final set, right in the middle of "Dirt Road Strut," the girl put some money on the bar and walked out the door. Just like that. Tom managed to get through the song, but he didn't sound so strutful by the end. When we were packing up, he kept looking at the door, as if any minute she'd walk back in, movie-style. Mike said, "You axed for water, man, and she give you gas-o-leen." Tom looked like the babysitter had sat on his Happy Meal.

Uncle John gave us each fifteen bucks, our standard for a Wednesday. Then, while John was taking out the garbage, Mike hit No Sale on the register and lifted another ten. I didn't approve, but what could I say? Out on the sidewalk, in the dense and cooling midnight air, Mike said, "She was too skinny, anyway. Did you see those ribs?"

This was the final summer before college. Mike and Tom and I had been classmates since junior high, but I didn't know them well. I had grown up on Clock Hill, in the shadow of the clock tower, which was erected in the fifties to create the idea of a community where five years before had been nothing but fields and woods. Mike and his mother lived in the Robinsonville part of our school district, not far from the Road House. Tom and Pete were Clock Hill kids — their father, like mine, was a white-collar guy at GE — but they lived on the Robinsonville side of the hill, and spent more time down there than I ever had. Until Mike dropped out, we all went to the new high school of low-slung brick and glass, just down the street from my house. That spring, when Mike put a note on the school bulletin board, "Bass Player Needed for Blues Band," I responded. I knew only one blues pattern, which I had cribbed from a Clapton record, but I could adjust it in tempo and key, and that was enough for the Sheiks.

The day after that Wednesday night gig, I walked over to Tom and Pete's place, as usual, so that Tom could drive us down to Mike's garage for practice. Tom had a '65 BelAir that his parents bought him. My parents could have afforded an extra car, too, but Dad said I would understand the world better if I had to buy one with my own money. Since it was summer and school was out, we arrived before Mike got home from the t-shirt factory, and played our kill-the-man-with-the-ball version of basketball at the hoop that Mike's father had long ago hung from the front of their dilapidated garage. The houses on that street were all on top of each other, but nobody seemed to mind the ruckus we raised.

Mike and his mother arrived together, as always. They shared an old white VW Beetle, and he picked her up on his way home from work. She was a nurse's aide at Our Lady of Mercy, the only mother I knew who worked. She was also the youngest, prettiest mother I knew. While we got cans of coke from their old rounded fridge, she showered and changed into tight-fitting jeans. She returned to the kitchen with her honey-blond hair parted down the middle, falling to her shoulders. Her shampoo smelled like strawberries.

"So, Austin," she said, "Do you have a girlfriend?"

Mike said, "Oh, yeah, Mom, she's a cutie. Her turn-ons include watersports and dancing, and her favorite food is filet mignon." The other guys laughed, and I threw my empty coke can at Mike. "Austin is completely faithful to her, aren't you, Oz?—at least until Miss August comes along."

I couldn't imagine saying this kind of thing in front of my mother, but Mrs. Davis just laughed. Mike was always talking about girls, making up songs about them ("I'm just a man whose erections are wood—Oh Lord, please don't let my girlfriend be too good"), but he never brought them home. Mrs. Davis asked me, "Whatever became of that nice Jill Hoskins?"—a girl Mike used to go with, before he lost all contact with the high school.

"Ragatology," said Mike. Tom and Pete laughed, and kept on joking, but I gave Mrs. Davis straight answers about who was dating whom, where people would be going to college, what we all thought we wanted to do with our lives. Just because she was cool didn't mean we had to act like dumb kids with her. Once in a while we saw her with a boyfriend, but it was never the same guy for long.

Then Mike said, "I've been thinking about the chorus in 'Wildcattin'.'" That was our cue to head for the garage, thanking Mrs. Davis as we went.

I never met Mike's father. My parents naturally socialized with the people around them, and that didn't include anyone from "off-hill." It wasn't like the Davises had petitioned to join in; they couldn't have cared less about bridge and golf. Mr. Davis had worked at the oven company. Tom said that every chance he got, he was off on a hunting or fishing trip. Then, one weekend when we were sophomores, he just never came home. He had headed out for a cabin somewhere in Indiana, and there was no word from him until two months later, when Mrs. Davis got a postcard from Denver. That was the last of him, as far as his family was concerned. Tom thought there was another woman, but nobody really knew.

Mike dropped out of school that spring, right after his sixteenth birthday, and got a job at the t-shirt factory, just a few doors down Industrial Drive from where his father had worked. This surprised me, because he was a smart guy; he definitely could have gone to college. He arranged all our music, and talked about things in ways that I hadn't thought of before. One time after practice Tom and I were talking about college. In less than two months, he would be off to Denison, and I would be headed for Duke.

Mike broke into our conversation. "College is the booby prize, man. College is high school with beds."

Tom smiled and said, "Sounds pretty good to me."

Mike said, "Congratulations! You may have already won."

When my father asked what Mike was doing with his life, I said, "He's making a living, Dad. College isn't the only answer, you know."

Dad looked perplexed, but he didn't push. He and my mother weren't thrilled about The Sheiks playing late hours down in Robinsonville, but I had always been such a good boy, straight A's and straight-arrow, that they must have decided to leave well enough alone.

Still, sometimes I wondered what Mike was doing, too. Far from seeming to think he was too good for the Sheiks, he was always talking about our potential. "The Sheiks are really gonna be something," he said. "If we just keep at it, man, the Sheiks are gonna **be** there." Sometimes after practice he'd spend an extra half-hour with me, going over the bass lines that I found especially tricky. He set up some rudimentary recording equipment in the garage, to make a tape that he planned to distribute around town, in the hope of getting us more gigs. Maybe he liked being able to shine in our barely competent midst. Or maybe he just didn't know how good he was.

The next night, Thursday, the girl was back at the Road House. Her name, Tom said, was Natalie, and she was from Wellington, a brick-and-ivy neighborhood tucked under its elms right next to Robinsonville; it was where the old money stayed, while the new money built big homes on Clock Hill. She went to the Country Day School, and she drank hard. I watched from the front that night as she slugged down a couple of beers and then some mixed drinks. I saw Uncle John raise his eyebrows, but since she spent her breaks with Tom, he must have figured she was all right.

During the first break, when I was getting beers for Mike and Pete, I stood next to Tom and Natalie for a minute at the bar. He asked her if she could bring some friends next time. Their voices descended into conspiratorial tones, and I couldn't hear what she said. I turned my attention to the Reds' game, got our beers, and walked over to join Mike and Pete.

"So," said Mike. "The bitch is back."

According to Tom, Natalie didn't have any friends. He said she was one of those girls who was too pretty for the other girls. The only child of socialite parents, she had her own Cougar, red with black trim, and she seemed to have free rein. She hated her snooty school, with its blueprints for college and marriage. As for boyfriends, Tom said she was too smart for most guys. The truth is, at that age most guys are stalking around with their hands straight out like Frankenstein's monster, in search of boobs, so maybe her boyish body limited her appeal.

But she was pretty, and she was smart. On Friday afternoon, when Tom and Pete picked me up for the ride to our practice at Mike's garage, there she was in the front seat. She said to me, "Hey, Seagull."

I answered, "What's up, Sweet Woman?" She gave me the kind of smile that could save your life.

When we arrived, Tom started pounding his little brother on the basketball court. Natalie and I stood among the tomatoes in Mrs. Davis' scruffy little garden.

She said, "You know what lyrics like that are called?"

"Like what?"

"Mistakes, like 'I didn't have no seagull,' or 'Scuse me, while I kiss this guy.'"

"Or 'He's got the whole world in his pants'?"

"Yeah." She laughed. "That's what Tom thinks, doesn't he?"

I laughed with her. I didn't know any girls like this.

"They're called 'mondegreens,'" she said.

"Mondegreens?"

"Yeah. There's this old song, about how they killed the Earl of Murray and they laid him on the green? Only somebody thought it sounded like they killed the Earl of Murray and the Lady—" She held out her hand, palm open.

"Mondegreen," I said. "How tragic."

"N'est-ce pas," she said.

Then Mike and his mother arrived. He pulled the Beetle right in under the hoop, ending the basketball game. When he got out of the car, he didn't acknowledge Natalie. He headed straight into the house, and Mrs. Davis had to introduce herself.

"Mike must have had a rough day," she said, looking at the kitchen window. "He didn't say a word on the way home." When we got to the door, Mike was coming out.

"Hey," said Tom, "How about a coke for a man who just demolished his little brother in a hot game of hoops?"

"You know where they are," Mike said, sliding between Tom and Natalie on his way to the garage.

Natalie said to Tom, "I should be going. You guys have to practice."

"But—"

"I can walk. And I mean it about the practice: you need it." She smiled. "You've got a big gig coming up." She gave Tom a peck on the cheek, and walked off.

Mike was tugging open the big garage door. Sometimes it stuck. This time he yanked it so hard that the rollers clanged against their stoppers and the windowpanes rattled.

"What big gig?" he said.

Tom unpacked his guitar from its perfect black case. "Natalie got us a job at the Wellington Country Club."

"Yeah, right. Like those rich farts would want to listen to the stuff we play."

"It's for the kids. They've got this youth program, Sunday afternoons—they have dances out at the teahouse, while the grownups are getting smashed inside. They usually have this doofus band—Nat knows one of the guys in it—and they had to cancel this week. She got him to suggest that the Sheiks fill in." Tom obviously thought this was the best news since the birth of Stony Jones.

"The teahouse," said Mike. He was sitting on his amp.

"You know—that glassed-in shelter thing out behind the clubhouse, overlooking the eighteenth hole."

"I remember." He had been a caddy for a while, until he got fired for "disrespectful behavior." According to the club, he made a pass at one of the lady golfers. According to Mike, it was the other way around.

"It's good money," Tom said. "And those are the richest kids in Cincinnati. Next thing you know, they'll have us playing at parties all over the Eastern Hills."

Mike didn't say anything. When we finally got around to playing, we couldn't hear him come in on the first number. He had forgotten to plug in.

There was a bigger crowd that night, a Friday crowd—guys from the factory with their dates and their paychecks, a few of the tougher kids from the high school. It was a sticky-hot Cincinnati evening. The better nightspots had air conditioning, but air conditioning was for wusses. These people were here for beer, and loud music, and the nearness of overheated bodies.

For some reason, the Sheiks couldn't find a groove that night. Tom stumbled over lyrics, and I kept falling behind tempo, which Pete, trying to compensate, would then push too hard. Mike was practically absent. I mean, he played his parts, but he hit the notes with all the expressiveness of a grocery bagger.

During our breaks, none of us said anything about how off we were. Maybe, I thought, this was just what it meant to be professional: even on bad nights, you muddle through. Tom and Natalie talked quietly, Pete and I sat at our table and drank our beers, and Mike stood by himself at the far end of the bar.

This continued until the end of the final set, when, while the rest of us were packing up, Mike didn't unplug. I didn't notice until I reached the bar and saw that Natalie was still looking up at the front window. Uncle John looked annoyed—he had already poured our final beers and announced Last Call, and he could hardly tell people he was closing while the live music continued.

Mike started playing something I'd never heard before—a medium tempo shuffle, loose-limbed and rangy, more soulful than anything we'd played all night. Then he stepped up to Tom's microphone. I'd heard him sing sometimes in practice, when he was demonstrating the timing of a song, or when we were debating the lyrics, but he'd never sung at a gig before. His voice was a gruff baritone, unembellished but strong.

"It takes a rockin' chair to rock," he sang, and on the guitar he filled in with a three-note lick. "It takes a soft ball to roll," he went on, and then the same answering riff. "It takes a song like this"—da-da-da—"to satisfy my soul."

At this point another voice rang out, in unison with the three guitar notes that followed "soul." "SATISFIED," Natalie sang in a clear contralto. Then she joined Mike for the chorus: "I ain't never been SATISFIED! I ain't never been SATISFIED!" Mike gave her a little smile. He moved on to the next verse, with Natalie chiming in after every line:

> Milk in the pitcher
> SATISFIED!

Butter in the bowl
    SATISFIED!
Can't get a sweetheart
    SATISFIED!
To save my soul
    SATISFIED!
I ain't never been
    SATISFIED!
I ain't never been
    SATISFIED!

By the time they got to the chorus, several other people at the bar had started singing the response, and with the final verse everyone in the Road House was shouting along.

I got a letter
    SATISFIED!
In the bottom of my trunk
    SATISFIED!
I ain't gonna read it
    SATISFIED!
Till I get drunk
    SATISFIED!
I ain't never been
    SATISFIED!
I ain't never been
    SATISFIED!

At the end, the whole place was roaring—except, I noticed, for Tom. He focused on his beer.

When Mike stepped away from the microphone and walked to the bar, he got a huge round of applause; Uncle John even slapped him on the back. Then John went about closing the place, while we packed up. I heard a couple of well-lubricated patrons on their way out, still singing back and forth to each other. Mike raised his beer mug to them. Then he helped himself to a ten from the register. I figured he had earned it.

Mike and Natalie didn't speak, though. As soon as we were ready, Tom ushered her and Pete and me to his car, and we were off in a hurry. From the back seat I looked out the rear window and saw Mike standing on the sidewalk with his chin on his upright guitar case, watching our car pull away.

The next day, Saturday, was blistering hot, and I took the bus down to the Robinsonville public library, where I read *On the Road* in the air conditioning. I was reading a lot that summer; I figured that soon, with all my college work, I wouldn't have time for it. I had my guitar with me, so I could walk straight from there to Mike's for practice. When I stepped out into the heat at three-thirty, I was still rolling across country with Kerouac. I heard the turning screws of a VW engine just before the dirty white Beetle pulled over beside me.

"Hey, Austin, you want a lift?" It was Mrs. Davis.

"Sure, Mrs. D." I got in, and found just enough room for the bass between my knees.

She wiped the sweat from her temple, and put the car in gear. "It's hot as the fifth floor of hell, isn't it?"

"Yeah. That's why I was in the library."

"The library. Imagine. I couldn't pay Mike enough to spend an afternoon in there."

"Oh, I don't know. Maybe if you offered him time and a half."

She laughed. "No, when he's not at the factory all he wants to do is play that guitar."

We came to a stoplight, and her voice got softer. "You know, Austin, some nights, when I can't sleep, I get up for a glass of water, at two, three, even four o'clock, and I see the light on in the garage. I go out there, in my slippers, on my tippytoes, to look in the side window, and there he is playing away—without an amp, you know—like he's in another world, with his eyes shut and his head swaying. A few hours later, I get up again, to wake him up for work, and sometimes I find him still playing in his bed. I mean, he's asleep, but his hands are still going." She took her hands off the steering wheel for a second, to demonstrate. "I can't stand to wake him. Sometimes I just stand there and—listen, you know?"

I nodded. We started up again.

After a few silent blocks, she said, "Austin, does Mike ever talk about his father?"

"No. Not that I've heard. I mean, we're pretty busy practicing usually, there's not a lot of talk."

"Of course." We had arrived at their house, and I had my hand on the door handle—that skinny metal handle in the old VW—but she wasn't through talking. She looked out the windshield at the house next door. Its sagging front porch, littered with broken toys and furniture, was badly in need of paint.

"Jesus," she said, "somebody ought to drop a bomb on this neighborhood, huh?"

I thanked her for the ride and got out. She went into the house. I was earlier than I'd planned, but the garage was open, so I went in and set up my gear, to warm up.

I ran through a series of scales, but soon I got distracted. The garage was full of stuff that must have belonged to Mr. Davis — all kinds of tools hanging neatly from hooks set into pegboard, hammers and saws and t-squares, wrenches lined up in order of size like schoolkids posed for their class picture. At the rear wall was a counter with cabinets and pigeonholes, coffee cans brimming with nails and screws and washers, sorted by size and type. The vice at the end of the counter squeezed a two-by-four that kept it from rusting.

"He loved this stuff."

I hadn't heard Mike come in behind me.

"It's great stuff," I said. "You could work on anything here."

Mike nodded.

The question popped out of my mouth before I could stop it. "Why do you think he left? I mean, it looks like he meant to stay. It's all so perfect."

Mike loosened the vice, pulled out the two-by-four, and slapped it lightly against his palm. "Maybe you just answered your own question."

He beat a little rhythm on the counter, then put the two-by-four back in the vice, and said, "You want to work on the intro to 'The Arkansas Stomp'?"

I really wanted to learn the song he and Natalie had sung the night before, but I strapped my guitar on again. "Yeah," I said. "I keep messing up that part."

"I know," said Mike.

That night was our final gig at the Road House. It wasn't supposed to be — we had signed on for the whole summer — but we hadn't figured that Mike would throw his guitar through the window.

It started in our first set, even before the Road House was full. Natalie was at the bar, and Tom was acting like she was the only person in the place, mugging for her, tossing her name into the lyrics. When we took our break, Mike tried to catch him on his way to the bar, and Tom shrugged him off. I could see that Mike was pissed, so I grabbed his arm and said, "Can we talk about it at practice Monday?" He gave me a dark look, then slowly removed my hand from his arm and walked to our table. "I'll get the beers," I said.

In the next set, Mike started acting out. On "Big Timber," one of our raunchier numbers, he didn't play at all. Tom gave him a quizzical look — the song didn't go far with only bass and drums — but Mike just looked back at him. On "Fencepost Blues," which Tom liked to do slow, so he could drawl out the refrain — "I'm straddlin' the fence, babe, should I jump or go back home?" — Mike pushed the tempo, making Pete and me follow him until Tom could barely spit out the words. In the pause afterwards, as Tom glared at him, Mike started a solo, something we'd never heard before.

It was a slow, gutbucket blues. Certain notes Mike seemed to hold until the moment when you thought they couldn't be held any longer; then he held the note a little more, bending it so slowly that it had become another note before you realized it. Somewhere in the middle, without thinking, I picked up a bass line, softly at first, then with growing confidence. It was a pattern I'd never played before, but it wasn't hard. Mike, deep in his solo, didn't seem to notice. Then Pete found his way into a little muted backbeat on the snare, and the three of us were off, into country I had never visited. I could feel the crowd hush. Tom backed away from the microphone and sat on his amp, arms draped over his guitar.

We built up to what seemed like the finale, with Pete working the cymbals while Mike drew out the last notes; then he gave us a nod that said That's as far as you go, and we dropped out. He lit into a coda, spiraling up to the top of the fretboard, his fist clutching handfuls of spitfire in close to his belt, then swooped down, slowing the beat with each falling note, lugging the whole song now, and all the feeling behind it, to a nearly unbearable dissonance; then, as if an afterthought, came the light, almost heedless strum of the resolving chord, hanging its hat by the door. Mike held it for just a moment, and even as the crowd started to applaud, he raised the guitar over his head, spun with it stretched out before him, and flung it through the window.

After the crash and scattering of glass, there was a moment of shocked silence; then the shouting applause began in earnest. Mike looked around, as if surprised to see us all there. He focused briefly on Tom, and Pete, and me. He glanced at Uncle John, and the bar. Then he took a big, theatrical bow, and walked out the door. He went straight to the VW, which was parked across the street, and was gone before we could even get out from behind our instruments. I went out and picked up the guitar, leaving Tom to deal with an outraged Uncle John.

Driving home, Tom said we shouldn't call Mike until he got over his sulk. He said he'd hold onto Mike's guitar, and Mike was sure to come for it soon. From my seat behind Tom, I could see only a dark sliver of Natalie's profile against the occasional roadside lights. We were all quiet then.

* * *

I was still in bed when the doorbell rang the next morning, and then Dad shouted from downstairs, "Ozzie, it's for you!" I threw on a t-shirt and a pair of jeans and hurried down to the front hall.

There was Pete, with Mike's battered old guitar case in his hand. "I'm going to take this down to Mike's," he said. "You want to come?"

I looked out into our driveway. There was no car, of course; Pete wasn't old enough to drive. He had come on foot, walking away from Robinsonville, to ask if I would go down there with him.

I looked at our front hall clock. "Petey, it's Sunday morning. He's not going to be awake yet."

Pete said, "Then we can just leave it for him."

"You're going to walk all the way down there just to drop off a mangled guitar? That doesn't make any sense."

Pete shrugged.

I looked at the clock again. "I've got to get ready for church," I lied. "Let's just wait until our next practice, OK?"

Pete nodded, and I watched him walk back down our drive, lugging Mike's guitar, his cowlick bobbing in the morning light.

We never had a next practice. When Tom called the next day, he reported that Mike had left town. It turned out that Pete did in fact walk down to Robinsonville, and what he discovered was that Mike had come home the night before just long enough to pack some things into the Beetle and take off. When Pete offered Mike's guitar to Mrs. Davis, she just stared at it for a minute, said thanks, and didn't invite him in. On the phone, Tom said it was just as well. Mike had been getting too weird, he said. It was time to be thinking about college, anyway.

And that was the end of the Queen City Sheiks. The big country club gig never panned out, of course: without Mike, we were just a bunch of teenagers playing kill the man with the ball. Tom said it was too late in the summer to look for a new lead guitarist. The three of us quickly discovered, or were reminded, that the music had been the whole basis of our acquaintance.

Once, when I was out in Dad's car, running an errand in Robinsonville, I drove past Mrs. Davis, who was walking on the sidewalk, her eyes turned down. She looked so immersed in her thoughts that I decided not to toot the horn.

As far as I know, Mike never went back for his guitar. But I don't know much. We didn't hear from him again. I went off to college. When I was home for Christmas, I heard that Tom was going out with someone from Denison. So Natalie had disappeared from our lives just as quickly as she had materialized. I also heard that Pete was playing with a new band, and I meant to go hear them; but I never got around to it. What would have been the point? That summer, I got a job working on campus, and I didn't go back to Cincinnati at all.

One night, though, I was sitting in my room in the mostly empty dorm, going through some old stuff, when I happened on an unmarked cassette. I popped it in my boombox.

At first, I thought the tape was faulty, or just an old blank: there was nothing but static. But then I heard voices, too far from the microphone to decipher. And then came the shout: "One, two, onetwothreefa!" and a clatter of drums, ending in a rimshot that brought the guitar and the bass tumbling in. It was "The Arkansas Stomp." The bass, most of the time, was a little behind the beat. But it was sincere as hell.

Foolhearted Man

"I tell you what," said Frank. "If *I* had the chance to escape, I'd be out of here faster than you can say 'alimony.'"

Frank pronounced the word "exscape." He was standing at our work station, sipping coffee from a mug inscribed "World's Best Dad," talking to Marie and Edna about me: at the end of the summer, I would be leaving the factory, taking off for my junior year in France. Just now, I was busy rolling out the next order, since the bell that signaled the end of our afternoon break had rung several minutes before. Edna and Marie were sorting the shirts Frank had cut before the break. Frank never went back to work until he saw Lily, our foreman, head over toward us at the cutting tables.

"Dream on," said Marie. "You couldn't stand to leave us, Frankie." He hated it when she called him that. "You wouldn't have nobody to shit on."

"Marie!" said Edna, looking at me, as if I'd never heard the word.

"You're just jealous," Marie went on, ignoring her friend. "You're thinking about all those French girls Lewis is going to meet."

Frank snorted. "French pussy don't smell any sweeter than American," he said.

"Frank!" said Edna, looking at me.

Frank cackled at his own wit.

"How would *you* know?" said Marie.

I kept rolling out the cloth. It was a huge order of v-necks for Ohio State. In the Date Due box of the order form, in big red felt-pen letters, was the command "STP," followed by several exclamation marks. This was the front office's idea of cleverness: it meant Sooner Than Possible. Which meant that Lily would soon be stomping over, bug-eyed and red in the face, waving her copy of the order above her frizzy white-blond head, raising hell with us — but with Frank above all. Frank had seniority at the cutting tables, and when there was hell to pay with Lily, he paid it.

In the summer, when all the college orders came in, two out of three were STPs; that was why they hired seasonal help like me. But no number of red exclamation marks ever hurried Frank. He just stood there with his coffee, smiling his crooked half-smile. On the plywood board of the workstation behind him was thumbtacked a cartoon of a guy doubled over in laughter, with the caption "You Want It When??!"

Frank said things like "Her and me went to the smorgasborg last night," or "I like them little cheese thingies so much I just stoled me some for later." Sometimes I wondered if he talked like that just to get my goat; he gave me a little sideways glance, as if to say, Take *that*, college boy. Almost all the workers at the Brillianteen Manufacturing Company were recent immigrants from the hills of Kentucky who had left their dirt driveways for a chance at more money in Cincinnati. They were already old hands at exscape, and I was just a beginner.

* * *

This was the summer of 1974, when Richard Nixon was

self-destructing week by week, like a man who can't make up his mind about a method of suicide. At home, my father, a business executive who had been a Nixon man since 1952, was in agony. "So," he said to me early that summer, "You think he's lying? He says he didn't know about that stupid break-in. You think he's lying?"

Dad could believe that the party hacks had made a mistake, hired the wrong guys, even that Nixon himself had signed off on some kind of nefarious business without knowing what it was about. "He's the leader of the Free World, for pete's sake, he's got more important things to do than send a bunch of petty criminals into some hotel." But Dad refused to believe that the President of the United States would lie to us; in his view, it was obvious that Nixon was being framed by the Democrats.

I did my best not to get into those conversations. It was easy enough at dinner, when Dad was just home from the office, too tired to talk about much. Mom would keep us focused on the food or the news from my perfect sister, who was married and teaching French in Pittsburgh. But in the morning, when he drove me to work while the dew was still thick on the lawns of Clock Hill, and it was just the two of us on the big sofa-like front seat of his Lincoln Town Car—those were the times when I had to be inventive to avoid The Subject. Did I think Dick Nixon lied? Damn straight I did. But what would have been the point of saying that to Dad?

Fortunately, it wasn't a long drive. The factory was two suburbs over, in a no man's land just beyond the boxy little houses of Fairfax. Every morning, Dad drove me there, while I kept up a steady chatter about the humidity, already dense at 7 a. m., or Pete Rose's chances for another batting title. The moment I dreaded was when he pulled the big car into the gravel lot of the factory. All my coworkers drove old Chevies and Fords; I didn't need them to know that I was a Town Car kid. I was glad that we usually got there by 7:20, beating the crush of workers who arrived just in time to punch the clock. But Frank was always there on the loading dock already, sitting in an old plastic chair with his coffee mug, watching us all come in.

When I had first started this job, back in May, they had put me on the grommeter. Every gym bag required two grommets — little circles of metal that held a drawstring in place. This meant somebody had to sit at this machine, take a bag from one stack, hold it in the right spot over a spike, pump a pedal that punched the metal into the canvas, move it to a second spot, pump again, and put the bag on another stack to be hauled away to the printers. Then take the next bag, hold it in the right spot . . .

Not only was the task excruciatingly boring; it also happened to be completely isolated, separated from the other workers by a high bank of machinery. Maybe it wasn't just happenstance; maybe it was conceived as trial by boredom. If you could make it at the grommeter, you were ready for anything in the factory. After a week, just when I was about to decide that I wasn't Brillianteen material, Lily appeared at my station waving an order form and saying that was enough gym bags for now; they needed me at the shirt-cutting station. I was saved.

Working with Frank, Marie, and Edna gave me a new life — and also a musical education. The sewing room was essentially a big shed, like an airplane hangar, with windowless cinderblock walls and a high metal roof. In that tin drum, each kind of work produced its own brand of noise—the muted sporadic whirs of the sewing machines, operated by thirty women at thirty little sewing stations; the whine of Frank's saw, slicing through layers of material that I rolled out on the cutting tables; the rumbling wheels of the carts carrying cut patterns from our tables to the sewing stations—but if you walked from section to section, as I sometimes did, delivering stuff we'd just cut, you moved from one sad-ass hillbilly song into another. No work station was complete without its own brought-from-home radio, and every one of them was tuned to WCKY, The Hot New Country, or WCPO, Home of the Brand New Opry. I never knew there was so much white soul on the air. Maybe some kind of filter kept it out of Clock Hill.

Frank was in charge of the radio at our workstation, and it blasted out songs about drinkin', drivin', and divorcin' all through the day. Sometimes he sang along in a brassy baritone.

> I was drownin' my sorrows
> They were learnin' to swim
> I was thinkin' of her
> She was thinkin' of—

Here, the pedal steel kicked in, so that you could fill in the blank yourself. Frank laughed every damn time. He had a whole assortment of laughs, ranging from the snort of derision to the cackle that punctuated his own jokes to the Big Laugh, which made him look just like that cartoon character, doubled over in an ecstasy of amusement.

I didn't see what he had to laugh about. Frank was about forty-five, with big yellow teeth and a peninsula of fine black hair slicked back down the middle of his head. In the morning, his freshly shaved jaw gleamed blue, but by quitting time it was grainy with black stubble. Marie told me he had been on the wagon ever since the divorce, five years before, but he could fall off any minute. He moved like a guy who had been an athlete once, as if he could still tear off an open-field run if he needed to; but he was going paunchy, and when he pulled up his shirt to show off his appendectomy scar, his fishy white belly looked like it hadn't seen the sun for years.

Frank was always in hock. He complained about his ex, Melinda, who did not understand the words "enough" and "money" in the same sentence. He complained about the latest malfunction of his '64 Fairlane, The Shitbucket. He complained about River Downs, where his horse was always Dogmeat. His only comment about the government was that they taxed his ass coming and going. Naturally, he was always desperate for Friday, when, as the lingo had it, the eagle flew. That was when Lily came around with our paychecks. When she got to Frank she always held onto his for an extra second or two before letting go. He gave her a little I-don't-need-this-shit glare, wrenched the check away from her, looked at it, and said, "The eagle has crapped again." There was a song on the country charts that summer called "Foolhearted Man," and every time it came on he shouted, "They're playing my song!" Then he cackled with glee.

I had a serious girlfriend that summer, and we spent every free minute together. Every night after dinner Mom let me have her car, a late-model Buick convertible, and I drove over to Kayla's house on the other side of Clock Hill. We could have hung out at my house, but I knew that Dad didn't approve: Kayla was several years younger than

I, and she wore halter tops. When her name came up at dinner, he said, "You mean that girl with the overheated drawers?"

He wasn't entirely wrong. When I went over to her family's house, we did lots of things — talked, listened to music, went for walks — but whatever we were doing, Kayla held on to me as much as possible. We always did the crossword in The Cincinnati *Post*, sitting on the old couch in their basement rec room, our legs and arms entwined. She wore her shiny brown hair in a short shag cut, and she favored a lemony scent; her eyes were hazel, and with her new contact lenses they looked a deep green. Perhaps as little as a year before, with glasses and a less stylish haircut, she had been a gawky teenager; but now, in tight jeans, there was nothing gawky about her.

In the evening, we usually watched TV — but thank God nobody ever asked us for synopses of the shows. I couldn't actually stay all night, but we didn't have a curfew, either. Often we fell asleep in each others' arms in front of The Late Show, and didn't tiptoe upstairs to the car until 2 or 3 a. m. Then we spent another thirty minutes saying goodnight, as the last crickets sang in the woods around her house. We had agreed somehow, without actually saying it out loud, that we weren't ready for sex — by which we meant old-fashioned intercourse. But we were getting closer all the time.

Every morning, I stayed in bed until the last possible minute, skipping breakfast, and threw on my jeans and a t-shirt as if it was part of a fire drill. I should have been exhausted by this routine, but somehow I wasn't. When I ran downstairs, my mother met me in the kitchen, holding out a brown paper bag that contained the lunch she'd made for me, and she gave me a questioning look — the closest she ever came to stating her disapproval. I thanked her for lunch, and kept moving.

At lunchtime, I took my sandwich to a perch up high in the rolls of new cloth, the area we called "the stacks," where I liked to read while I ate. Sometimes Kayla rode her bike down to the factory to spend that half-hour with me; there was a bench under a water tank out behind the building where we could sit in privacy. She always brought me this butterscotch pudding that she knew I loved. Then we could make out for fifteen minutes until the noon bell rang. Her mouth tasted of milk and sugar.

One day in June, from his chair on the loading dock, Frank saw us saying a tender goodbye at her bike. When I returned to our work station, he caught my eye, nodded in the direction of the parking lot, and said, "Young man, what are your intentions?"

"What do you mean?" His little smile made me shuffle my feet.

"You know what I mean. Ain't no nookie without its price. What are you willing to pay?"

Marie broke in. "It ain't none of your business, Frank Thibault, and you know it." She turned to me. "Don't listen to him, Lewis."

"I'm just trying to help the boy out," Frank said, all innocence.

"Right. You're just jealous because you're an old fart."

He gave her a wounded look. "I may not be as good as I once was," he said. "But I'm as good once as I ever was."

"Frank!" said Edna.

He gave me a look, and tapped one of his big front teeth with a fingernail. I got back to work on the order I was rolling out.

One day, Frank had a lunchtime visitor of his own.

From my perch in the stacks, I had a good view of the picnic tables on the little front lawn of the plant. There on one of the benches sat Frank and a young woman with hair the color of the copper crayon in the box of sixty-four. He seemed to do most of the talking. At the end of our lunch break they parted, and I watched her walk towards a car. Nobody in Clock Hill would wear those frosted jeans, but she carried herself with style.

When I got back to the cutting tables, Frank met me with a stony face.

"I seen you lookin' at her," he said. "You keep your eyes to yourself."

I never knew when to take him seriously, so I just got back to work on the order I had been rolling out before lunch. A few minutes later I got a chance to ask Marie who the copper-haired woman was.

"That's his daughter," she said. "Brandy."

"Nice name, ain't it?" Frank was standing behind us. "The wife didn't think Whiskey was a good name for a girl." He cackled. "Anything else you want to know, Slugger?"

The wife, apparently, had tired of his drunkenness years before; she was in touch now only when the alimony was late. Brandy worked at the 7-Eleven in Fairfax. She had just completed her GED, and had been accepted to UC for the fall semester. "She's real smart," Frank said. "She got her old man's brains."

"Good thing she didn't get his looks," said Marie.

One day when I was helping Edna count shirt fronts before sending them over to a sewing station, I started talking about college. How boring it was, sometimes. How I had to take this stupid Geology course for my science requirement. "Igneous, metamorphic, and sedimentary," I said. "That's all I remember. A whole semester, a notebook full of notes I'll never look at again. Rocks for Jocks, we called it." I noticed that Frank had turned off his electric knife. "Now," I said, "when I drive through a highway cut, like the ones on Columbia Parkway? I can tell which layers of rock are igneous, which are metamorphic, and which are sedimentary. But how's that going to help me if there's a rockslide?"

Edna said, "Well, it's nice to know the names of things, ain't it?"

Frank didn't say anything, but I felt his eyes on me. A few minutes later, when he needed me to sort the patterns he had just cut, he called out, "Hey, Rocky. Come over here and tell me what all these layers are. This one's ignorous, ain't it?"

He laughed, a medium guffaw, and I smiled, but I didn't rise to the bait. I really was sick of school, and as the summer wore on I got more and more doubtful about the idea of a whole year in France. Why did I need to go away, when things were going so well with Kayla? College itself was starting to look pretty stupid, now that I got a paycheck. If I stayed at the factory, I could afford to rent my own place in Fairfax. Kayla could visit any time. French was a dumb thing to study, anyway. I had just picked it up because I used to help my sister with her vocabulary, and I liked the sounds of the words. I didn't know a single French-speaking person in Cincinnati. One steamy day in July, Marie asked me how to say "It's as hot as new love" in French. I didn't know — the idiom threw me — but Frank jumped right in.

"Hey, I know French. Commontalley-voo? I took it in junior high. It's like English on drugs. When they answer the phone, they say 'Allo?' When they bump into you, they say 'Pardoan.'"

I said it with the right accent. I couldn't help myself.

"Yeah," Frank said. "Like that." He laughed. "Orvwahr, mes amis," he said, and he went back to work.

By mid-summer, Nixon was in deep shit. He had been doing his utmost all year not to release the tape recordings of his conversations in the Oval Office, claiming executive privilege but sounding like an eight-year-old caught with his hand in the cookie jar. Almost every day in July, The *Post* carried headlines about incriminating new evidence. Down in the basement with Kayla, I noticed them briefly before turning to the crossword.

At the dinner table, Dad took the defensive. "You think the Democrats don't do the same things? It's just politics. The only difference is that these guys got caught." He was sure it was just "these guys," Ehrlichmann and Haldeman and Kleindienst, who got overzealous in some Prussian desire to make absolutely sure their boss got re-elected — as if he could lose to that wimp McGovern — and misled the President in the process.

"Don't get me wrong," Dad said in the car the next morning, as if the conversation was just continuing from the night before. "A CEO is still responsible for the people he hires. Mr. Nixon" — Dad always called him Mr. Nixon — "is guilty of mismanagement, no question. But if that's an impeachable offense, then I'm Marie Antoinette." I didn't try to respond, and it didn't matter: Dad really seemed to be talking to himself.

It was always a shock, stepping from the air-conditioned car back into the warm, damp morning, then into the bright linty air of the factory — but I found myself looking forward to it, as if my real life began when I walked in there and felt the metallic thunk of the clock punching my card. I made a game of punching in at exactly the same time every day, so that my card would carry a perfect blue row reading "7:21" over and over. All my plans for the summer—studying French politics, reviewing my grammar, immersing myself in Balzac—had vaporized in the heat. It was all I could do, with my mother's steady reminders, to apply for a student visa and fill out a plan of study. My passport photo was a wild-eyed thing, hair corkscrewing in every direction, a young poet drunk on absinthe.

When I wasn't at work, I was with Kayla, doing our daily crossword, making nice with her parents, and, most evenings, making out in the basement, in front of the flickering tube. One of the songs on the country charts that summer had a refrain that went "My body's got a mind of its own," and sometimes I found myself singing along. One day after lunch Frank heard me—I didn't realize I was that loud—and he turned down the radio. He said, "Hey. Where was that pretty little girlfriend of yours today?"

I said she couldn't always make it.

"Have you two been pitchin' woo?" he asked.

I wasn't even sure what that meant, but Edna said, "Frank!"

He tapped his tooth. "Well," he explained to Edna, "That's what happens—the more you see of 'em at night, the less you want to see 'em in the day." He turned to me. "Am I right?"

I blushed, and Marie jumped in. "Tell him it's none of his damned business, Lewis. Tell him to keep his horny nose out of it."

Frank laughed. Then he turned back to me, serious again. "You haven't, have you? I can see it in your face.

You read too much, Rocky. Please tell me you're not being all patient and gentle with her. Women *hate* that."

Marie said, "You better take notes now, Lewis. If anybody should know what women hate, it's Frankie."

Frank couldn't help laughing a Big Laugh at that. Then Lily appeared with a new order and a glare, and he cranked up the music again. By then, it seemed like every day brought a fresh explosion from Lily, who must have been under pressure from the front office. While we sorted a double-size shipment of sweatshirt material, Edna explained that this happened every summer, with all the college orders. Every year, the front office talked about automating more of the work—which naturally scared the workers—and then called on everyone to work extra hours instead. Edna said that in spite of appearances Frank had special pull with Lily, because he was so adept with that knife. He was especially pleased about the extra pay, because Brandy had already taken all the college loans she could, and he didn't want her to keep working at the 7-Eleven.

The bell rang for the afternoon break, and Frank and Marie came over to join us. Edna continued our conversation. "Brandy's the first Thibault to go to college."

"Not that she *wants* to," added Marie.

"Really?" I asked.

Frank gave Marie a black-eyed look, and said, "She just wants to play house with that boyfriend of hers. I'm gonna make sure she don't end up in a piss-hole like this." He picked up his coffee mug and headed out to the loading dock.

* * *

On the last day of July, the House Judiciary Committee approved three articles of impeachment. In the next few days, Dad didn't say a word at breakfast, and we listened to big band music on the drive to work. At the dinner table, Mom kept the conversation alive; Dad made just enough social noise to be polite before retiring to his chair in the den, where he read the evening paper. On August 5, the president had to release tapes showing that he'd known about the cover-up since Day One. That night, Dad finally spoke.

"The man shit in his own nest," he said. That was all he said. He didn't usually swear.

Now we were into the sultriest time of the year — haze in the morning, mid-day sun crashing off windshields in the parking lot, afternoon humidity so thick you had to lean forward a little just to move through it. Occasionally a flash thunderstorm rattled on our tin roof, and the next time we looked outside we'd see the steam rising from Industrial Drive. It felt as if summer could never end.

On the morning of August 8, a Special Report broke into the music at our workstation: that evening the President would address the nation on television. At 9 p. m., on the sofa with Kayla, I insisted on watching the speech. It was full of the usual evasions and self-justifications, but then he spoke the impossible words — "Therefore, effective noon tomorrow . . . " — and he actually managed a wan smile. The commentators went on past midnight, replaying the moment again and again. Kayla rested her head on my shoulder. I couldn't stop watching.

In the Town Car the next morning, we listened to the radio. It was wall-to-wall talk about Nixon. Should he face prosecution for the charges against him? Dad said, "I hope they crucify the lying bastard."

At work that day, Lily asked us to stay late, so when Mom picked me up, I drove her home, grabbed a snack, and drove myself back to the plant. It was a pain, of course, but there was also pleasure in the urgency of it, the clarity of what had to be done. And there was beauty in how well we could work together, when we had to. As soon as I finished rolling out the cloth for an order, Frank traced patterns on it with his tailor's marker, then fired up the knife and started cutting. While Edna and Marie sorted and counted the shirts he had already cut, I rolled out the next batch of material on a second table. Sometimes I pushed the rollers too fast, leaving ripples in the layers of cloth, but Frank knew how to work through them smoothly, avoiding snags by keeping consistent pressure on the knife. A helicopter was carrying Nixon away from the White House lawn. In the heat of the late afternoon I worked up a sweat, but I didn't mind.

At 7:00 we took a dinner break. Near the end of it, I looked up from my book to see that Brandy was sitting with Frank at a picnic table. They seemed to be having an animated conversation. He returned to the workstation late, and then he just stood there, looking into the fluorescent air, his hands kneading the cloth he was supposed to be cutting. Edna, Marie, and I stopped our chores. Finally, he noticed that we were watching him.

"She says she ain't goin' to college. She says it's a waste of money and time." He paused after each sentence, as if he were responding to a language instruction tape. "She's gonna get married. She says I can't stop her."

Edna and Marie seemed to know that there was nothing to say just yet; they waited for Frank to get back to work. I didn't have that much sense.

"It's her life," I said.

Frank looked at the cloth beneath his hands. After a long pause he spoke, without looking up. "You might want to roll this out again, Rocky. Somebody's gonna have a hard time cutting it." Then he turned and walked through the stacks, made the small jump off the loading dock, and disappeared. In a minute we heard the crunch of tires on gravel.

I thought the steam in Lily's face was going to blow the blond frizz right off her head. She ran to the other building and was back in minutes, dragging an older guy, an evening-shift janitor who sometimes did some back-up cutting. But Frank was right: the guy kept snagging the knife on those ripples, and eventually we had to throw out that whole table of cloth. Lily said we'd just have to stay until we got that order done.

Marie said, "Lil? We have to find Frank."

Lily's shoulders sagged. "We've got to finish this order tonight." Then she let out a little puff of air. "Who's going to find him?"

When I stepped down from the loading dock, the last light was fading. I hadn't noticed that the days were getting shorter. Ordinarily, I would be downstairs with Kayla by now. The obvious place to start was the 7-Eleven.

Brandy seemed to know who I was. She shook her hair from her face and said, "I haven't seen him." Then she looked down and began straightening a box full of peppermint patties.

"We've got to find him," I said. "Lily is all over us, because this order just has to be finished today or we lose the whole UCLA account, and—"

"Try the Third Base," she said.

"Excuse me?"

"The Third Base Bar, on Worcester Pike." Another customer came in, and she said, "May I help you?"

"Last Stop Before Home," said the faded sign above the door. Exhaust from a rumbling air conditioner splashed on the sidewalk. Inside, the dimly lit room resounded with country music. It was so smoky I had to sneeze.

"Rocky!"

He was sitting in a corner, under an old black-and-white TV that showed Gerald Ford's mouth moving silently. There were several empties on his table. He looked bad: fluorescent light gleamed off his balding head, and his beard was so dark that when he spoke his teeth seemed to shine out of nowhere.

"It's beer-thirty," he said. "Pull up a chair."

I sat down across from him. What good would it do to take him back to the factory drunk?

"Where's that poontang of yours?" Before I could answer, he waved me off. "Oh, I know you wouldn't want to bring a sweet piece like that to a dump like this." He pointed his bottle at the bar. "This place is even sorrier than it was five years ago."

I told him what was happening at the factory. He didn't look surprised.

"So Sam couldn't hack it, eh?" He laughed. "I bet Lil's havin' a shitfit." This

made him laugh harder. "Everybody misses old Frank. Well, that's just a clusterfuck, ain't it, Rocky?" He was winding up into The Big Laugh now. I looked away.

Then he seemed to sober up. "So they sent you to get

me. To fix up this little excapade of mine. Well, you know what, Rocky? I refuse to be fixed."

Another song came over the speakers, and he smiled. "They haven't changed the damn jukebox in five years."

I shrugged. "It all sounds the same to me."

"Oh, no, Rocky. You're not listenin' good. Wait, wait." He held up his bottle. "Hear that? That little growl at the start of the refrain? Nobody does that like Merle Haggard."

I nodded, and listened to the rest of the song. Frank held up his bottle at key moments, like a conductor's baton. I started to notice the growl—half angry, half joking.

"So," he said. "Did you talk to Brandy?"

"She was busy. She told me to look here."

"You should talk to her. Maybe she'd listen to you, bein' that you're in college and all."

"I'm not going back," I said.

He looked up. "Like fun you're not."

"I'm not."

He gave his bottle another flourish. "Well then," he said. "Let's toast to all the fuckin' failures in the room."

I told him I had to get back to work.

"Suit yourself, partner. Here's one for the road." He took a big swallow. "And here's one for the ditch." He started laughing so hard that he couldn't even take the second drink. When I stopped at the door and looked back, he was still laughing.

It was well after dark when I got back to the factory. Inside, it could have been four in the afternoon—the same shadowless overhead light, the same staticky cotton-dust air. Edna and Marie were sitting on an empty cutting table with cups of coffee. Sam had disappeared. Nixon was back home in San Clemente.

"Did you finish the order?" I asked.

"We did enough," Marie said. "Eventually Lily realized that Sam just wasn't going to get it done in one night. She sent him home. Did you find Frank?"

I told them. Marie said, "That old sonofabitch." I looked at Edna, but she didn't say anything.

It was too late to stop at Kayla's, but too early to go home. I drove Mom's car all over the eastern hills of Cincinnati, with The Hot New Country on the radio, loud.

The next morning when Dad dropped me off, there on the loading dock, in his usual spot, stood Frank. He lifted his coffee mug to me in greeting. The skin under his eyes looked bruised, but I couldn't read his face. I went straight to the clock. 7:22.

Marie told me I had a new job that morning. Apparently the latest order included a big shipment of gym bags, and that meant grommets. Meanwhile, there was a new guy, this kid from the other building, rolling out cloth on one of the cutting tables. Marie looked apologetic, but I knew it wasn't her decision.

At the grommeter all morning, I heard the high wail of Frank's radio, but I couldn't see or hear my old companions. When I looked for Edna and Marie at the morning break, they were out at the snack truck. I didn't wander as far as the loading dock.

At lunch, though, he was standing near my usual perch in the stacks. "Hey, Rocky," he said with that half-smile, "How do you like the vomiter?" I wanted to lay into him, but then he said, "Whoops—looks like you got company."

He nodded towards the picnic tables. Kayla was just coming up on her bike.

She had never looked better. Her skin was a little flushed from the ride, and the green of her eyes glowed above her lightly freckled cheeks. She took a small paper bag from the bicycle pannier: butterscotch pudding. Without speaking, we went around back to our bench.

I told her about the night before, and apologized for not calling, but she just shook her head: she understood. Then I started complaining about the grommeter — how tedious it was, how much I had left to do, how they had brought in another guy for my old job, and it looked like I could be stuck there for weeks —

"Weeks?" she said. "You're going to be gone in ten days."

"I don't know," I said.

I looked out across the back lot. There was a weedy patch of gravel and dirt, then the hurricane fence of the building next door, where they made — I didn't even know what they made. It was just another factory.

Kayla said, "Don't get stupid, Lewis." I started to object, but she said, "Just hold me, and shut up."

I heard the news two weeks later, on the S. S. France, steaming towards Le Havre. I was so busy meeting people, trying to wake up my dormant French, that I wasn't paying attention to the little pamphlet of daily news that someone put together from the ship's radio. So it took a minute to register when the cabin steward, a burly middle-aged guy from Marseille, said, "Vous avez entendu? Nixon a été pardonné."

The whole summer rose up in my mind, like a flock of

birds filling the sky. I saw that shameless lying bastard, announcing his utter disgrace with a smile. I saw my father, squeezing the wheel of his oversized car. I felt Kayla's head on my shoulder. I heard the whine of the pedal steel, and Merle Haggard kicked in with a growl. The steward was waiting for my reaction. All I could do was laugh.

BECAUSE BECAUSE BECAUSE BECAUSE BECAUSE

The Thing about the Highway

Late afternoon, the end of March, iron cold. She stands at the window, shading her eyes against the sun. The little front yard lies deep in snow, the crabapple tree is bare. All she can see of the neighborhood — power lines, driveways, the silhouettes of little houses — is black and white. She tries to imagine green grass, green buds under all that snow. When a car goes past, it makes the ensuing stillness seem more still.

She has been in with the kids all day. It's impossible to take the stroller out in this cold, over the icy sidewalks. The baby is teething, demanding constant attention; his four-year-old sister lies on the floor and draws pictures of spaceships like flying houses, then fills them with sixty-four colors. The mother makes a silent promise to spend more time with her, soon.

But when their father gets home at last, she meets him at the door. "We're out of Huggies," she says, although she knows there are more under the bathroom sink. "Anything I can pick up for you?"

"No, thanks." He is already down on the floor with the

girl. "This is *Wizard of Oz* night, snooks. Are you ready?" He doesn't watch his wife leave.

For the past few weeks, she has been taking the car as soon as he gets home—out to do some errand, out to pick up last-minute items for dinner, out. After his commute, the old Toyota carries his scent of sweat and cologne—but at least it's warm. With the heat cranked up high, she opens the window a couple of inches, so that currents of hot and cold stream around her. She heads straight for the highway.

The thing about the highway is that it takes you west, away from the river, away from town. She doesn't turn on the radio; she doesn't want to hear anything but the wind. She likes jockeying for position in the traffic, keeping up with the fastest BMWs and Audis on their way to the western suburbs. She likes looking into the windows of the other cars, imagining the lives of the drivers. Are they intent on a martini and slippers? Or on their way to a rendezvous in a dark and quiet place the wife doesn't know about?

Lines from *The Wizard of Oz* ring in her head. *What makes the elephant guard his tusk, in the misty mist, or the dusky dusk? What makes the muskrat guard his musk?* She sees Dorothy and her ragamuffin magi make their way to the gates of Emerald City, and she hears the angelic voices: *You're out of the dark, you're out of the woods, you're out of the night.* Just a year ago, she watched it with her daughter, reveled in it all again—and felt pole-axed by the ending. She had been so immersed in Oz, the golden roads and talking scarecrows, the Lollipop Guild and the ruby slippers, that she completely forgot it was all a dream. What was she doing back in Kansas, with the dishwater neighbors and family? She looked at her daughter, to see if the girl was disappointed, too.

This Was the Deal

The baby is howling in the kitchen; he can't hear anything else. But he doesn't expect to hear the car soon. Ever since they moved to Detroit from New York, last October, she has been fidgety and sad. He knows she misses the buzz of the city. He knows that her life now is constrained in ways that remind her of her own mother, which they swore would never happen to them. But this was the deal they made. New York might be a good place for a young couple, but you couldn't raise kids there. He is making more money now, and even though things are tighter than they planned, they agreed that this was the next step. As soon as he gets his promotion, they can buy a second car, maybe a bigger house. Then it will be her turn—whatever she wants to do. This was the deal.

He gives the baby some Zweiback crackers, which immediately stop the crying. That was what his own father said about raising him: "You used to cry like it was the end of the world, but we just kept giving you Zweiback. Man, I wish I had bought stock in that stuff." He never thought he would be emulating his father. But the old man wasn't always wrong.

He sits at the kitchen table and watches his son gum the crackers. The late afternoon is gauzy and still. He gets up and turns on the radio, to drown out the sounds of Bert and Ernie from the living room. While he's at it, he pours himself a scotch.

Lake of Dreams

She drives west, past Dearborn Heights, Inkster, Livonia. When the city highway gives way to interstate, she looks at the green destination signs—Ypsilanti, Ann Arbor, Lansing—and takes an exit that leads to some nearby town or suburb she has never visited before. Then she drives every street she can find. Since the days are finally getting longer, every evening she drives further.

In the pale light of early spring, the suburb of the day seems to be dressed in formal attire, English and impeccable. The houses luxuriate deep in their snowy lawns. She knows that if she were to keep driving, eventually these places would give way to country estates, where the gatehouses are bigger than her home and the homes themselves invisible beyond hillocks and stands of evergreen. Then those homes too would recede behind her as she drove on into the country, out into the flat unattended world of field and farm and blue horizon.

Once, when she was in junior high—back in another lifetime—she did a project on the moon. She learned that the moon's elliptical orbit is always getting a little larger, swinging out further from the earth every year, so that eventually—long after we're dead—the pull of gravity will be such that the moon will reach a point beyond which it can swing no further. Like a ball on an elastic string, it will come crashing back to the earth, and that will be that.

It was just a project, but she fell in love with the moon. She studied all the phases, and charted them on a calendar. She learned that the word "month" came from moon; so did "menstruation," which they had just covered in Health. Growing up in Ohio, she had never seen the tides, but she knew they were governed by the moon, and twice a day she felt that pull. With a map on her bedroom wall, she studied all the mountains and seas that had been plotted and named: Mare Nubium, Sea of Clouds; Mare Imbrium, Sea of Rains; Lacus Somniorum, Lake of Dreams. And that was just on the near side of the moon. Because its rotation coincides with its orbit, we never get to see the other side. Even after the project was over, she went out into their little backyard at night before bed and observed the moon's position, following its course across the suburban sky. Her mother said it was a pearl in a black velvet box; but she knew there was no box out there. That was just sky, on and on.

Da-Dunt-Da-Dunt-Da-Dah-Dunt

He tries putting the baby to bed. It's early yet, still before dark, but it's time for the movie. If he pulls all the shades of their little bedroom and shuts the door behind him, it is dark and quiet in there, and the boy might just drop off to sleep. God knows he has cried hard enough to be tired. The father still marvels at these kids—how hard they do everything, how fully themselves they are, every waking second. When they're hungry, all the world is food; when they're cranky, every mote of dust is an irritant, incapable of being swept away. And yet, when on some rare occasions he does manage to sweep it away, they brighten so abruptly it gives him whiplash. What mote of dust? What are you talking? It's a beautiful world. Even when they finally crash—as the baby is doing now, thank God—they sleep so intently that he can watch for long minutes. As the tiny blue vein in the boy's temple pulses, you can almost see his bones lengthening, his muscles knitting. You can practically hear the little heart's command: I got to grow, get out the way, I need my rest.

By the time he gets back to the living room, the movie has begun. His daughter is lying on her belly on the shag carpet, head propped in both hands, three feet from the screen. He tells her to move back, but she doesn't even register his presence. So he gets down on his knees behind her and, taking her ankles, drags her whole body several feet back. Her head never leaves her hands, and her eyes never leave the screen. But when he tries pulling the drapes, to cut the glare of the setting sun, she says, "No, Daddy! More light!" He opens the drapes and sits down on the sofa behind her.

He had intended to tell her about seeing *The Wizard of Oz* at about her age, to warn her about the scary parts. He had nightmares for weeks, thanks to the Wicked Witch, her chanting soldiers, and those horrible flying monkeys. Sometimes, even now, when things are going badly at work and he expects his boss to appear at his cubicle, he hears her theme music—da-dunt-da-dunt-da-dah-dunt—and sees those damn monkeys swarming the sky.

But it's too late to explain anything now. Dorothy is still in Kansas. She has just run away, with Toto in her arms, and here she is talking with Professor Marvel, the traveling wise man, whose sign says he has read fortunes for the crowned heads of Europe. The father had forgotten about this part, this phony old man with his crystal ball. He is so obviously a faker, conning Dorothy into believing that he can see into her life. How can she take him so seriously?

What If Everything Changes?

She keeps turning corners. The shadows on the lawns are growing deeper, and lights start coming on in the windows of the big houses. The air rushing in at her window is fresh and cold. She can't stay out here much longer; she can't leave him with the kids all night. But the car is so perfect now, she is so comfortable, she'll drive just a little more. She punches the cigarette lighter, not because she intends to use it—she gave up smoking when she first got pregnant—but out of old habit. She just wants to pull it out and look at the red-hot coil. When it pops up, she lights an imaginary cigarette, takes a deep, soul-warming puff, then breathes it out into the night.

The night! It's getting dark fast now. She turns back towards the highway. The kids should be in bed by now, and he often puts them to bed anyway, since she has to watch them all day. He's good about things like that. Fairness, dividing the chores, trying to keep everything in balance. So why does she always feel half a step off the beat?

She knows it is her fault. Night after night, her fault. Didn't she say the vows? For richer and for poorer, in sickness and in health, in boredom and in suburban Detroit. She was brought up to honor her promises. But what if you don't know what you're promising? What if everything changes?

She is about to get back on the highway when she sees that she's low on gas. Usually he fills the tank as soon as it gets below half—but she has been driving a lot lately. She has more than enough grocery money. She pulls into the station just before the ramp, asks the attendant to fill it and check the oil, and gets out to stretch her legs. The air is shockingly cold—but it feels good. In the blue-black of the eastern sky a crescent moon is rising. She doesn't know if it's waxing or waning.

There is nothing she wants more than a cigarette.

Inside the station, she sees that the attendant is no more than a kid, wearing a greasy Tigers cap with the bill curled into a frown that shades his eyes from the fluorescent lights. She wonders what his story is. Is he an underachiever who just wasn't cut out for the college track? What does he want out of life?

She asks for cigarettes, and then throws in a pack of Juicyfruit. She is sure that her fair, freckled face has turned a hectic red; under the heavy down parka she can feel the prickling of sweat where she recently shaved her armpits and legs. But the kid just hands her her Winstons, and makes change without looking up.

She starts the car, and punches the lighter again. She'll just smoke one here in the peace of the station. The car is facing west, so she can watch the last colors of the day wash away. The horizon is gold, topped by candy-corn orange and an unearthly blue. Behind her, the moon must be coming up.

Turning and Turning

Professor Marvel, that old humbug, has fooled Dorothy into believing that in his crystal ball he has seen Auntie Em clutching her broken heart, longing to see her again; Dorothy has swept Toto up in her arms and hurried back to the farmhouse. A storm is coming up, rattling the fenceposts and hurling tumbleweeds down the dusty roads. When she gets back to the house, there's no one around, and she can hardly hear her own cries over the roar of the wind. A twister is spinning on the near horizon. She runs to the storm cellar and pulls at the door, but it's jammed, or locked from inside. Back at the house, when she opens the screen door, the wind tears it right off its hinges.

Darkness has fallen in the living room. When he turns on the lamp beside the sofa, his daughter doesn't seem to notice. The house is turning and turning now, cows and boats and neighbors sailing past the window.

What If He Knew?

The cigarette is impossibly good. The smoke opens her lungs, clears out her veins, helps her see better in the gathering dark. She had forgotten how good this is.

The gas station kid comes walking toward her car. He is loose-limbed and skinny, in a gray sweatshirt and greasy jeans. He ought to wear more in this cold. Through the half-open window he says, "Got a light?" She can't see his eyes under the cap.

She looks toward the office. "Don't you have matches in there?"

He smiles. "I prefer a car lighter."

She punches it in.

"I can watch the pumps and the register from here." He says this in response to a question she hasn't asked. He leans back against the fender, his butt just in front of the side mirror. She doesn't step out, or invite him to sit in the car. She's just being nice, giving him a light. She flicks her ash outside the car window. If he wants to do his teenage cool-guy dance, that's his business.

What if he knew that she has two kids and a husband at home? He doesn't have to know.

A Wounded Animal

After putting his daughter to bed in her own little room down the hall, after another nightcap and a long stare out the window at the empty driveway, he lies down on the sofa to wait. He falls asleep. He dreams of salmon as big as trombones, leaping from fast-running water in perfect little rainbows.

Then he hears a sound—a whimpering cry that seems

to come from offstage somewhere. He begins to awaken, and wonders — was that just part of his dream? But then he hears it again. It's like something is just outside in the yard, a wounded animal. He hauls himself up and fumbles to the window, but there's nothing out there, just a scatter of light on snow. He closes the drapes and goes down the dark hall to their bedroom, keeping a hand on the wall. By the green glow of the nightlight he sees that the baby is peaceful.

Maybe that noise was something in his dream after all. He has never put much stock in dreams. He gets a glass of water from the bathroom tap, knowing that he will be dehydrated in the morning. Then he hears the cry again, and realizes — of course — that it's coming from his daughter's room.

She is writhing in her bedclothes and moaning, "No, no, no." He turns on the bedside lamp and awakens her. "Honey, honey, it's all right."

It is not all right. She will not tell him what she was dreaming. She will not allow him to leave. He says, "Want me to sleep here with you?" She nods, sniveling. He kicks off his shoes and climbs in beside her, still in his button-down shirt and dress pants from the day before. In the crook of his arm, she is asleep in seconds. He knows that the boy will be awake and crying soon. He listens to the furnace laboring under the house.

What Makes the Hottentot So Hot?

The gas station kid finishes his cigarette and lingers by the car. He makes a few remarks about the cold. She can tell that he's trying not to sound like some jerkwater high school kid, and it makes her feel for him. She is only seven or eight years older — but she can't help wondering about his mother. Is she at home now, waiting on her baby? Is she disappointed in him? What does she wish for her boy, and how much of her life is mortgaged to that wish?

She keeps her silence, and finally the kid mumbles something about taking care of things in the station. He shambles back toward the office without thanking her for the light. He's got a pigeon-toed walk. She punches in the lighter again, and pulls another cigarette from the pack.

By now the only light is the garish brightness of the office. When the lighter pops up, she looks at the cigarette in her fingers, then tosses it out the window, unlit. She puts the car in gear and heads for the highway. One sign says West, Ann Arbor; the other says East, Detroit. If she goes away from the city, there will be so much less light pollution. It will be like driving into a black velvet box.

Hearts Will Never Be Practical

Before long, with his daughter's little head limp against his shoulder, he loses all feeling in his arm. But he doesn't try to move her. He wants to stay awake, to hear his daughter's breathing, to listen for his wife's return. She says they should never lie down to sleep with their kids: it encourages a bad habit of dependency. He listens to the bedside clock flip each new minute over.

They should have lived together longer before marriage. But his parents couldn't stand it that they lived together at all, even for the few months after she dropped out of college and stayed with him at the little off-campus apartment. When they planned to visit his family for a vacation, his father made it clear that they would not share a bed under *his* roof. So they did not make that visit. He could be just as stubborn as his old man. But it was too painful, month after month, to think of his mother wanting to see him, wanting them reconciled. They might as well be married.

He should have made sure that she stayed in school—or that she took some classes, at least, even after she got pregnant. But she didn't see the point. They wouldn't be in New York long. How was she going to keep up with classes when she had a baby at home? They couldn't afford day care, and this was a crucial time for him at work. His father had helped him get this job, and he had to prove he could hack it. There would be time for her to go back to school soon enough—as soon as he got his feet on the ground.

The transfer to Detroit meant starting all over again, with a different boss and new expectations. He knew that things weren't the same for her—how could they be? Kids and work: you couldn't focus on your partner the way you once did. Their sex life dwindled. But you had to be realistic. He thought the daughter was a blessing: she gave them a new shared concern, something to talk about, a reason they belonged together. And the son: well, they didn't want to have an only child. Only children miss out on so much.

Is there another man? He doesn't think so. But where the hell does she *go* on these evenings? At first he asked, of course; and she accounted for her errands, and brought back the appropriate purchases. Every morning he offered to pick things up on his way home, so she wouldn't have to go out later; but every afternoon she discovered something they needed. It was probably just a phase. It would change when the baby was less demanding, and of course when the kids started going off to school.

Hearts will never be practical, the Wizard told the Tin Man, until they can be made unbreakable. The Tin Man wanted one anyway.

His arm is now completely asleep, and tingling painfully. He moves it ever so carefully out from under his daughter's head, watches her stir and settle, then slips out of her bed and turns off the lamp.

She has driven past Jackson and Ann Arbor. There hasn't been a highway sign for a while; she could be halfway across the state by now. There is nothing in the world beyond her headlights.

Then, rounding an uphill turn, she sees the moon again, a white sickle punched out of black construction paper. How can that be, if she is still driving west? She knows how: the moon has passed its apex, and is setting now.

The boy is still sleeping. In the kitchen, the father turns on just the range light, finds the bottle of scotch and a glass, and sits at the table. He wants to put on some music, the Stones, *Let It Bleed*; but, as the album notes say, "This music should be played LOUD." He takes his bottle into the living room, where he parts the drapes and stands at the window for a minute. Then he puts on his shoes and steps outside.

It's cold, and he is wearing nothing over his wrinkled dress shirt, but he doesn't care. He bends down to settle the bottle into the snow on the little front stoop. His breath plumes out in front of him. Across the street, the Mitchells' porch light burns. He steps out into the snow, his wingtips crunching with every step. Under the one bare tree of their little front yard, he drops to his knees.

When she steps back into the house, there is just enough pale light through the drapes to make out his sleeping body on the couch. She is tired, so tired, but she has never felt more awake.

"Hi, Mommy!" Their daughter is standing at the entrance to the living room, wearing only a t-shirt and panties. He shouldn't let her sleep like that. The little girl goes to the window and finds the cord to the drapes. This must be something she just learned. She looks at her father, comatose on the couch. She looks at her mother, as if to say Now? Her mother nods, and morning floods the room.

She has never seen this room before. The dust on the bookshelves, the knickknacks, the walls disappearing in corners. They will talk. There will be tears. Why couldn't she stay in Oz?

THE BAT

When one of her students makes an error in class, it causes Penny an actual physical pain, somewhere in her chest. Not a serious pain — it's more like hitting her funny bone — but it makes her wince, all the same. She tries not to show it. She has learned not to say "no" to these students, not to correct their errors for them. Instead, she repeats the incorrect sentence, with an interrogative lilt and a slight emphasis on the error — "We *doesn't* have chicken today?" — in the hope that the mistaken speaker will catch his own error.

It hurts because she loves the language so much. Growing up, back in Wisconsin, she went every Sunday to hear the sermons of her father, a Lutheran minister, and marveled at his ability to hold a congregation in his spell simply through the force of words. At the dinner table, he conducted little impromptu spelling bees for her and her older sister, and when she got one wrong she felt the weight of his disappointment on her shoulders like a sack of something moist and ungainly, something hard to spell, like sorghum. When Tomo says, with a hopeful face, "We *does* have chicken today?" she winces.

This is her first teaching experience — a ten-week immersion, four hours a day. Her students are mostly Asian, older than she, and they are all male. They have come to New York, to this brightly lit room in a brownstone on the Upper West Side, to learn the language of international trade. When Penny brings in a poem—just to start the class with something more interesting than grammar drills— they look at her with uncomprehending smiles. They would rather die than be impolite to the young woman with the yellow hair. But she can tell, she thinks, when the smiles are phony. Even a poem chosen for its simplicity, Frost's "Nothing Gold Can Stay," seems to leave them cold. Is it the mere fact that this is a poem, by definition frivolous? Or has she chosen unwisely, bringing to these ambitious entrepreneurs a poem that denies the staying power of gold? They smile frozenly—as if, in the home of a host they hardly know, they have just eaten something revolting.

Except for PJ. "Miss B?" he says. He is the only student who calls her "Miss B," even though she has urged them to use this name, knowing that her actual name would be hard to pronounce. The other students either manage never to use the direct address or they simply say "Miss," as if she were a Victorian governess. But PJ doesn't hesitate. "Miss B?" he says. "What is Eden?"

He pronounces it "E-**den**," with such a stress on the second syllable that for a moment she doesn't know what he's asking. Then she realizes: even in this poem chosen for its brevity and simple language, its presumably universal sentiment about the loss of paradise, there is a world of culture beyond their grasp. So Eden sank to grief.

"Well," she says, seeing that her other eleven students care not a whit about Eden, "Perhaps we'll get to that later." PJ offers a disappointed smile.

PJ Huang is the kind of student she imagined, when she first took this job—open, inquisitive, eager to learn a new culture. She had thought she could give them not just the rudiments of Business English but the whole world implicit in that language, the world of Shakespeare and Lincoln and Emily Dickinson. Only PJ seems to care. After class, when all the others have folded their notebooks, snapped shut their briefcases, and filed out of the room, speaking their own languages in low conspiratorial voices, PJ lingers at her big metal desk. He is taller than most of them, but otherwise similar—dark spiky hair, big black-rimmed glasses, and a wardrobe described by Penny's friend Sally as "Geek Central, Asian Branch"—black pants, black leather shoes, white socks and a white dress shirt, shiny with polyester, short-sleeved for summer.

"Miss B?" he says. She is erasing the blackboard, gathering her books and papers. She nods. "Is now later?"

She stops shuffling her things. "Excuse me?"

He is smiling broadly. "Is now later?"

She doesn't think she gets the joke.

"You say, we get to E-den later. Is now later?"

"Oh!" She laughs. "I meant, later in class sometime."

Judging by the way his smile fades, this isn't enough of an answer. So she adds, "But yes, now is later than when we discussed it. Right?"

"Right," he says. He doesn't look convinced. He stands there for a moment, and she returns to gathering her papers, giving him his chance to leave.

"Don't you wonder what they're like sexually?" says Sally. It's Friday afternoon, and they're having their ritual drink at The Blue Parrot. Penny finds this below-the-street-level bar too dark and smoky for an afternoon drink; she wants light and air at the end of her week. Sally tells her she's being

Midwestern. Sally, who arrived (from Ohio) six months earlier than she did, is an expert on all things New York. "It's not dark and smoky," she says, "it's just a bar. This is what a bar is, in our country. Repeat after me: b-a-r, bar."

At least it's air conditioned. Penny had no idea that New York could be so tropical. Her classroom is suffocating—but the students don't seem to mind. Maybe they're used to this kind of weather.

"So don't you wonder?" Sally says over scotch and water. "I mean, it's like you've got this classroom full of International Coffees. Don't you want to taste some?"

"No!" says Penny, laughing. "They're my students!"

"Exactly! It's verboten, right? Doesn't that make it sexier?" This is a conversation the two of them have been having ever since they met, ten weeks ago, in the seedy little lobby of their building, where the mailboxes are. That was Penny's third day in the city, and already she was eager for a friend, even if Sally didn't seem like a natural soulmate. Sally has big red hair and favors clothing with predator prints. Her first conversational gambit was "So, what do you find sexy?" Penny's response—the moment in "Rebecca" when Olivier kisses his fingers and presses them to the forehead of Joan Fontaine—made Sally laugh so hard that she almost wet her leopardskin pants.

Penny does not mention PJ. Mr. Waddington, founder and proprietor of The School for International Adventure, has made it clear that there is to be no fraternizing with the students. He is a tall, dour man with his thinning gray hair slicked straight back, and she, for the moment, is his only employee. The School for International Adventure keeps a low overhead. When he has enough students to make a class fly, he calls an employment agency for someone like Penny—a liberal arts graduate, new to the city, ready to work for next to nothing. On her first day, he gave her a book full of grammar drills and made it clear that she was replaceable: hundreds of Pennys arrive in New York every week. "I pay you to teach them English," he said. "Their private lives, and yours, should remain just that—private."

That night, she indulges in another Friday ritual: a bubble bath and a Harlequin. Back in Kenosha, she never took baths. She was too busy, it took too long, the bathroom she shared with her sister was seldom unoccupied. After a certain age, she didn't want to be in there when Maxine came buzzing through—Maxine the beautiful, the princess, the egg with two yolks. Penny knew that she was herself not unattractive—but when Max was in the room suddenly her eyes were too small, her thighs were too big. Penny competed by not competing. She wore her dusty blond hair in a straight shoulder-length cut; she dressed in jeans, or—now that she had to look nice for work—a rotation of straight skirts and sensible sweaters. She never wore perfume or jewelry. Her boyfriends, in both high school and college, were serious boys who sang with her in the choir, boys who were going to work in the family business. She dated one of them, a sweet, dull fellow named Ben, during the year after graduation, when she was living at home, working at the college library, waiting for her life to begin. She thought about the Peace Corps, just for the adventure—but Maxine, beautiful Max, was getting married that summer, and Penny just had to be there to help plan the wedding. When, the following spring, Maxine gave birth to a baby boy, Penny surprised everyone—including herself—by announcing that she was moving to New York. She knew this would upset her father—and that he wouldn't say so out loud.

Now, on the far reaches of Morningside Heights, the main feature of her dingy little two-room apartment is a clawfoot bathtub that sits in a corner of the kitchen. It is her favorite conversation piece, when she speaks on the phone with her parents or friends back home: "The bathtub is in the kitchen!" Kooky New York! She doesn't mention the cockroaches, the uncleanable little broomcloset that houses the toilet, or the absence of natural light. Instead, the story is that she lives above a Hungarian bakery, that she can walk (twenty minutes) to work, and that she has a bath-tub — go figure!--in her kitchen. She doesn't add that when she bathes out in the open like that—even though the kitchen is not large — she feels more naked, somehow. Her thighs feel bigger.

But on Friday nights, she tries to make a virtue of ne-cessity. She doesn't have a TV, and it's too early for bed. It's too hot to sleep, anyway. In this little fourth-floor apart-ment with windows on just one side, there's no cross-ven-tilation. On weekend nights, when the street noise is louder and later than usual—is every car in the city re-quired to blast its music? — there's no use even trying to sleep. Therefore, a cool bath and a Harlequin. She never read this stuff in college; she was too busy with real books, with her thesis on The Invisible Woman in the Novels of Ford Madox Ford, which won her honors and the high-est praise of Dr. Dunwoody. But now, in New York — why not? She has a bathtub in her kitchen. She teaches Asian men that we doesn't have chicken today. She might as well relax with the adventures of Rowena Thornehill, the English spinster whose humdrum life is transformed by a noble savage. When Rowena is in a fix, she is always *superb*. Under the bare fluorescent light of the kitchen, the pulpy pages curl.

Monday after class, PJ lingers at her desk again. He has this trick of just appearing there, while she is gathering her worksheets, so that when she looks up, suddenly there he is. "You know," he says, "what means PJ?"

"What means PJ?" she says, still sorting papers.

"Yes!" he says, and waits.

This can't be bad. They're still in the classroom. It will help his English. "No," she says, "what does it mean?"

"Pajama!" he says, practically shouting, and bursting into laughter. "PJ mean pajama!"

She can see that he's expecting a response, so she laughs too. Is this his idea of a joke? Or could his name actually be Pajama? She remembers the poor kids in Faulkner named Montgomery Ward and Wallstreet Panic. She tries to laugh in the right way. He says, "Bye, Miss B!" and walks off.

What makes PJ so forward, so unlike the rest of her students? Mr. Waddington had told her that Asian men would not be likely to speak up, especially in the presence of a Western woman. When she tries, nonetheless, to get them to talk about their jobs, she gets a deeper silence than usual. They all look down at their desks. But PJ's hand shoots up, and he starts riffing on the beauties of free enterprise. He has apparently made a bundle in some kind of import-export business. "Show me da money!" he shouts. "Show me da money!" The other students laugh, and it takes her a moment to realize that he is quoting from a movie.

Walking back to her apartment in the heat and glare of the late afternoon, through the grimy, litter-strewn streets that lead to her nondescript block, her mind drifts to the cool, clean feeling of winter back home. When you went for a walk, on a bright afternoon, you would see your breath

rising in front of you in a reassuring plume. In the neat suburban yards, you would see tracks in the snow, leading off
into the woods, and wonder what made them.

* * *

Saturday is Laundry Day. This is one of the things she likes
least about New York — having to haul her soiled clothing out
in public, where anyone can see. Not that her basket is full
of kinky lingerie — her underthings are cotton, slightly blue,
thanks to many washings — but she still hates displaying herself this way, in front of all these people she has never met.
So when she opens her apartment door, a big plastic basket
full of whites in her arms, and there he is, standing in the dim
light of her fourth-floor hallway, she is less than pleased.

"PJ! What are you doing here? You scared my eyebrows
off!" This is weird. He didn't call ahead of time, or buzz
at the downstairs intercom to get in; he is just here, and it
looks as if he has been standing here for a while. Of course
it's easy to have someone let you in downstairs — but why
didn't he knock? What is he doing here in the first place?
She hasn't bothered putting in her contacts, because her
eyes are tired, so everything is a little fuzzy.

When she tries to pull the door shut behind her while
balancing the big laundry basket under her chin, he steps
forward and says, "I help!" As if he has come with just this
mission in mind. He takes hold of the basket and gives it a
friendly tug, but Penny does not let go.

PJ repeats, "I help!" and pulls again. He seems to think
that she has simply misunderstood, that she is just trying
to find her balance. But she has no intention of letting go.
They do an awkward pas de deux in the narrow hallway,
until Penny pulls so hard that she bumps into the wall,

stumbles, and loses her grip. PJ is still tugging, too; the basket lurches up between them and its contents go flying.

"Damn it, PJ! What are you *doing?*"

"Solly! Solly!" He releases the basket, now half-empty, and scrambles to pick up the strewn clothing. "Solly!" he keeps repeating. She rushes to grab a pair of panties at her feet, and doing so tips the rest of the basket over her shoulder, spilling more of her unmentionables. Her face is burning. "Solly!" he says. She drops the empty basket and collapses on the stairs behind her, on the verge of tears — and all she can do is laugh.

He seems puzzled for a moment, like an infant in the second after a fall, not knowing whether to scream or giggle, and then he starts laughing, too. "I solly!" he says again.

"I sorry?" she says. She can't help it.

He looks confused again. Then a light dawns on his face, and he makes a slight bow. "I *am* solly," he says.

"Good. Listen, PJ — "

"We have saying," he says.

"We have saying?"

"Yes. We have saying. I translate." She can tell that he has prepared this little discourse. "Saying is, 'Feces' — feces, yes?"

"Yes." There's no stopping him now.

"'Feces will be excreted.'" He smiles. "You get?"

It takes her a second. She's pleased with his use of the future tense. "I think so. The truth will — come out?"

"Yes!" He beams. "Feces will be excreted!"

She doesn't know what this saying has to do with anything, but she is starting to think that maybe she shouldn't expect things to make too much sense. PJ seems to have completed his little speech, and she has laundry to do. She allows him to walk with her as far as the laundromat, at her street corner, and then, when she stops at the door and he just lingers, apparently ready to go in with her, she says, "It was nice of you to come by, PJ." She says it in her clearest Game-over tone, as if it were the end of a date and she were saying "I'll call you." PJ just stands there. Is she not being clear enough? This tone always worked with Wisconsin boys. He stands there. She can't just turn her back on him; he might follow her in. "I have to do my laundry now, PJ." He nods. "I'll see you in class, OK? Don't forget that worksheet on irregular verbs."

Suddenly his face gets strange—as if it doesn't know what emotion he feels. His eyes seem to run through several possibilities, like a computer trying out combinations. She sees, for the first time, that the skin around his eyes is smooth: he is younger than the other students, perhaps only a few years older than she.

"I go now," he says. "Worksheet, yes." He turns on his heel and walks quickly away.

In class the next week he is quiet, and she avoids calling on him. He's probably just embarrassed; a little time will solve it. At the Blue Parrot on Friday, she can't help mentioning this episode. Sally is fascinated.

"Ooh," she says, "Do you think he's pissed? Maybe you insulted his ancestors or something. Do you think he needs to, like, save face now? What if he commits, like, a ritual disembowelment? How cool would *that* be?"

So much for confiding in Sally. Penny changes the subject to her friend's latest conquest—the guy with the pet ferret, which really shouldn't be illegal. They're cleaner than dogs, and you don't have to walk them.

As the course nears its end, she wonders if she has helped her students at all. She can see no change in their writing, which is still littered with errors of verb tense and number, and (except for PJ) they continue to speak only when called on, to garble the simplest constructions. Again and again, she experiences that little pain in her chest. She must be a terrible teacher.

She has been thinking, vaguely, about going home. Who is she trying to fool? This isn't her kind of place. The heat and the noise are ridiculous; she hasn't slept well since May. She's not going to get a real job without another degree. When she asks Mr. Waddington about the next class, he just says he's working on it. Will he even want her to continue? She can't bear to ask. Her parents, on the phone, never apply any overt pressure — but she knows they would love for her to come back home. She could probably find a job back at the college, shelving books, just for a while, as she thinks about graduate school. Her mother says Ben was asking about her at church last week. Her only real obligation is the course, soon to be completed. Oh, she has a lease — but she could find someone to take it over: in Manhattan, even a little dunghole like hers would go quickly. Once the course is done, she has no idea how she's going to afford it, anyway. There is nothing to hold her here.

Monday after class, PJ lingers at her desk. She hasn't even looked up; she just knows he's there. Every light on the dashboard is on. She doesn't want to encourage him. She doesn't want to break the rules. She doesn't want to provoke a ritual disembowelment.

"Miss B?" he says finally. "You eat dinner?"

How could she say no?

They take the subway downtown. There's one good thing about the subway at moments like this: it's so loud and distracting, you don't have to talk. PJ has simply taken the lead. They must be headed for Chinatown. Penny has been there just once—her first week in New York, before work began, when she was trying to see all the famous neighborhoods. She knows it's not just Chinese anymore: once you get beyond the tourist facades, the red dragons and golden palaces, there is every kind of Asian immigrant and refugee known to this country. She realizes, to her dismay, that she doesn't even know what nationality PJ is. That isn't her job, of course: her job is simply to teach them basic English. But this is embarrassing. In the insufficient air conditioning of the racketing subway car, she is aware of a bead of sweat running down her side, rib by rib.

She follows his lead, out into the early evening. There is still plenty of daylight, but shadows are deepening, the lights of commerce growing brighter by the minute. She can't help being rapt by it all. People are sitting on the steps of buildings, standing in groups of three and four on the sidewalk, hovering around food venders on the corners—roasted nuts, fried pockets of dough containing strange vegetables, bits of meat on little sticks. It's all so different from her own neighborhood. Up there, no one lingers on the street; everyone is hurrying to get somewhere else. And there are so many more words down here. BREAKFAST SERVED ANY TIME ALL DAY. IF YOU LIVED HERE, YOU'D BE HOME NOW. NEW YORK LOTTO: HEY, YOU NEVER KNOW.

Of course, many of the signs are in Chinese. At least, she assumes it's Chinese. She wants to believe that they are not as tacky and commercial as the signs in English. She invents her own translations. Wise Man Saves at Good Fortune Bank. You Will Meet Handsome Stranger at Panda Inn.

"When is next class?" he asks, after they order. The walls of the little restaurant are such a sulfurous green they hurt her eyes. She tries not to look.

"Tomorrow morning," she says. Why would he have to ask?

"No," he says. "*Next* class." He makes a rolling arm motion towards the future. "*Next* class."

"Oh," she says, "the next *course*?" He nods. "I don't know," she says. "There may not be another course. I mean, I may not be teaching it."

He looks concerned. Does he want to take another course? "I mean," she adds, "I may be going home."

"Oh!" he says. "New York not home?"

"No!" She laughs. "Can't you tell? Most of the time, I can't stand New York." She takes a drink of water. "The thing is, I can't stand Wisconsin either." She has never actually spoken either of these sentences before. "I mean, it's *nice* and all, it's where I'm from, you know, but—I just can't go back there. My father would want to pay for everything, and I'd have to move back in with them, and I—it's just—I can't afford to stay here, either. You know?"

Could she *be* any less articulate? Their food arrives, and she is glad for the distraction—the neat, efficient waiter, the steaming platters, the perfect mound of rice.

They begin eating. His dish seems to be something crunchy. Didn't he order quail? Do you eat the bones? She has a plate full of something so stringy it keeps sliding off her chopsticks. She always asks for chopsticks, and always wishes for a fork.

They say little until the food is gone. He doesn't seem to mind the silence.

"So, PJ. Where are you from?"

"Brooklyn," he says.

"No, I mean—where are you from originally? "

He takes from his pocket a marble, deep blue, with tiny continents painted on in green. Holding it between finger and thumb out over the little table, he points with a nubby fingernail to North America.

"U. S. A.!" he says. "U. S. A.!"

Then he hands the marble to her—and she doesn't know what to do. She shouldn't accept it—but she doesn't want to make a scene. She slips it in her breast pocket.

After a pause he says, "You know what means bat?"

Is he talking about baseball?

He holds his hands a certain distance apart. "Fly in night. Bad eyes."

"Of course," she says.

"You like?"

She laughs. "Bats creep me out. You know, we have this whole mythology about bats—I guess because they're nocturnal, and they're black, and they have those sharp little teeth." Penny shudders in spite of herself.

"I am bat," he says.

"Excuse me?"

"I am bat. We say, when person go—goes—from home, he is bat. Bat is not bird, yes? Is also not—like mouse?"

"A rodent?"

"Yes. Not bird, not rodent. I leave from home, stay America, not live like my people. Not bird. But also not rodent." Holding his hands back to back, he makes quick little flapping gestures. "Bat."

The check arrives, and, after her brief protest, PJ pays it. Then he walks her outside.

The heat and humidity have eased: it's a balmy, delightful summer night. People are out strolling, eating Italian ices. PJ reaches a street corner a step ahead of Penny, stops, and points at something in the distance, down the open avenue. When she sees it, she cannot help catching her breath. Thirty blocks away, brilliant against a blue-black sky, there's the Empire State Building, top floors lit up red, white, and blue.

They walk quietly to the mouth of the subway. She has been dreading this moment. What will he want from her now? She thinks, *Be superb*.

"I take E train," he says, polite as any Wisconsin farm-boy. He makes a slight bow. "Good night, Miss B."

On the phone, Sally says, "He is totally playing you, girl." Penny finds a reason not to meet her for the weekly drink.

In the final days of class, PJ is quiet. He seems to have done his homework—he is always ready when called on—but he raises no questions or digressions. Every day after class she expects that he will be lingering at her desk. She shuffles her papers as usual, waiting for the rest of the class to clear out—and when she looks up, she finds that the room is empty.

The final class meeting arrives. She had thought that she'd be relieved. No more awkward silences, no more dis-appointment of her cultural efforts, no more pains in her chest. No more weirdness with PJ. She has made her brave big-city effort, and thank God it's over.

Instead, when the students shuffle out of the room for the last time, what she feels is a sudden hollowness, a shortness of breath. They've hardly begun! Tomo is still having agreement problems! Suddenly, sinkingly, she can't bear the thought that she won't be seeing them again.

PJ stays behind.

"You look bad," he says. "Unhappy."

What can she say?

"You go Brooklyn," he says.

She decides to take it as a question. "No, I've never been to Brooklyn."

"You go," he says.

It's odd: she expected Brooklyn to look different, somehow. It has always seemed distant and foreign to her—beyond the bridges and the river, beyond the pale. When she comes up the subway stairs into the sticky afternoon light, it looks and feels just like her neighborhood in New York.

In Manhattan, she corrects herself: Brooklyn is New York, too.

The address he gave her is on an ordinary street—Korean grocery, Greek pastry, turbaned cabbies at the taxi stand. He told her that he had an opportunity for her. "Show me da money!" he said with a laugh. He asked if she was interested in giving private lessons. Immediately, her heart clung to the possibility. Maybe, with the right contacts, she can set up her own little business. She already has the grammar drills, and there is hardly anything else the school provides—except for tax requirements, which she might now be able to finesse. Perhaps, in her own lessons, she can go beyond Business English; it can be true cultural exchange.

Still, she doesn't know quite what to expect at this address PJ has provided. Was it vague because his English wasn't adequate to the description, or because he meant it to be so?

The first voice that comes through the staticky intercom

is incomprehensible—a woman's voice, she thinks—but is that English? No, she has no idea what the language is. She announces her name. Surely PJ told them she was coming? When she asked why he wasn't coming with her, he said he had to work. There is a pause on the other end. Have they given up on her? Then the same voice says: "Yes?" She offers her name again, and says that PJ sent her. The door to the building buzzes, and she enters the dark foyer.

No air conditioning here, either, no lobby to speak of—just a narrow staircase and a smell of garlic and spices that Penny cannot name. When she gets to the third floor landing, 3D is open, and there in the doorway stands a dark-haired little Asian girl in a cotton pinafore.

"You're Miss B?" she says.

Penny nods.

"Come in, please."

Penny steps into a dark apartment with no entrance hall. It takes a moment for her eyes to adjust. This place is even smaller than her own—just one medium-sized room, with a galley kitchen on one side and a large bed on the other, a sofa against the third wall facing two windows with the shades pulled down. Maybe this is their way of trying to keep it cool. If there is a bathroom, she doesn't see where it would be. The furnishings are plain but perfectly neat.

"Have a seat," the girl says, gesturing to the sofa. She couldn't be older than seven or eight, but her manner is that of a little adult.

"Are your parents home?" Penny finally asks—although the answer can only be no.

"My mother is out—doing the shopping." The girl's English is perfect, unaccented.

"I can come back some other time," Penny says, moving back toward the door.

"No. Have a seat, please." She gestures to the sofa again. "Would you like some tea? Earl Grey? Oolong?"

Hot tea on a day like this? "Um, Oolong would be fine." She sits, and the girl turns to the stove, lights a match, puts a kettle on. She pours loose tea from a tin into a perforated metal ball that she places in a blue and white china pot. Then she turns to Penny.

"Did my father tell you what we want?"

Her father? Penny shakes her head.

"We want my mother to learn English."

The tumblers are falling in place so slowly that Penny still can't speak.

"She says she doesn't want to learn. She says she's fine. She's so stubborn. She's been here five years, and still, when she goes to a store, she points at things, as if she was some dumb tourist, she holds out her money so the storekeeper can just take the right amount. She says the Korean grocery guy doesn't speak English, either, and he still likes her money. She doesn't know: when someone speaks English to him, he speaks English. She's so dumb."

The kettle whistles, and the girl fills the pot. "I don't mean dumb like a retard. I mean dumb like a mule."

They must share the bed. Maybe the bathroom is out in the hall. Everything is so neat.

"So," she says, "Will you teach her? I used to try, but she won't listen to me. He says you're a great teacher. He brought me a poem you gave them."

Penny's heart lifts. "Does your father live here too?" She knows the question is rude, but the girl seems ready for anything.

"No." She arranges little blue cups on a lacquered tray. "We don't know where he lives. They don't speak. Once in a while, when he knows she won't be here, he comes by. He knows when she is out. I think he watches." Penny can't help looking towards the street. With the blinds drawn, the afternoon light turns the windows into faintly glowing tablets.

The girl goes on. "He left when I was three. Almost as soon as we got here." She pours the tea, brings the tray over to the sofa, and holds it out to Penny. "Will you teach her?"

The whole thing is outrageous. First, he ingratiates himself with her in class. Was that all just a ruse, to win her over for this? He tells her that story about the bat—omitting some crucial facts, obviously—in order to win her sympathy. He sets her up with this errand, suggesting that it's all in *her* interest. And then, to top it all, he has the nerve to try to manipulate her with this poor little girl, his own abandoned daughter? Just because he feels guilty? Does he think he's going to get all the credit? No way will she do this.

Just as she reaches for the little blue cup, there is the sound of a key at the door. It opens, and an Asian woman enters, wearing a simple summer dress, arms full of grocery bags. She stops and looks quizzically at the stranger in her apartment. She might be just three or four years older than Penny. Even in the darkness of this room, it is clear how tired she is.

The little girl sets down the tea tray and says, "Ma!"—and then a flood of clicking consonants, vowels stretched in strange and singsong rhythms. Penny thinks she hears the words "Miss B."

The woman puts down the groceries. Then she starts speaking, in little staccato bursts. She sounds exasperated. The words ricochet off the walls. The girl replies. When she talks like this, she looks just like a little PJ. Penny looks dumbly from speaker to speaker.

Finally, the woman shrugs, and turns to face her.

Penny stands. She can feel her future stretching out before her like a sheet of white paper.

She holds out her hand.

"Hello," she says.

Extremities

Patrick and Melvin are sitting at the Village Tap after a particularly stubborn Roto-Rooter job. That pipe must have been clogged since 1957. It's another gray February afternoon. As usual, they are talking about sex.

"Hey," says Melvin, "I wouldn't kick *her* out of bed for eating crackers. Know what I mean?"

He is talking about Kathy Mandeville, and Patrick knows what he means. Kathy has always been cute, and now the word is that she's showing some skin again—on her ring finger. Melvin goes on.

"I always thought Eddie Mandeville was the north end of a southbound horse. Know what I mean?"

Patrick knows. It's a small town, Cransford, Vermont. They all went to school together, and Kathy has been working at the hardware store ever since. Patrick has stayed out of there lately.

"So," says Melvin, "You still shootin' blanks?"

Patrick puts down his bottle. "I am *not* shooting blanks. It just hasn't—happened yet, that's all." He scrapes the dish on the bar for the last shreds of peanut. "You can't rush these things."

Melvin nods. "Ain't it a bitch? Back in the day, it seemed like if I just *looked* at Marie the wrong way, she got pregnant." He and Marie have three kids, all in their teens. "Hey," he points the bottle at his bearded chin, "maybe you and Laurie need a little help from the Melvinator."

"We're doing fine, thank you very much. Keep the Melvinator in your pants. We just have to keep trying."

"Yeah? How's your NPW these days?"

Melvin is a statistics guy. NPW is Nookie Per Week. There's also the OPE, fondly known as the Opie: that's how many times, in a given sexual episode, you achieve the big O. According to Melvin, you ought to keep the ratio around 3:1. Lately, Patrick has been flatlining. But once should be enough, he figures, if he puts his heart into it. Melvin would question his understanding of anatomy.

Patrick checks the clock. "I gotta go." He puts a five on the bar. "See you tomorrow."

Outside, it's already dark, and Patrick almost falls on the ice next to his pickup.

Fact is, he's not convinced that Laurie is trying very hard. She's thirty-five, after all; it's not like she has forever. But it's hard to pry her away from her work. She is an editor of scientific texts—work that would seem ideal, because she can do it at home. But she always has some impossible deadline, some crazy number of pages to do by Friday; it never lets up. Patrick tells her that manmade deadlines are always flexible; they're just her boss's way of getting more work out of her. The real deadlines are the ones we get from our bodies.

She may not be trying, but he certainly is. Three times a week, at the crucial moment, he shouts, "Baby! Baby! Baby!" If she wants to hear this as a term of endearment, let her.

Patrick Henry Hobsbawm is not your average butt-crack plumber. He keeps his shirt tucked in. He is the only plumber in town—unless you count Melvin, his doofus assistant. Patrick never gets drunk on weekdays. He stays awake in church. Sometimes he watches public TV. When the Fire and Rescue guys are stopping traffic on Main Street to collect spare change in buckets, he always gives. And not just a showy handful of pennies: we're talking folding money. He gets up early every damn day, puts on the coffee, and takes Tess for her walk.

This is not as easy as it sounds. Like the next morning, when it's five below zero and Tess is taking her own sweet time. Patrick is used to the daily tour of the bushes and trees; he can deal with the ritual inspection of alien landing spots on the soccer field; he even puts up with a certain amount of lunging after squirrels. Tess never tires of going after squirrels. Sometimes he takes her hunting, just so she can chase the little suckers. Although she's getting on in years, she is still strong enough to knock a man down with a single leap—all in fun, of course. If he needs to, Patrick can calm her with a hand on her neck. But on days like today, when the only thing he can see through the crease between his beanie and his scarf is the cloud of his own breath, he has only so much patience. Tess has been squatting for ages. High in the bare branches of the maples, enormous black birds are fussing about something indecipherable.

"Come on, Tessie! Squeeze, for Christ's sake!" They shouldn't still be giving her that Mighty Dog stuff. If it was up to him, she would have been on the dry food for years, and now she'd be getting the older dog formula. But

Laurie won't hear of it. Laurie refuses to accept that Tess is no longer a puppy. "How would *you* like to be put on the Older Guy formula?" she says. When she puts it that way, he shuts up.

Tess isn't his dog, after all. Sometimes he has to remind himself. She has been Laurie's for eleven years—eight years longer than he has been. Patrick knows, in the end, that he has no claim. Just as he knows that Laurie can't really *see* Tess anymore, not as Tess is now. For Laurie, Tess will always be a golden puppy, romping through a park like this one, terrorizing the squirrels, leaping into the pond to retrieve a stick again and again, until she has gnawed it to splinters.

Just now, the pond is frozen solid, and no one is romping. When Tess finally produces something and turns to sniff it, Patrick pulls from his pocket one of the plastic sacks he always brings on these walks. This new town law is a pain—but Tess likes the park so much better than the fenced-in back yard of his little house. They lean over the little steaming pile together.

Looking up, he sees it. The long blue box lying on its side. For a moment he stares, then straightens up and swears softly into his scarf. There are two Port-a-Potties in this park, and across the way one of them is lying at the foot of the other, flat on its back, like a beached blue whale in the snow.

He and Tess walk over. Naturally, it's the Gents, which always gets more use. A lot of women are reluctant to use these "comfort stations." You wouldn't catch Laurie dead in one even if her eyeballs were turning yellow. Sometimes, just to keep the wear even, Patrick switches the signs. Without opening the door, he knows that he will find it awash in excrement. He loops Tess's leash over a fencepost and tries to set the thing upright, but he should have known better: he immediately tweaks that spot in his lower back. Goddamn kids.

Patrick is the one who got these Port-a-Potties put up in the first place. That was two years ago, when the sheriff padlocked the johns at the old snack bar. They were the only bathrooms in the only park in town, and the town council in its infinite wisdom had decreed that they just weren't safe anymore. Kids were using them for drugs and sex and God knows what-all; the town couldn't afford special security just for the park. So Patrick and Melvin went door to door, taking up a collection. He knew a Port-a-Potty guy who gave them a special deal, provided they take care of the maintenance themselves. Once a week for two years now he has picked up the pump truck at the County Sanitation Department, suctioned out both of these units, hosed them out, refilled the chemical solution, and taken the truck to the waste treatment plant. It's a small price to pay for a decent park.

Back in the truck, with Tess in the passenger seat, he uses the cell to leave a message with Melvin, who will certainly not be awake yet. Then he heads home, and cranks up the Hot New Country. It's Jo Dee Messina, singing "Foolhearted Man." Patrick wails along in falsetto, and Tess starts howling, too.

"Remember to burn that mop when you're done." Melvin is sitting on the fence by the parking lot, watching Patrick swab out the mess. They are both on their lunch break, and they've managed to get the crapper standing again. After that, Melvin is purely an observer. By some freak of chance, the vandals have struck at the optimal moment, just before the weekly visit of the pump truck. They must have been pleased with their handiwork.

"Remember the time we left the flaming sack on the principal's porch?" Melvin laughs. "Man, the look on his face — I'll never forget that. That was just what the dude needed." Melvin's theory is that people don't get pissed off enough. He says that eighty per cent of cancer cases arise from unexpressed anger. His own permanently pissed-off father lived to be a hundred and one.

Laurie says it would be better for everyone concerned if Melvin found a real job of his own; she says this assistant position keeps him from "actualizing himself." Patrick says, "Oh, he's about as actual as I can stand." Seriously, what would Melvin do? He's got five mouths to feed and a mortgage to pay. He urges Patrick to stay out of the baby-making business. "I mean, they're great and all, don't get me wrong, but — *man.*" He says this last word with a whistled exhalation, closing his eyes. "You know what I mean?"

In fact, Patrick knows that for all his talk Melvin is absolutely dedicated to Marie and the kids. He notices, when they're all together for Sunday skating here at the pond, that when Melvin's with his kids there is something different in his laughter. It doesn't depend on jokes or pranks or witticisms; it's nothing like the desperate cackles of the guys on the morning radio show, or the nervous titters of polite conversation. It's something from deep in the chest, the simple pleasure of a father cracking up with his kid.

Patrick keeps mopping. He and Laurie are not married, and this makes him crazy. They met when she was walking Tess in the park, soon after she moved to Cransford. She had broken up with some guy in Burlington, and she was looking for a fresh start, away from the city. It wasn't long before she moved into his little house. Patrick didn't blame her for wanting to get out of that condo. He sure didn't want to spend nights there, and it was stupid to keep driving back and forth all the time, paying two mortgages. Besides, people ought not to live alone. Life is too short. Too many cars on the road contain only a driver, too many items at the Price Chopper are packaged for one person to pop into the microwave and eat in front of the TV. He hates sleeping alone. And there's Tess: that condo was no place for a dog, and one busy person couldn't walk her enough.

There is no external pressure to get married. His parents had both died by the time he was thirty-five; Laurie visits hers, in Florida, just once a year. After all the divorces of the eighties and nineties, people in Cransford have stopped thinking that marriage is such a necessary solution. But still. Patrick can't help thinking that if they just keep *trying*, pregnancy will seal the deal.

"That's just stupid," Laurie says, as they're getting ready for bed. "It's like tipping cows."

Patrick nods, a memory warming his mind—but he doesn't say anything. Laurie has never been amused by his Tales of Wayward Youth. Right now, she is putting on the old flannel nightgown—never a good sign. He always turns the heat down overnight, and she is terribly susceptible to cold. He used to get a kick out of teasing her about the blankets and comforters piled high on her side of the bed. You'd think that maybe she'd want a little human warmth, a little 98 point 6, but no—she said his hands and feet were too cold. Actually, she said his *extremities*. She was always using sixty-four dollar words, correcting his grammar. He told her that he may be dixlexic, but he could make her plumbing work. It was funny at the time. He used to make a big show of warming his feet by the vent. Now, he just climbs into bed, thinking about the park.

The next morning, he puts the coffee on and bundles Tess into the truck for their five-minute ride. The drive is too short to get the heat going, but at least they're not out in that merciless air. In the wan morning light, the whole neighborhood steams. Patrick notices which houses are stirring, sees the blue light of television screens through living room windows.

At the park, he pulls up in the little lot and leaves the engine running, so the cab will be warm when they return. Then he sees that it has happened again. This time it's the Ladies that's down—the one he didn't mop out yesterday. Just looking at it makes his back ache. When he walks Tess past, he can tell from her sniffing that the interior will not be pretty. He and Melvin will have to give up their lunch break again today. It must have been done late, in the darkest, coldest time of the night. What kids are so intent on this?

After walking for ten frigid minutes, they sit in the warm cab for a while. This time of year is just a bitch. It's too damn cold to go hunting. Football season is over, and the Celtics suck again, and it's still months before the Sox begin their annual tease. Tess buries her snout in his side, snuffling for the pocket of his parka. "Oh, you think there's something for you in there?" She makes her little whine, that reedy sound he has come to understand as excitement, not pain. "What makes you think that?" His hand goes to his pocket, and she draws her head back, absolutely still, eyes fixed on the invisible hand. "Ah-ha!" he shouts, pulling forth a dog biscuit. "The magic Milk-Bone!" She snaps it cleanly from his fingers.

Out in the park, there's old Mr. Fromm, the all-weather jogger, bundled up like the Michelin Man, doing his laps. A jet of exhaust rises above his every step. People are strange as hell.

Three days later, the vandals strike again. Only this time, it's not just one of the crappers: both of them, male and female, are lying flat on their backs, perfectly parallel, like a married couple in a bed of white linen. And someone has left a signature: on top of the Gents, coiled up perfectly on the door like something you'd buy in a joke store, there is a fresh human turd.

Even Tess seems surprised. Patrick can't help thinking how cold the kid must have been.

"That's disgusting," says Laurie at dinner, as she serves meatloaf to Melvin. He comes to dinner just once a week, when Marie and the kids are at her mother's. Marie's mother can't stand Melvin.

"Yep," says Patrick, "it was just laying there like nobody's business."

"Or somebody's," says Melvin, and they laugh.

"Lying," says Laurie. "I fail to see the humor. I mean, besides being revolting, it's completely unsanitary."

"Oh, I don't know," says Melvin. "It's so cold out there, I bet all the bacteria was frozen sterile."

"Were," she says. "People are such animals."

"You got that right," says Melvin.

She looks at him sideways. "Oh don't give me that 'state of nature' stuff again."

"Well, you got to admit that the way we live now isn't exactly natural. I mean, for thousands of years people just took care of their needs out in the woods, like all the other animals. They weren't so uptight about it all."

She puts down her fork. "Do you know what the average life expectancy was for a human being in the year 1900?"

"Nope," says Melvin. "But I have a feeling I'm about to find out."

"Forty-five. And I'm talking about this country, not some far-away loin-cloth place. Forty-five. A hundred years ago. And do you know why?"

This must be something she edited recently. Patrick hates it when she puts down her fork.

"They didn't have enough sex?"

She rolls her eyes. "Hygiene. They had livestock living in their houses. They didn't have indoor plumbing. Most people died of infections — simple contagious diseases."

"Well," says Melvin, "at least it was natural. They weren't depending on all these pills and machines to keep them going. All this diet and fitness shit, just to stay alive a few more years." He pats his beer gut. "You know what I always say: live fast, die young, leave a beautiful corpse."

"Oh, so you want to go back to a forty-five year life span? Let's see, that would mean you've got what, two years to go?"

"Nope, that's Patrick. Me, I got three more years to raise hell."

"Who wants coffee?" says Patrick. He knows that the longer this conversation goes on, the lower his NPW will be.

Even though at first he supposed that there must be a crew of vandals, Patrick finds himself thinking of just one kid. The next morning there is nothing amiss in the park, but after Tess does her business they sit in the warm truck longer than usual. Patrick has started bringing his insulated coffee mug, so he can savor it while they watch the light rise, a little bit earlier each day.

There just isn't any evidence of kids having fun. You'd think there would be beer bottles, or cigarette butts, whatever it is they do these days—but there hasn't been anything like that. You'd think, if they were goading each other on, there might be more than that one pile of shit.

He has started imagining this kid. Thirteen or fourteen years old—old enough to stay out really late. Maybe it's not a question of age, if the parents are clueless enough. But the kid would have to be big enough, physically, to knock these things down—or to work out a system for doing it. Patrick imagines this kid—one of those loners, maybe a little overweight, with dark hair and a terribly pale complexion, dressed all in black, with those big ugly shoes.

He looks out over the empty kiddie area—the jungle gym, the monkey bars, the swing set. It's not nearly as impressive as some of the new ones. When he took Melissa to the clinic in Burlington that time, how many years ago, he didn't feel comfortable in the waiting room, so he sat on a bench outside. It was an early spring day, and the kids on recess from the school across the street were swarming the playground, wild with all the months of being caged up indoors. Whose bright idea was it to locate Planned Parenthood right across from a school? The playground bristled with wooden towers and ramparts, bright plastic platforms with ladders and slides and firemen's poles. Patrick sat there feeling drained. It made no sense that he should be so depressed. He knew he couldn't tell Melissa what to do with her body. He knew they weren't ready. It wasn't that he had some deep religious objection. He just didn't see how you could look at a picture of a fetus, all those amazing tiny working parts, and decide it wasn't human. He also knew, with every instinct, that this would be the end for him and Melissa. He has never told Laurie.

When Tess snuffles at the pocket of his parka, he realizes that his coffee has gone cold. Laurie will be wondering where he is.

The next day, both crappers are down again. It's like the kid is timing it so that just when Patrick thinks it's over, he finds a fresh outrage. He is getting tired of this game, tired of the midday mopping. His back hurts. Melvin, sitting on the fence while Patrick mops, says, "Hey, you know what we need? Metal stakes. Know what I mean?"

Of course. There's a provision, with these Port-a-Potties, for just this kind of problem. They rest on wooden skids, and you can basically nail the damn things into the ground. Back when Patrick and Melvin set them up, it didn't seem necessary. Now, all they need is some long metal stakes. This means going to the hardware store.

There's no denying it: Kathy looks good. Melvin goes straight to the counter. "Hey, Kath. How's it goin'?"

"Can't complain."

Patrick smiles and heads for the back room, where they keep the heavy-duty stuff. He was pretty sure, once upon a time, that Kathy was interested in him. But he was with Melissa then. She could have done better than working a cash register—but this was what you did if you had your kids young and you wanted to stay in Cransford. In all the years that he's been coming into the TruValu, she has always been helpful and friendly—even when she was going through hell with Eddie, who gave her two kids and then fell in love with Jack Daniels. There were times when her makeup couldn't disguise the bruises.

Patrick finds eight stakes and hauls them out to the register. Melvin has disappeared.

Kathy rings up his bill. "How's Laurie, Pat?"

"She's good." He fumbles for a credit card. "I seen where Bret was high scorer again last week."

"Yeah, he had a good game. I wish I could get him to concentrate on his homework the way he does on his jump shot." She still has that smile.

Patrick laughs. "Well, you know kids." Where the hell is Melvin?

When he gets back out to the sidewalk, he finds his assistant deep in a spirited conversation about organic farming with Clayton Johnson, the night watchman at the school. They're against it.

Laurie would have given him hell for that "I seen."

It's not easy getting the stakes into the frozen ground at the park. But Patrick doesn't get to use the sledgehammer often. It's going to take some serious muscle to budge these shitboxes now. Melvin sits watching.

"Now, Kathy Mandeville," he says. "There's a fertile-lookin' woman. You know what I mean?"

The next day, pipes start bursting all over town. Patrick is always amazed at how surprised people seem, how clueless they are. It's not like they've never seen this kind of cold: it happens two or three times every winter. And yet here's Mr. Thornton, who still hasn't insulated the plumbing for the mother-in-law cottage he rents to the college kids behind his house; and here's Mrs. Milner, who has once again neglected to shut off the pipes leading to her outdoor faucets. Patrick wonders how some people manage to get through the day without hurting themselves.

But that's all right: it all adds up to more work for a hungry plumber. Besides, Patrick likes fixing things. After replacing the pipes at old Mr. Graebert's place, he notices that the outside door to the mud room isn't closing right, because they added it to the house without laying a foundation; frost has heaved the cheap wooden flooring so that the frame is all out of true. He gives it a temporary fix with a screwdriver, by moving the metal plate where the door meets the frame. Mr. Graebert is amazed and delighted, but Patrick knows that it's no big deal. Come summer, somebody's just going to have to move it back again.

That week Laurie takes her annual trip to Florida, to visit her parents. She plans it for this season every year, and who can blame her? It's a thousand degrees below zero. Alone in their bedroom at night, Patrick piles up the comforters. He's wearing his long johns, and Tess is curled up at his feet. It's late, but he's not sleepy. He reads for a while — a book about baseball — and finally turns out the light.

But he can't get comfortable: his back is still aching. He's never noticed before how lumpy and uneven this old mattress is. After trying every possible position, he lies there stiffly, listening to the joints of the house pop with the cold.

He snaps on the light, and Tess looks up. "Sorry, girl." He throws off the covers and pads to the bathroom. The tile floor is icy. He knows that Laurie keeps some sleeping pills in here somewhere. He starts trying drawers, pawing through lotions and cold medicines and — and — a circular container of little pills, one for each day of the month. At the bottom of a drawer, there are several of them. Several months of his life.

* * *

He pulls on socks, a flannel shirt, jeans, a sweatshirt, a sweater. Tess clambers down from the bed. From a cabinet in the kitchen he grabs a half-empty bottle of Johnny Walker. Boots, scarf, parka, gloves, beanie, keys. "Come on, Tessie. We're going out."

The air knifes into his lungs. The sky is perfectly clear: there's a half-moon, and the stars are tiny white stones. The truck starts up like a charm. He doesn't bother waiting for the heat to kick in, doesn't turn on the radio. There's nobody on the road. The headlights carve out gouges of empty air.

A block away from the park, he leaves the truck on a neighborhood street. With Tess's leash wrapped around his wrist, he can carry the big flashlight in one hand, the bottle in the other. But he doesn't need to turn on the light. He can see that the Port-a-Potties are still standing, silvered by the moon. He and Tess walk over, and he sits down in the snow, his back to the Gents. He doesn't care how wet it is. He doesn't care who the vandal is. He takes a long pull on the bottle, then coughs. The whisky burns, all the way down. Tess lies down in the snow beside him.

"Goddamn her, Tess. God *damn* her. Why would she do that? Why would she fuckin' *do* that?"

He takes another drink. There's no wind; the park is completely still. Aren't there supposed to be night birds, or something?

"She *knows* I want us to have a baby. She said she wanted one, too. But she didn't, did she, Tessie?"

Tess looks up at him. He goes on.

"You know what the worst thing is?" He drinks again. "The worst thing is, she's right."

He starts to laugh. How could he not have seen that?

"How could I not have seen that, Tess?"

For a minute, this is a total crack-up. He can't stop laughing. Then he does.

"But why would she not have *told* me?"

Tess doesn't answer.

Then he sees headlights approaching through the dark neighborhood. They pull into the little parking lot, some fifty feet away, where they stop, and go dark. Patrick can see enough in the moonlight to know that it's a pickup. He doesn't get up. He sets the bottle carefully upright in the snow, takes the flashlight in one hand, and lays the other on Tess's neck.

When the driver opens the door of the truck, the dome light isn't enough for Patrick to make out much. A dark figure takes something from behind the seat, climbs out of the cab, and shuts the door with a thunk that resounds in the thin night air. It moves toward the Port-a-Potties, boots crunching on the snow. Patrick waits. Under his hand, he can feel Tess restraining herself. When the figure is close enough that he can hear its raspy breath, he hits the button on the flashlight.

There in its beam, carrying a crowbar, is Melvin.

"Drop it, or I'll shoot!" says Patrick. Might as well make him soil his pants.

Melvin drops the crowbar, then squints at the light. "Hobs? Is that you?"

"If it's not, you're in deep shit."

Melvin grins.

Patrick takes his hand off Tess's neck. "Get him, girl!"

Tess takes him down.

After they finish off the Johnny Walker, Patrick says, "Now get the hell out of here, Melvin. You got work to do tomorrow. I'm sendin' you out on every pipe call we get."

They both know this isn't true — but Melvin seems to know when not to push his luck. He picks up the crowbar and clears out.

Patrick is too drunk to drive home just yet. He sits back down. His butt is already as wet as it's going to get. Tess settles back into the same spot beside him.

He takes off a glove and puts his hand on Tess' flank. It's warm; he feels it rise and fall. He had thought he would be with her until the end. He had been wrong about that, too.

"Hey, Tessie, you know what we should do tomorrow?"

She looks up at him.

"We should go shoot at some squirrels. We should go scare us some of those little fuckers. What do you say?"

Tess is one hundred per cent in favor.

A Second Life

Si muore un po' per poter vivere. ~ Paolo Conte

When the towers went down, I couldn't help thinking of Giancarlo. I watched them crumble, from my own window—the view of those towers was one of the main selling points for this apartment—and like everyone else I was horrified, I was outraged, I wondered what would happen next. But I also thought about a boy I once knew, in another lifetime. The first boy I kissed.

I know it's wrong to relate that disaster to a chapter in my little emotional life. But this is the way it felt.

He said it was destiny, that kiss. For months he had been badgering me, saying it was bound to happen, I might as well give in. And I had been saying No way, dream on, laughing in spite of myself at his limitless self-assurance, his idea of "destiny." And then he just leaned in, as we sat on the broad wall that surrounded our little city, and he kissed me. I let it happen. What was I going to do, slap him? He was my friend. And I admit, I was interested, I wanted to know what it would be like. It was soft, and a little strange, like kissing your brother. But when he leaned in further, and his hand started roaming, I pushed him away, and sputtered something like "Oh no, my friend, not on your life!" He didn't persist; he just smiled. He was a handsome boy, Giancarlo.

He always said that one day he was going to marry me—one day, that is, after he had completed all his "adventures." I told him he was crazy; I wouldn't marry him if he was the last man on the planet. He thought I was saying that just to be contrary, just to flirt. Sometimes he made me so angry.

There had always been three of us, ever since primary school—Giancarlo, Umberto, and me. It's hard to say exactly what brought us together—maybe just chance, the fact that we happened to be in the same class year after year. But there was also the way we felt about that school: we hated it. We understood that the teachers were our enemies, and we took it as our duty to beat them any way we could. Giancarlo especially. He devised elaborate schemes for cheating on tests and papers, and he made me and Umberto swear a solemn vow that if any of us was caught, that person would never, never betray the others.

It's a little painful to remember how I felt about Lucca at the time. It is such a lovely little city, with its narrow flagstone streets, its red tile roofs, its cool dark churches and odd, asymmetrical piazzas where the men stand to talk about politics and prices and girls. And all of this is encircled, embraced, by those fat city walls. They were broad enough that in the late nineteenth century, when the cannons were no longer needed, the city leaders planted the ramparts with shady plane trees, and turned them into a promenade. There was even room for a paved lane, so that carriages—and later, cars—could go up ramps at certain points for the most scenic drive in town. Those massive walls kept the city safe—first from mortal enemies like those dogs from Pisa, and later from the encroachment of suburban development. When people ask me why I became an urban planner, I tell them about the walls of Lucca—how they created a space, gave it integrity, by imposing strict limitations. Umberto and I grew up outside the walls, in comfortable homes in the hills, and came by bus every day to the school. For us the walls were an emblem of civic pride. Giancarlo's family stayed within them, in an old urban villa.

I can't say, now, that I understood everything he felt and feared at the time. I was, after all, going through my own little adolescent crises; and what did I know of boys? I knew that my own little brother was a monster who enjoyed nothing more than tormenting me. But at least he enjoyed it. Giancarlo was clearly miserable. His father was a lawyer, a very busy man; for a while, when we were children, he was mayor of Lucca. In middle school, Giancarlo's house was the place where the three of us gathered after school, before Umberto and I took the bus home. In his big only-child bedroom we ate snacks, listened to music, and talked endlessly, plotting the downfall of that stupid school.

After a while, Giancarlo didn't invite us anymore. Eventually he told me why: one day, when he stopped by home for something during school hours, he heard strange noises from his parents' bedroom, walked in, and discovered his father having sex with their maid. And that wasn't the worst of it: gradually he understood that his mother knew this was going on and did her best to pretend it wasn't.

His mother was tall and elegant, always dressed in couturier dresses, with high heels and a scarf, even at the height of summer. In the early days, when Umberto and I stopped by their house after school, she was always there, with a tall glass of some kind of iced drink. I thought it was brilliant that she didn't have to work; my own mother, a school-teacher, was always fiercely correcting papers. Whenever I was there, his mother made much of me, straightened my hair, fussed with my humdrum clothes. At first I liked it, since my mother was too busy for such things, and I always had to share her attention with my brother. It felt like I was the daughter Signora Bellini never had. But after a while I couldn't help feeling that I was being treated as a daughter-in-law in training. She might as well have measured my hips to gauge my potential for bearing children. When Giancarlo stopped inviting us over, I was relieved.

Are you destined to become yourself no matter what, because of your genes? Because of the way you grew up? Because of your education, your social class, your town? I used to thank God that I hadn't been born in Pisa, where they were so snobby about their precious Campo Santo, or in Prato, with that funny accent. Or is destiny something more than the accidents of birth, something over which you have control? And if so, do you exercise that control every day, every minute, in everything you do? Or does the chance come just once or twice in a lifetime, in a moment that changes everything?

I fretted over this kind of question back then, when my parents announced that we were moving to America. This was in the mid-seventies, a terrible time in Italy. Domestic terrorism was at its height, striking unpredictably at any symbol of power or luxury. They kidnapped the children of the wealthy, torched villas, and eventually murdered the mayor of Rome, who was found in the trunk of a car after the authorities refused to pay his ransom. My parents, who were comfortably bourgeois if not exactly symbols of power, decided that this was no place to raise their children. My father had always been fascinated by the Anglo-

Saxon world, that culture of phlegm and self-control, so different from the operatic indulgences of Italians. Besides, he knew it would be good, in the coming global society, for his children to be educated in English. He had business contacts in America, and so he arranged the move to San Francisco, in time for me to be a junior in high school.

My reaction, at first, was *Nooooo!!!* What teenager wants to leave everything she knows — her friends, her town, her language? I sulked for days. But what could I do? Children are hostages of fortune.

My farewell with Giancarlo took place on the walls. We had a favorite spot, a bastion where a plane tree stretched its broad limbs so wide that we could climb out and get a little privacy from the cars and the people always passing by. On a clear day, from that branch, you could see out to the wall of the Appenines, behind which lay Viareggio, and the sea, and then everything beyond that — Spain, the Atlantic, the tall cities of America. Giancarlo liked to show off by climbing out too far, where the branch narrowed and stretched beyond the wall, forty feet above the gravel below. I shouted at him what an *idiota* he was, how he ought to climb back in — and of course I loved every minute of it. I called him *la scimmia* — the monkey — and he obliged by capering and hooting and scraping his side with a long, loose-hanging arm. He called me *testa seria* — Serious Head. Life for him was an absurd game, and you just had to play it at break-neck speed. But on this day he sat quietly, looking off toward the sunset. It was May; the flowers of spring had faded, and summer grasses spiked up like green flames through cracks in the wall.

"San Francisco," he said. We all took English, of course, but still it came out as *Sahn Frahnseesco.* "That's where it's really happening. You're so lucky. You're going to have such great adventures." He made a teasing pout. "Before long, you're going to forget all about poor old Giancarlo, stuck back here in the Middle Ages."

"Giancarlo who?" I said.

He gave me a shove, and that smile. "Go on, then, get out of here, see if I care. You'll be back." He stood up on the broad branch. "When you get back, I'll be mayor of Lucca, and at every gate to the city the guards will have a command saying 'Don't let Chiara Caldi in, unless she's ready to marry His Honor!'"

In the months to come, I wasn't too surprised that I didn't hear from him. Giancarlo had never been much of a writer, and it wouldn't be like him to "keep up," anyway. But from Umberto I received long, chatty letters about the latest absurdities at school, the ridiculous tests in geometry, how so-and-so was punished for mimicking a teacher. In those first months, when my English was so bad that I couldn't even tell anyone how homesick I was, those letters, written in Umberto's careful, clear Italian, were my lifeline. His references to Giancarlo were brief, and often critical—which made me realize that the two of them had never been natural friends; I must have been the glue that held us together. He reported that Giancarlo had made a three on the history exam, which was no great shock: he wasn't stupid, by any means, but he was proud of not studying. And he always hated history above all other subjects. "Who cares about the past?" he said. "The more you study it, the more you're stuck in it." His parents were convinced that our leftist teachers were persecuting him, and decided to send him to a boarding school in the north. It was the kind of school, Umberto said, where if you paid, you passed.

Gradually, I got caught up in my new American life. Not that I liked it. I hated that school, and our dumpy little house in Daly City. I spent hours in my tiny bedroom, listening to Edoardo Bennato and looking out the window onto the fenced-in back yards of our neighbors, with their pathetic little shrines to the Madonna and their geraniums planted in white gravel. I couldn't believe we had left Italy for *this*. But I realized, eventually, that I could either rot my life away moping or I could learn English so well, do so well at that school, that I'd get into a good college, get a degree that would get me out of there, get me back to Italy. It never occurred to me that I wouldn't be going back to Lucca: it was the place where my heart belonged.

And so I started spending more time on my homework; I got a tutor for English; I even joined the student council. I gave myself over to bake sales and pep rallies, although I hardly knew what "pep" was, or why I should have it. My letters to Umberto became shorter, less frequent; I started to feel that writing in Italian was cheating. Naturally, his letters came less often, too.

So it was a surprise, one day after school, when I came home and got Umberto's letter about Giancarlo. He had been in a terrible accident, had sustained burns over ninety per cent of his body. It had happened in Verona, and he was in a hospital there, in critical condition. Umberto was fuzzy on the details—because he didn't know them, or because he didn't want to tell?

Of course, I wrote to Giancarlo immediately, at his Lucca address. Long-distance phone calls were rarer then, more expensive; I didn't want to ask my father. I was supposed to be living in the present, becoming more American. Besides, I didn't have a number for the hospital, and I didn't want to talk to Giancarlo's parents. But the fact that I didn't call ate at me, all the same.

Eventually, through other Lucca friends, we learned what had happened. At least, we got a version of the story. It was too horrible not to be true.

It was the Easter vacation, and Giancarlo was on the way home from his new school in the north, traveling with a friend, both of them on motorcycles. Maybe the motorcycles themselves, with their suggestion of both wealth and rebellion, were part of the problem. The two boys left their school late in the day, and discovered that they wouldn't be able to make it home by a decent hour, so they stopped in Verona to spend the night. Why they didn't stay at a cheap hotel is beyond me—Giancarlo could easily have had the money—but they didn't. They had sleeping bags; they could camp out somewhere, get enough sleep to get back on the road in the morning. It was part of the adventure.

On the banks of the Adige, not far from the center of town, they found an old warehouse, crumbling from disuse. There was a storm fence blocking access, but someone had cut a large opening, so it was easy for Giancarlo and his friend to get through, locking their bikes outside. The ground floor was filthy with rubble and trash, but to their surprise it was empty. It was dark and quiet. It seemed the perfect place to stay for a night. They didn't know that it was a common hangout for druggies and bums; they didn't know it was so quiet only because there had been a police raid the night before. If they had known, they probably would have stayed anyway, thinking their timing was perfect. They bedded down in their sleeping bags.

It happened around three in the morning. I know the story from various sources—from Umberto, from other Lucca neighbors, from newspaper clippings. I never managed to ask Giancarlo. This is what I heard. Around three in the morning, while they were sleeping, someone came to the warehouse. A group of men, apparently. Maybe they were drawn by the motorcycles parked by the fence. The story that made the newspapers was that it was a group of neo-fascist terrorists, men who had taken it as their mission to cleanse Italian society of all its "impure" elements — drug users, homosexuals, prostitutes, bums. Maybe they stopped by that building often.

Giancarlo awoke to some noise. He hadn't been sleeping well; it was warm for Easter, so he had pulled himself out of the sleeping bag, to lie on top of it. There was a rustling, and some low voices, then quiet. Then he heard a splashing, and felt something wet, like a bucket of water had just been emptied on him. In the moment that it took to register the smell — gasoline — he heard several familiar clicks. Cigarette lighters.

And then it was chaos. Giancarlo was lucky. Because he was out of his sleeping bag, because he was already partly awake, he was able to jump up and tear off his shirt, throw himself in the dust and roll around, flailing instinctively until the flames were out. His friend was less fortunate: he was still in his nylon sleeping bag, which went up like a match. Frantically, he did what he could to pull it off, ran from the building, and jumped in the river. They found him the next morning, a kilometer downstream.

Giancarlo was taken to the hospital — lucky, again, if you can call it luck in such circumstances, because there was an excellent burn center in Verona. For forty days he was in critical condition — so I couldn't have called him, anyway. Later, after he had made it past the original danger, they started the many operations needed to reconstruct the skin that had suffered the worst burns, on his legs and the backs of his hands.

But this is just the beginning. This isn't why I thought of him when I saw the towers fall. Why is this story so hard to tell?

That summer, when my family went back to Italy for a visit, I was able to go to Verona and see Giancarlo at the hospital. That day trip was a big deal, in its own way. Umberto said he couldn't go. My parents were busy with the many little chores that always occupied them in our brief returns to Italy, so they let me take the train to Verona by myself. I was sixteen. Maybe they figured it was time for me to have such independence. Maybe they knew that I wanted to see Giancarlo on my own.

The trip out, the three-hour train ride and then the bus from the city center to the hospital, was easy. I remember feeling like a grown-up, as I asked for directions around that massive modern complex, making my way to his room. But seeing Giancarlo himself: nothing could have prepared me for that.

He was in a special aseptic room, because the burns had destroyed so much of his skin. As fragile as it is, the skin is still a shield against bacteria and infection; when it is compromised, the body lies open to every floating germ. His room was sealed, accessible only to hospital personnel wearing masks. The only way to visit him was to sit by a window in the wall, where there was a speaking panel in the glass, like those things you see in prison movies.

When I got there he was in bed, where he spent most of his time—not only because he was still weak, but because movement was so painful. He was dressed head to foot in a loose white garment that must have been especially made for burn victims. His handsome face was almost unchanged; there was just a streak of burned skin along his neck, reaching up along his jaw. He said it made talking painful. Still, he said he was glad to see me. He asked about Sahn Frahnseesco.

I must have talked a lot. I hardly remember. By the end of our brief visit—the nurse said he shouldn't be disturbed for more than thirty minutes—it seemed that I had hardly stopped talking. I know he said something about how miraculous the recuperative powers of skin were, how he would eventually regain full function. He said something about starting a second life. But I can't remember how he said it.

What I remember most, of all the strange experiences that day, is the train ride back to Lucca. All the way back, I sat by the window and cried—and if you had asked me why, I couldn't have answered. Through tears, I watched the countryside stream by. Italian countryside, mine and no longer mine. What could I do for Giancarlo, anyway? Within days I would be headed back to America. I would start my senior year in high school, and I would get into an American college, and my life would move ahead like that train.

For a while, I kept in better contact with Umberto, and I even received a note about Giancarlo's progress from his mother. Within a few months he was out of the burn center, back home with his parents, still wearing special protective clothing, but starting to get around on his own. For the time being, while he regained strength and flexibility, he had to drop out of school—and Umberto reported that of course this was OK with Giancarlo. I wondered, though. He had taken such pleasure in his very hatred of the school. Where would that energy be directed now?

I guess I should have known that even before the accident Giancarlo was into drinking and drugs. It didn't occur to me, because Umberto and I were so squeaky clean, and Giancarlo never got high in our presence. Maybe he liked having us as one part of his life, the part where he stayed on the straight and narrow. But after we caught the bus back to our homes in the hills, we never suspected what he might be doing within the old walls at night. And then when he went off to that school in the north—well, what can you know about another person's life? I didn't know. But of course I wondered, later, if I could have made a difference.

Instead, I rode that train into the senior year of high school, into AP courses and SATs and applications for college. It was easy to get swept up in all of it—especially if you didn't really want to listen to the voices that buzzed around the edges of your mind. I received the usual warm, newsy letters from Umberto, who was talking about becoming a priest. That infuriated me: why would he give up on so much of life? Wasn't he becoming just what we had always hated? I wasn't surprised that the letters didn't say much about Giancarlo.

The next summer we didn't go back to Italy. I was upset: how could we abandon our home so completely? But my parents said there wasn't time or money for it. I had been accepted to an expensive college in Massachusetts, and there was so much to do, so much to prepare. I had to admit, they were probably right. Thanks to immersion, my English had improved immensely—but still I was nervous, wondering how I'd measure up. Every day I did the crossword puzzle in The Chronicle. I assumed that Giancarlo was healing. I was sure I'd get back to Italy the following summer, once I had settled into college. I promised myself that I'd go on my own if I had to.

And then came freshman year. Talk about a runaway train. Besides physics and math and history and my beloved nemesis, English, I was still learning a country. When people asked me how I liked college, I never knew what to say. It was like being asked how you like life: you learn, after a while, to shrug and say "Fine." I still thought about Lucca every day. There were occasional good letters from Umberto, who had started seminary, and I wondered how Giancarlo was getting along. When I was most exasperated with a problem set, or a paper, or a dumb little flirtation with the guy down the hall, I consoled myself with the thought of how good it would be to get back there in the summer, to sit on that branch with Giancarlo and talk about all the nonsense we had both been through.

It was February when the letter came. The second semester had barely begun, and the thrill of college was starting to wear thin. The ground had been deep in snow since November, and it seemed like years since we had seen the sun. I had had a long day of classes. And so I was especially pleased, upon returning to my dorm, to see a letter from Umberto. I tore it open right there by the window of the mail room, to make the most of the dwindling afternoon light.

Inside, there were just a few lines from Umberto—something about how terribly sad it was, how he would write again soon, when he had more time, and knew more. And there was a clipping from the local newspaper. Son of prominent Lucca family dies in accident.

He had been out on his motorcycle. It was late at night. The paper didn't say anything about drugs or alcohol—but it didn't require much imagination. He had ridden the bike up the ramparts, as he had done many times before—and somehow straight into a tree, causing him to be thrown over the wall, down to the gravel below. He was dead on arrival.

I staggered out into the courtyard of the dorm, clutching those scraps of paper, and sat down, cross-legged, in the snow. I don't know why. Anybody in that four-story dorm could have looked out a window and wondered what the Italian girl was doing, sitting there in the snow. I don't know how long it was before I noticed that my jeans were soaked through, my butt was frozen, and the court-yard lights had come on. I didn't care. I sat there a while longer.

And that's what I thought about when I saw the towers fall. Maybe this is self-indulgent and "Italian" of me; I don't care. This is who I am, even though I have lived in New York for almost twenty years now. Everything in my life radiates back to that moment, sitting there in the snow with my butt getting colder and wetter by the second. I can't say that I knew it then, not in so many words — but that is when it became impossible for me to go back to live permanently in Italy. I wasn't going to get stuck in that history.

And yet here I am, telling the story.

I've never let another summer pass without returning to Lucca. I always visit Umberto, and spend a night or two in one of the guest rooms attached to his church. Over the years I've become used to seeing him in the black shirt and white collar — but I still give him grief about it. I tease him about Oriana Minucci, his high school crush. But I see that he has made his choice. He could have done worse.

I always make some excuse to get off by myself, and Umberto always lets me. He knows what I want to do. I go up on the walls. Cars aren't allowed up there anymore. I sit and look out, to an empty spot on the skyline.

Mystery Kid: The Final Episode

Max Keller is standing by the window in his usual spot, with one eye on Sue the bartender and the other on the traffic light down at the intersection below. On a prematurely cold October night, that light is the only thing in motion out on Main Street in this little New Hampshire town. Green yellow red green yellow red. Max keeps hoping it will throw him a different combination.

But he'd have to be drunk for that to happen, and there's no drinking on the job. That was the first rule Bob was absolutely clear about: "No booze for the personnel." Bob likes words like that, "personnel." He has a rule for everything — how you get docked for every minute you're late, how to tuck in your shirt, no visible tattoos, always wash your hands after using the can. Bob has a thing about germs. He doesn't believe in shaking hands. Every time the phone rings, he pulls out a Handi-wipe and gives the receiver a good going over before saying hello. But how is he going to know if you washed your hands or not? Max always runs a little water in the sink after flushing, just in case Bob is near the door.

Max works security. Which means that he wears this t-shirt (neatly tucked in) and he checks IDs at the door and stamps people's hands, and he stands here by the window with his arms crossed like Mister Clean, and sometimes, if somebody gets a little difficult, if he absolutely has to, he asks them to take it easy. Most of the time, after people stop showing up at the door he doesn't really have much to do, especially on a night like this. It's a Sunday, and almost everybody in town is at one of the sports bars with the multiple TV screens, watching the Sox in the playoffs. This is a music bar, with just the one old TV over Sue's head.

Somebody should tell this band about the music part. Most of the time Bob manages to book somebody decent, a group that can at least count to four in unison. These guys, it sounds like they just met downstairs and said Hey, let's take a whack at a song or two. If you can call this a song. Bono said all you needed was three chords and the truth. Seems like this guitarist knows more chords than Mel Bay, but he hasn't found two that like each other yet. In the pools of light cast by the coffee-can spots in front of the dinky stage, there are six or eight people standing, dangling bottles of beer by their thighs, trying to sway to the beat.

Max is supposed to "circulate," pick up empties, make sure everybody knows he's there, like the lunchroom lady in elementary school. Bob says the only reason he has a job is that it's the law: any place serving booze has to have somebody in a Security t-shirt. Bob has apparently had some little run-ins with the Liquor License people. He says you never know when they'll show up, looking for the smallest excuse to shut you down.

Max looks over at Sue, behind the bar. She's quartering a lime with a serrated knife, placing the wedges in a glass dish, looking up at the game as often as she can. Even halfway across the room, he thinks he can smell the burst of fresh citrus. When she moves, she steps in and out of the track lighting so that her short blonde hair takes fire again and again. Is it just his imagination, or is she looking extra restless tonight? Max thinks he can see the tension in her neck, above the collar of the pink polo shirt that says "Bob's" in friendly script above her left breast. He isn't sure how old she is—forty?--but she's sharper and more energetic than the twenty-year-old girls who used to be in his classes, before he dropped out. She has those crinkles around her eyes when she smiles, those little lines that look like wisdom. That sad little triangular smile. Max has only been working here for six months, and he doesn't know much about his employers, but he can tell that they have been married a long time. Bob does all the talking, Bob makes all the rules, Bob hires the bands and manages the sound board and counts the receipts; but Sue rules the bar. They don't have children. Sue is a huge Red Sox fan, and she chats with Max sometimes about their chances. Bob doesn't even remember his name. That's another rule: no fraternizing on the job.

This band calls itself The Zombie Virus, and Max has to give them credit: they picked the perfect name. They've been sleepwalking through the same song for God knows how long, the traffic light has been through fourteen changes, and they just keep clanging along. One thing Max has noticed: the weaker the material, the longer the song.

It makes him think he should get his guitar out again. With a little practice, he could do better than these guys. That was one thing he learned from his dad. Most of the time, his father did nothing but work and worry, work and write checks, work and make sure to take his daily walk in order to stay healthy enough to work some more. When he saw Max come home with another handful of comic books, he said, "When are you going to stop being such a *kid*?" But once in a while, on a rainy Sunday afternoon, he pulled out a scarred old guitar and played some spirituals he had learned from his own father, whom Max never met. "We Shall Gather at the River," that sort of thing, played in a loose, chunky style that hypnotized Max: how did you make something so beautiful come out of a box? When his father sang, in a sweet reedy baritone, he went somewhere else for a while, over the hills. Max always wanted to go there, too. For his thirteenth birthday his father bought him a cheap used guitar, and he learned enough to play along some—but after a while he didn't want to play that old cheesy stuff, and then in the final year or so his dad stopped playing.

Max isn't talking tonight, anyway. For the past few days he's had a canker sore near the back of his tongue, like a big raw pothole in his mouth, and it hurts every time something touches it. Every time he eats or drinks, every time he speaks, it rubs against his teeth and rouses a little shock of pain that rattles his skull. Even the vibration of the bass in this goddamn band makes it hurt, rumbling through his mouth. If you wanted to make yourself understood during a song, you'd have to shout, and shouting hurts even more. But Max isn't much of a talker even when his tongue is perfectly sound. He'd rather daydream.

* * *

Mystery Kid is on a precipice, and he can't see what he came here to find. It's after ten o'clock, and he has just materialized here; he's trying to get his bearings. This must be the River Road. Out here on the edge of town, beyond the suburbs, there are no streetlights; it's so dark he can see the glimmer around his own body, the momentary sheath of light that accompanies him every time he translates from one place to another. In the ordinary light of day it's so subtle that not even he notices. Now, in the dark, it sheds just the faintest gleam, which helps him start to see—pebbles at his feet, tufts of grass beside the road. There's supposed to be a full moon tonight. Must be behind the clouds.

Where is the girl he came to save? He doesn't know who she is, or why she would be out here in the dead calm of a late-October night. But he knows that it's a girl—it's always a girl, beautiful in a way that most people don't notice, unappreciated by her husband, weary of her tiresome life. In his mind he hears The Girl theme, a single plaintive oboe rising above the strings.

Could he have arrived too late? He knows that several feet from where he stands, in the inky nothing beyond the shoulder of this dusty road, a cliff plunges two hundred feet to the river. At least once every year this place makes the headlines: a daredevil kid who was too drunk or too stupid or both, a brokenhearted lover who could bear it no longer. His eyes strain against the dark. If he can just reach her, he can whisk her away from the brink. He just has to be able to take her hand, or touch her arm, any kind of contact between his skin and hers. He waits—for his eyes to adjust, for the clouds to release the moon.

Around ten thirty a guy comes to the door, alone, and Max goes over to take his five bucks and stamp his hand. He manages to do all of this without saying a word, which isn't hard, since it's all so automatic. The guy is medium height, and pretty skinny, as far as Max can tell through his big down coat. Max always checks when guys come in on their own, because they're the most likely to cause trouble, and he wants to know if he can take them. Not that he's supposed to: Bob has made it clear that there is to be no physical contact unless absolutely necessary. This guy doesn't look like a problem. He has thinning brown hair and those fashionable little rectangular glasses; he looks like a grad student down on his luck. He heads over to the bar, and Max goes back to his spot by the window. The Zombie Virus keeps spreading. Green yellow red.

A few minutes later, when he looks over to see what's up at the bar, Max notices that Down Coat has struck up a conversation with Sue. Or *at* Sue. In fact, he looks pretty animated. He's pointing to the TV above her head and gesturing insistently. Max can't tell if Sue looks happy or not. Bob isn't at the sound board; he's probably out back, making up some more rules. It's not like he needs to monitor the board too carefully: with a band like this, you just turn it to Earsplitting and let it rip. Max circulates over towards the bar, and picks up some empties at the closest table, fifteen feet away. If this damn band would ever finish a song, he might actually be able to hear something.

Down Coat keeps pointing to the TV screen, which is crowded with men in costumes, running around on a field. Tonight is the third game of the ALCS. Max has already decided that he can't bear to watch. He was born in Yaz's last summer, and his dad used to tell him that the Sox were his birthright. You can never give up on the Sox, his dad said. Someday, sooner or later, hell or high water, they'd win it all. Someday King Arthur would return from Avalon; someday Elvis would turn up at a diner in Montana — and not White Jumpsuit Elvis, but Black Leather Elvis from the first comeback show.

But the Sox have already lost the first two games, and it's just too obvious that they're going down again. Max doesn't want to look. The memory of last year's Game Seven is too fresh, too painful. He watched it with Samantha, and she was astonished at how hard he took it. She said he never showed that kind of passion about *her*. He realized that she was right, and before long they just drifted apart. For a while he had thought she was the one. This year he's not getting burned by the Sox again.

Down Coat seems to be yelling now. In the mirror behind the bar, his mouth is a dark O against the sudden brightness of his pale skin. Max looks at Sue, who is watching Down Coat with care, drying a glass with a bar towel but not taking her eyes off him. He's shouting and waving his arms at the TV, and Max is almost on top of them, but with the band banging away it's like a pantomime, it's like fish in a tank.

And then suddenly, finally, the band stops. They've actually finished a number, and they're taking a break. The whole room seems to lighten, as if they have just moved into a better neighborhood. Except that Down Coat is still shouting, and now Max can actually hear some of it. It isn't pretty.

Mystery Kid's eyes have adjusted as much as they can, and still he can't see more than five or six feet in the darkness. He knows this is the right place — but he doesn't know why. He just gets these feelings, and tonight the feeling told him the River Road.

Mystery Kid isn't like some of those other guys. He doesn't have super strength, or blinding speed, or x-ray vision; he can't spin webs or elongate his body in ridiculous ways, and he doesn't have any razzle-dazzle equipment, a Mystery-Mobile or a magic lantern. He is simply able to translate himself immediately from one place to any other place on earth, with a nod of the head and the barest little shimmer of the ethereal envelope that surrounds him. It's not a headline-grabbing skill. Sometimes, in fact, it just freaks people out. People don't always react so well when you materialize in front of them. They don't always love it when you disappear from in front of them, either, although that's usually less of a problem, because, after all, you aren't there anymore. Of course, when you have to go back for something you left behind — it's easy to leave things behind, because you've got to be holding something, with actual skin contact, for it to be translated along with you — then people tend to look at you funny.

Still, Mystery Kid has had his share of successes. There was the time he saved the mayor's daughter from Incendo-Man, by materializing just when she was about to get torched, grabbing her wrist, and translating her back to City Hall. He got the key to the city for that one. And there was the time he rescued the poor but lovely goose girl from the clutches of the Bog People, just as they were about to swallow her up in a nightmare of slime. And then there was the extended episode with the Angrynauts, who kidnapped the entire high school cheerleading squad and isolated the girls on a high-powered boat in the middle of Lake Santo. The Kid had to use his pin-point location skills that time, because he can't swim. And then he had to get all seven girls to touch some part of his skin, so he could transport them out of harm's way. It's not always such a bad special power.

But right now he is at a loss. It's just so ridiculously dark and quiet out here. There is no sign of The Girl. He's wary of venturing off the road, because he knows that one false step could send him hurtling off the cliff, and he's not keen on mid-air translations. If you don't have your feet firmly set on something, you can't be sure where you'll materialize. You might pop into some other mid-air space, still in free fall; you might show up in some strange country where you don't speak the language and they're not exactly happy about the sudden appearance of a lean but muscular guy in a purple and gold suit with a big black MK on the chest.

Sometimes he thinks he should have a sidekick, someone to share his dark secrets. But he has always been a loner. He has to be, doesn't he? That one time, with the goose girl, he started to let his guard down; he started to think that maybe he could have a normal life. But then, just as he was about to reveal his secret identity, he realized: he is not a normal person. There are too many bad guys out there who wouldn't hesitate to strike at him through a loved one, a family member, an associate. He cannot allow himself to get emotionally entangled. He kept his mask on.

Finally, a cloud drifts away from the moon, and suddenly Mystery Kid can make out the whole scene before him, in a cold clear light.

Down Coat is shouting. "It is high! It is far! It is . . . *gone!*" On the screen above him, a couple of Red Sox are standing at their defensive positions, hanging their heads. Another one is squatting, scratching in the dirt like a dejected Little Leaguer. A Yankee is circling the bases at a trot.

Down Coat takes a swig from his bottle, and holds it on high, like the Statue of Liberty. "I love it! Don't you love it?"

Sue doesn't say anything, and he doesn't seem to require a response. "Remember all that stuff Red Sox fans were saying this spring? This was going to be the year! Right? The same stuff they say every spring! As if just by saying it they could make it come true! It's like Peter Pan or something—like, 'Just focus on the second star to the right, everybody, and we'll get to Never Land!'"

He isn't really talking to anybody in particular, but he keeps asking questions.

"OK, so here it is October, right? So what's happening to the Good Ship Lollipop? Game One: Yankees crush Schilling." He pronounces it "Yang-kees," just to be extra annoying. "Schilling was going to be the Messiah, remember? Well, his ankle is shot, man, he's done for the year. So now what do they say? 'Don't worry, we've still got Pedro!' Game Two: Yang-kees rock Pedro. Hell, they've *always* been his daddy." He does a little "who's your daddy" dance.

Max looks at Sue. This must be killing her, but she just keeps drying the same glass. The members of the Zombie Virus sidle over in a little clump, looking for beer during their break, and she takes their orders. At the bar, out of the spotlight, they look like clean-cut kids, like they just got out of Calc class. Down Coat seems glad to have a bigger audience.

"But wait!" he says in a newsreel voice, holding the bottle like a microphone. "It's not over yet! We're going back to Fenway! The Sox are magic in Fenway! So what if we lost the first two games? We can't lose in Boston! There's no place like home, there's no place like home . . ." He clicks together the heels of his grubby running shoes.

On the screen, the camera pans through the crowd.

"Look at those idiot Red Sox fans! They're *crushed*, the poor babies! When are they going to learn? Ladies and gentlemen," he says with a flourish, "I give you Game Three!"

Max can't help looking up. The scoreboard on The Wall is bulging with the numbers the Yankees are putting up. No wonder the Sox are hanging their heads.

Down Coat bangs his bottle on the bar. "Yang-kees rule! Yang-kees rule!"

Then he seems to notice that no one is joining in. He turns to the Zombie Virus. "Don't tell me you guys are Red Sox fans."

The Zombies look a little uncomfortable, but they stay in their own little huddle at the bar rail, as if they were calculating pi to a hundred places. Max moves in closer.

Down Coat is still talking, addressing the TV now. "Just one more night, Red Sox So-called Nation! No one in history has *ever* come back from being behind three games to none! Ever! One more night, and then you get to spend another winter pissing and moaning about The Curse, and how it'll be different next year! Admit it: you were born to lose! You're like a dog chasing a car: you wouldn't know what to do with one if you caught it!"

Sue's mouth is pursed tight, and she is gripping that glass like she wants to throw the guy a little chin music. But then she goes back to fussing with things behind the bar, wiping the counter. Maybe this is just her way of dealing with assholes. But maybe she really wants Max to step in? He can't read her face. He moves up to the bar, in between Down Coat and the TV. He gets a whiff of bad cologne.

Down Coat finally notices him. "What are *you* looking at? Oh, wait: you must be a Red Sox fan."

Max shrugs. Even without speaking, he's aware of the raw spot on his tongue.

Down Coat looks at him harder, watery blue eyes behind the fashion specs. "Yeah, I can see it in your eyes. The undeniable look of a loser."

When Max still doesn't say anything, Down Coat starts strutting in front of the bar like the cock of the walk, his hands gripping his coat where the lapels would be, if a down coat had lapels. He begins to chant.

"Who's your daddy? Who's your daddy?"

Max looks at the Zombies, who are just watching, as if this is the best show of the night. He looks at the TV screen, where another Yankee is prancing around the bases. He looks at Sue, whose eyes seem to cry for help. Then he decks the guy.

In the quicksilver moonlight on the River Road, finally, there she is. The Girl. She has been out on this precipice every night of her married life. Mystery Kid swoops into action. The music soars. He rushes to the cliff's edge and reaches for her hand, for the clean unimpeachable contact of skin on skin.

But she draws back. Doesn't she want to be saved? He barely grazes her hand, and, losing his footing, finds himself lurching, over the lip of the cliff.

Down Coat is on the floor by the bar, rubbing his jaw. His glasses have been knocked off, and he's groping for them with his other hand. Sue has pulled herself up on the counter in order to look down at him; her feet are dangling above the floor behind the bar. She says, "Are you all right?" The Zombies are standing there with their mouths hanging open. From out of nowhere Bob appears, shouting, "What the hell is going on here? No fights in my bar! Where's my security man?"

Seeing Bob, Down Coat, who is still on the floor but has managed to put on his glasses, reaches into his shirt pocket and pulls out a laminated card. "Alcohol and Tobacco Board," he says, with a grim little smile. "You just lost your license."

And Max? Max just wants to vanish. He wants to be anywhere but here.

And now he is in free fall. It's ridiculously cold, for October. The moon is as bright as a streetlight. When a cloud passes over, there remains just the faintest glow, all around his body.

TRANSLATOR

It starts in the dark, with a call from Central. Spangle gets it on the first ring; he sleeps like a cat, always expecting trouble. In the big bed next to him Ginger rolls over, away from the phone. Trudy, down the hall, probably didn't even hear it. The blessed sleep of the young. Even before he speaks, Spangle knows what it will be.

"Yes?"

"I'm sorry, Spangle — "

"It's not your fault, Penny. What is it?"

"Another one down by the wharf."

"Method?"

"Meat cleaver."

Spangle winces. "How long?"

"Two-three hours. That's Dozier's best guess."

"Of course."

"Chief Clancy — "

" — wants me there immediately. I know."

"Sorry, Spangle."

"Not your fault, Penny. Tell Clancy I'll be there in fifteen."

"Yes, sir."

*Not that Clancy is even awake, at his own suburban home. Penny knows better than to disturb **his** beauty sleep. It's just* *his standing order: trouble in town, and there had better be a detective on the scene, pronto. We can't have another one of those cases where the press arrives first, now, can we?*

Spangle gets up without turning on a light. The green face of the digital clock by the bed reads 2:17. He pads softly to the bathroom, and splashes his face with cold water. Another one down by the wharf. Not Penny's fault, of course. But whose fault is it?

Max groaned, closed his laptop, and pushed himself away from the table with its stack of manuscript, beneath the skylight of his little attic room. Why did it always have to start with a phone call in the dark, in the breathless present tense? Why was there always a sympathetic female dispatcher with a name like Penny? What the hell kind of name was "Spangle," anyway?

Max knew he shouldn't worry about such questions; it wasn't his job. His job, Giampiero said, was to make it American. The Spangle novels were set in Milwaukee, where Giampiero had never been. He needed Max for authenticity.

In fact, being American was Max's only qualification for the job. He had never translated anything before, and his Italian was only *mezzo mezzo*. Already, he wondered: when he wrote that Ginger "rolled over," did that make her sound like a dog? When Spangle asked "How long?" meaning "How long has the body been there?" did it sound like he was asking about the length of the cleaver? Was "cleaver" even the right word for *coltello da colpo*?

Giampiero had told him to "go with his gut," to trust the words that sounded good together. After all, he said, "*traduttore traditore*" — the translator is always a traitor. A translator *needs* to betray the original, in order to capture the spirit of the whole; a good translation is always indirect. "Real details no matter, Max. Reader must to forget real life, get lost in story. Character must to get loster."

"More lost."

"More lost, yes. And then to get found again. Exact words no matter."

But Max wanted to get it right, word by word. He had studied his list of "false friends" — words that looked like they should mean one thing while they actually meant something entirely different. *Morbido* meant "soft." *Casuale* meant "by chance." *Molesto* meant "annoying." What could he do but go word by word? If he screwed this up, he'd have to go back to his ridiculous little life. His interminable graduate degree, his patient but quizzical parents, his apartment with no Mary in it. He wasn't at all sure where his gut would take him, but he didn't want to go back.

Giampiero Verraldi had enjoyed a moderate success with his first two books, but now he had visions of breaking into the Anglophone audience for airport novels, and he didn't want to pay for a real translator. He actually called them "airport novels," as if it was a genre he'd studied in his university days at Bologna. So he had given the job to this young American who had done such good work in his wife's language class. Max couldn't complain: the weekly cash from Giampiero was paying for this little rooftop room he was renting above the Strada Nuova. Except that he *could* complain, because the book was a tissue of cliché, and he didn't know what he was doing, and his impossible deadline meant that he'd never be able to get out and take a walk around the city. He needed to get with it. He opened his laptop again.

Was "beauty sleep" OK, even though the original just said "sleep"? Was "standing order" an accurate way to describe the Italian police procedure? Was "pads" the right word for the way Spangle stepped to the bathroom?

He went for a walk.

How would you translate the miracle that is Venice in January? The wintry sunlight that suffused everything with gold; the Sheherazade palaces, rising implausibly straight from the sea; the hundreds of humpback bridges, bracketed over canals; the cries of the gondoliers, looking for customers even in the damp cold of the off-season—and everywhere the water, lapping against the ancient pilings, washing through the city like a pulse. When a boat passed, you could hear the waves that slapped the stone quays, because there was no automotive traffic to muffle the sound. And yes, you could smell it, too, a mixture of brine and sulfur and something past its expiration date. You would have to be the most incurable romantic not to notice this odor—but you would have to be blind not to appreciate the beauty that went with it.

Max wandered toward Mariana and Giampiero's place, in a narrow alley not far from Santa Maria dei Miracoli. He had met Mariana six months before, when things had gone so wrong with Mary that he just had to get out of Atlanta. He had gathered his meager savings and come to Venice, justifying the trip by taking a language course at the Istituto Venezia. As if perfecting his Italian would help him with his dissertation on the "slippage of language" in the sacred poems of John Donne. At the end of the course, Mariana invited him and his four classmates from the Classe Avanzata out to a pizzeria for dinner, and there he met Giampiero, a big gray-haired guy in his forties, maybe ten years older than his tall, elegant wife. Upon learning that Max was a grad student in English, he had said, "I have a job for you, my friend!"

Max was buzzed in to their building and climbed to the fourth floor, where he found the apartment standing open—the welcome of someone too busy to wait at the door. Instead, he was greeted by Archy, one of the two gray cats of the house. Or was this Mehitabel? On an earlier visit Max had seen that they were both clearly Mariana's cats: she fed them and cooed to them, reciting Neruda's "Ode to the Cat."

> There is no unity like his,
> the moon and the flower
> have no such cohesion;
> the cat wants only
> to be a cat,
> and every cat is a cat
> from whiskers to tail,
> from sniff to the live mouse,
> from the dark of night to his golden eyes.

Max squatted to give Archy (he *thought* it was Archy) a how-do-you-do rubdown, as Archy (well, it *might* be Mehitabel) wound about his knees. And then he walked in. "C'e' qualcuno?"

A voice from his right led him into the kitchen, where he found Giampiero standing at the long central table, dicing onions with the two-handled blade called a *mezzaluna.*

"Max!"

Even in an apron, there was no doubting Giampiero's masculinity. He had the barrel chest and belly of a former athlete who doesn't work out anymore, a cook who enjoys his own creations. He seemed to know everything about food, from the names of tiny poisonous mollusks to the specialties of Ecuador—or at least, he was ready to announce an opinion about everything. French cuisine was overrated. Americans used too much salt, and they compensated by using too much pepper. The low-carbohydrate craze would soon come to an end. Who wanted a skinny woman, anyway?

He beamed his crowd-pleasing smile at Max. "Mariana is out," he said. "She shops for—something." He pointed with the blade to a shiny pink lump on the table before him. "Rabbit," he said. "I cook."

Max tried not to think of Thumper.

Giampiero wiped his big knuckly hands on the apron. "So, how is going the translation?"

"Great, great. But listen, I was wondering, how did this guy get such an unusual name?"

"I get this from song—'star-spangled banner.' Wonderful name, no?"

"Yes. But it's kind of strange. You know, the reader might wonder about it."

"Does not matter. Reader does not care. Book starts, phone call, body at wharf, Spangle goes. This is what matter, no? Suspense!" It sounded like "sauce pans."

"Yeah, but—"

"Does not matter," Giampiero said. "Book starts! Spangle already has name! Not to think too much, Max! Just write! Deadline, yes?"

Max nodded. "So, um, I was just out for a walk. Tell Mariana I came by?"

"Certainly. But why not stay? Eat rabbit!"

"No, no, I've got work to do. Deadline, you know?"

Giampiero smiled. Archy or Mehitabel came in and leapt up on the table, sniffing towards the lump of ex-rabbit. Giampiero shooed him off with the half-moon blade. "*Via, cazzo di gatto!*" The cat jumped down.

"Besides," Max said, "there's all of Venice to see."

"Oh, Venice." Giampiero threw a backhanded wave at the air, and saw that Archy-or-Mehitabel was back on the table. This time he grabbed the cat by the scruff and tossed it to the floor. "Venice is dead city. Full of ghost. Venice make you sad."

"It doesn't make *me* sad. We Americans love all this old stuff. It's why we come here. We don't have any of this."

"Ah, if you have it, then it make you sad. This is why I put Spangle in Milwaukee." He pronounced it *Mil-wow-kee*. "Nobody knows Milwaukee. No history. No ghost."

Max thought he could say a few things about the settlement of the upper Midwest, maybe even about the ghosts of a few Indian tribes—but he couldn't remember their names. The Pabst? Giampiero wouldn't want to hear about it, anyway. If he wanted to think the U. S. was a blank slate, that was his prerogative.

Back at the apartment, Max was glad to find that Sonia wasn't home. Not that he didn't like Sonia; she was a pure delight, a seventy-five year-old dynamo who often rented her spare room to students from the Institute. She gave him a key to her place, offered him soup and conversation, and never remembered his name. He just wanted a little quiet; he wanted not to have to explain himself, for once. He didn't want to tell his parents, again, why he wouldn't be getting married after all. He didn't want to explain to his dissertation advisor, again, why he was so far behind schedule with his research. He didn't want to tell his friends why he didn't answer their e-mails, why he'd grown this scruffy beard with the patch of white at the chin, as if he had always just spilled his milk.

He saluted the dancing lady. In the living room of Sonia's little rooftop apartment, there was a tailor's mannequin right in the middle of things, surrounded by drawings and swatches of cloth, always wearing Sonia's latest creation. She was a costume designer for a little dance theater on the Giudecca, the long spiny island on the southern edge of Venice, and she was always in the midst of a project, trying out materials on her mannequin. She liked to work late at night, after Max had gone to bed in his little room. He was an early riser, so some days they hardly saw each other, which was ideal, really, for both of them. It was a small rooftop apartment; their differing schedules gave them some privacy. But when he stepped out in the morning on his way to the bathroom, he always saw the results of the night's labor: the dancing lady would be freshly dressed. Just now she was sporting a top made of old bicycle tires sewn together — like a darker, svelter version of the Michelin man — and wings, blue wings, made from dozens of rubber gloves that had been dyed in the bathtub and strung together so they dangled like shimmering feathers. Sonia liked to use found objects, industrial leftovers, vestiges of something else. She said the source of all art was the Lost and Found. Max went back to work.

Kneeling over the body, Spangle can't restrain a little gasp. The blade seems to have landed just once, severing the carotid artery, and there is blood everywhere, all over the face. In the beam of his flashlight, everything is suddenly too bright, crim-

son on skin that has gone ghostly pale. Spangle's stomach takes a quarter turn. He's a big guy who loves to eat, and he has no trouble with his digestion; but he's glad that his last meal was hours ago.

He crosses himself, and thinks of little Trudy, under the covers in her pink room, posters of magnificent horses guarding her sleep. He thinks of Ginger, in her bathrobe now, making coffee for his return. He wishes she would stay in bed—but she knows that he will want company after a night call like this. Sometimes he needs to talk—and sometimes he takes her back to bed. He isn't always gentle on these nights.

God, Max thought, this is so full of shit you could compost a farm with it. It was so patently a wish-fulfilling image of Giampiero the good husband who would keep the world safe from the ravages of unreason. Little Trudy in her pink room! How sentimental could you get?

But as he looked over what he had typed, he also thought he was getting the hang of this thing. "Crimson on skin that has gone ghostly pale," that wasn't bad. He was starting to see Spangle in his mind's eye, like a character in an old movie, always in dark places with one bright source of light.

There was a knock at his door. "John?"

It was Sonia—sprightly, polite, clueless as ever. She asked about his day, talked about her day, in rapid-fire Italian, not seeming to expect a response, and then, finally, got to the point: she asked if he would be taking his dinner there at the apartment. His deal with her said he had the right to use the kitchen anytime. "Not that it makes any difference," she said. "I just wanted to plan my evening."

Max smiled. What she wanted, he knew, was to invite her lover to the apartment and have a little time with him alone. She had told Max about her love life: she was seeing a younger man. A seventy year-old. He had brought her flowers recently, and then, when he saw the flowers that were already in a vase on her dining room table (which Max had brought her as the gesture of a good guest), he had told her he was jealous. Well, Max's roses *were* nicer than his tulips. He could tell that Sonia enjoyed her lover's jealousy.

"I'll be dining out," he said.

She smiled. "With — what's her name — Maria?"

"Mariana."

"Yes."

"No. I mean, yes, that's her name, but I won't be dining with her. She's having dinner with her husband."

Sonia just looked at him, still smiling. What did *she* know? She hadn't even met Mariana. Much less Giampiero. Max thanked her for the visit, and headed out for dinner.

The night was thick with mist, as often happened in January: the damp cold of the sky mingled with the vapor coming off the canals, and covered the city in a shroud. *Il nebbione*, they called it, the big fog. You could step out to the corner *tabaccaio* for a pack of cigarettes, burrowing a tunnel through the fog as you went, and twenty minutes later, on your way back, the same tunnel would be waiting for you, like a rent in the fabric of time. When you couldn't see beyond the cloud of your own breath, this small city became even smaller.

Max walked past Santa Maria dei Miracoli, and then he turned north, towards San Zanipolo. Before long he was lost in a welter of narrow passageways. Even though he knew the city fairly well by now, it was almost a given that he would get lost on a night like this. It would be no use taking the much-folded map from his pocket: maps only help when you know where you are.

Suddenly the narrow *calle* opened on nothing but blank darkness. He could walk no further, because he had arrived at the water's edge, the open lagoon. Somehow he must have circled around behind the old hospital of San Marco; this was the Fondamenta degli Incurabili—the quay of the incurables. From this bank for hundreds of years the irremediable cases had left the hospital on their last ride, headed for the cemetery island of San Michele, just a few hundred yards offshore. In the dark, Max had to imagine the island, floating out there with its mortal burden. He lit a cigarette, as much for the light of its glow as for the warmth of the smoke in his veins.

He had stopped smoking two years ago, for Mary. She hated the smell on his breath, and the butts in his apartment and car; she nagged at him, sweetly, about the effects on his health. He wouldn't want their kids growing up in a house full of smoke, would he? Quitting had been torture, not because his body craved the nicotine but because his hands wanted something to do. As soon as he got to Venice, he started again. What good was Italy if you couldn't smoke? It occurred to him, looking out into the mist, that Spangle should be a smoker.

The next day, when Max stepped into the living room, ready to salute the dancing lady, he found Sonia already up, bustling around the living room. She smiled. "Tom! Are you ready to go to the theater?"

Did she really not know his name, or was this just her idea of a joke?

"The theater?"

"Yes! Rehearsal today! Hurry, we have to catch the vaporetto in ten minutes."

She acted as if they had already talked about this. Maybe it was part of that monologue she had thrown at him the evening before at his bedroom door. Well, Spangle wasn't going anywhere. Max got his coat.

On a vaporetto, one of the long, flat-bottomed waterbuses that were always motoring up and down the larger canals, you got a whole new perspective on Venice. This was the way it was meant to be seen—from the water, a little uncertain, bobbing with the rhythm of the waves. As they churned across the sound that separated the heart of Venice from the Giudecca, Max watched the towers of the city recede. He could call them all by name, and the names were as pleasing to him as the spires themselves—Santa Maria Gloriosa dei Frati, San Nicolo' dei Mendicanti, Santa Maria dei Carmini, bell towers that had called the faithful to worship for centuries, and also looked out for enemies coming across the lagoon.

If only Mary knew he was on his way to a dance theater. His trouble with Mary had been—well, the trouble had been manifold, but the best single image of it was that Max didn't dance. In the early days, they joked about it. Mary said they should go out dancing in town, she loved dancing, it was the best way to cleanse yourself of all the stress of a day; and Max said it was just the vertical expression of a horizontal desire. The first time he used this line, she laughed, and they wound up horizontal. But then she kept wanting to go out dancing, and he didn't want to, didn't know how, said that the way people threw them-

selves around a dance floor to that hip-hop noise was ridiculous. She said couldn't he just cut loose for once and
stop being so hyper-critical? He said he'd have to get really
drunk for that to happen; did she want him to be a lush?
She wouldn't mind, she said, if he'd be a little lusher.

They arrived at the theater, a converted warehouse
with rough brick walls and a gleaming wooden dance
floor. Next to a coffee vending machine, six or seven people
of various ages were sitting and talking, sipping espresso
from small plastic cups. There were two guys, and the rest
were women, all of them dressed in jeans and sweatshirts
and sneakers. Except for the tiny cups, it could have been
a coffee klatch in suburban Cincinnati. Sonia introduced
Max to everyone, and he smiled and took a seat near the
stage, hoping to be invisible. He wondered where the
dancers were.

Then one of the women got up, took off her shoes, and
stepped onto the stage. Bare feet planted, legs spread wide,
she threw out her arms, bent from the waist, and touched
her palms to the floor. Her long gray-streaked hair tum-
bled around her face. One of the men followed, taking little
warm-up leaps behind her, like a cartoon animal too happy
to remain on the ground. Within minutes the whole crew
had abandoned their cups and taken the stage, a flutter of
calisthenics and running in place. Then, without any signal
that Max could see, they all fell still, bodies limp. Over at
a console in one corner of the room, Sonia hit a button,
and a chorus of woodwinds began. The troupe exploded
into motion, and Max watched, agog, as they capered and
soared, coming as close as bodies can to being music.

When it was over and the dancers were resting, human
again, Sonia came over and sat next to Max. "Not bad, eh,
Todd? Wait 'til you see it with costumes."

Spangle lights up a cigarette and takes a silent drag.
Looks like another morbid casual molestation.
He can feel his beard growing.
He blows out a long plume of smoke.

"Max! How is going the translation? Is good book, no?"

They were sitting at dinner with Mariana, who had just brought a steaming bowl of pasta to the table.

What should he say? That the whole thing was a hopeless stew of cliché? That he had hit a little block? He cleared his throat, but Mariana spoke first.

"Don't you know it's bad luck to ask a writer about his work in progress? Who wants cheese?" Her English was smoother than her husband's, honed by years of working with Anglophone students at the institute.

Giampiero harumphed. "Max is no writer! Is translator only. Translator's job is to disappear. Yes, cheese." He gestured at his tagliatelle. "So, Max?"

"Well," Max said, "What makes a good book, in your view?"

Giampiero smiled. "First, bloody mess. Must to start with bloody mess, like world. Then, smart detective—but not too smart. Maybe stupid sometimes. Then, pretty girl. You know? Must to have romantic interest. In movie, Julia Roberts. Plus, happy ending. Reader want happy ending."

"And what makes an ending happy?"

"Detective must to solve crime. Clean up mess, no? Must to have girl. Big meal with good wine. *Bistecca fiorentina*, a nice Amarone."

Max didn't mention that it might be tough to get a good

bistecca fiorentina in Milwaukee. Instead, he asked, "When you say 'have girl,' you mean, like, once? Or like 'til death do us part'?"

Mariana broke in. "He means 'possess.'"

Giampiero cut her a look, not smiling, then turned to Max. "For happy ending," he said, "once is enough."

Suddenly one of the cats leapt up on Giampiero's shoulder, and he shouted and jumped to his feet, causing his chair to go flying behind him. The cat, of course, dug in its claws to hold on, draped now around the back of his neck. Giampiero shouted some more, words that Max had never heard, untranslatable. He seemed to rediscover some of his old soccer moves, juking and jiving at his end of the room, bumping into a potted plant that crashed from its shelf to the floor. Archy — or Mehitabel — hung on like death. Finally, Mariana got up, walked over to stand beside Giampiero, leaned in such a way that her own back was available as a pedestal, and the cat simply stepped down, leaping lightly to the floor, where he licked his chest as if nothing had happened.

Mariana said, "Archetto! Would you like a little nice cream?" Giampiero glowered and said nothing.

That night, Max got up at he didn't know what time. Let's say it was 2:17. He had to use the bathroom. Maybe he had drunk a bit too much wine at dinner. He stepped out, a little wobbly, into Sonia's living room. He could feel the whole city floating. Santa Fosca, Santa Lucia, Santa Maria della Salute. He thought he could hear canal water lapping at the foundations of the building.

He found himself in a room full of moonlight. In front of him stood a silhouette, a woman with wings, the madonna of the bicycle tires. He approached her, and asked her to dance.

Spangle has never been loster. He will never know whose fault it is. He sleeps with a golden retriever named Ginger, and hates it when she rolls over and plays dead. Little Trudy dreams of horses with magnificent shlongs. The house is full of sauce pans.

When he flirts with Penny, she says, "No way, buddy. Why don't you get with it?"

Citgo

The Dream Part

After the dream, Winters got up without waking Becky and shuffled to the bathroom in the dark. It had seemed so real. He was in a maternity ward, because *he* was about to give birth. Amidst the gleaming steel equipment and the floating blue clothes of doctors and nurses, there was Becky at the side of his bed, saying, "Well, you're on your own now, big boy."

In the bathroom, he didn't turn on the light. He searched with his hands, and was relieved to find that his middle-aged gut was unchanged. Relieved, and then strangely disappointed.

At the breakfast table the next morning, he described it to Becky — except for the part about what she had said. And the part about being disappointed.

She looked up from the newspaper. "So: want another waffle? Now that you're eating for two?"

"Don't mind if I do," he said, and patted his substantial shirtfront. "Junior needs his nourishment."

She dropped a waffle in the toaster. "Sweetie?"

Uh-oh. "Sweetie" was never good.

"Are you going to do something about the woodchuck?"

"Yes," he said. "I am definitely going to do something about the woodchuck. Right now." He stood up. "Where's my blowtorch?"

She sighed.

"What did we do with the AK-47?"

She waited.

"Do we still have that sack of Agent Orange out in the garage?"

Then he paused. Always a mistake.

"Soon?" she said.

He sat down. "I'll get one of those Hav-a-Hart traps today. Heck, it's Sunday, I'll get two. Maybe while I'm at it I can catch me a better job."

The woodchuck lived under the breezeway that connected their little house to its garage, where there wasn't any foundation, just gravel over the hard Vermont clay. Winters had never actually seen it coming or going, but he had seen the spot where the gravel had been dug away to make a dark burrow, just below their mail slot, and he had watched neighborhood dogs stop to sniff there, straining at their leashes. And of course he had heard about the creature's depredations: it tore into Becky's little garden of cucumbers and zucchini, no matter what kind of fencing she built, and it wreaked havoc in the Shacketts' blueberries and the Marriers' flowers.

Most of all, though, it ate his apples. Every evening, when Winters stood at the kitchen window doing the dishes, he looked into the back yard and saw the woodchuck standing on its hind legs in the same spot, just at the edge of the woods, with an apple in its forepaws, munching away. It practically said "Howdy!" and "Thanks!"

Winters finished his waffle, took his breakfast plate to

the sink, and looked out there. Nothing but woods. The woods weren't deep, just a little belt of maples and poplars that ran about a hundred yards down a rocky slope before bottoming out at the back side of the apartment complex on Pine Street. They stood on land that wasn't worth clearing, even this close to town, where property prices were shooting up by the month. Becky, who was in real estate, said those woods made their property much more valuable than it would be if it just backed up immediately on that ugly building. In a few weeks, you would be able to see straight through the bare trees to the lights of the apartments, and watch the headlights of cars prowling in the rear parking lot. Now, though, in October, there was still a screen of leaves. Winters liked to imagine it as a forest that went on for miles.

He wondered where to put a trap. Right by the breezeway? Maybe there was a whole family of woodchucks in there, a whole woodchuck town. Wouldn't they suspect that something was afoot? "Look, honey, somebody brought us a cage! With peanut butter crackers already laid out for us! How thoughtful!"

He put on a jacket and stepped out into the front yard. Obviously, instead of peanut butter he should use apples. There were so many of them—dozens every day, fallen overnight, whether there was a breeze or not. Who knew that such a scrawny, ill-tended tree could produce so much fruit? He had bought the tree for six bucks, at an Arbor Day sale down at the elementary school, and planted it in their bare little front yard, hoping that someday it would provide shade on a hot July afternoon. At the time, this seemed like a ridiculous act of faith, because the thing was just a dark yardstick, without a single shoot. That was when he and Becky had just moved into the little house, after years of renting and saving for their first home, so they could start a family. Maybe he should have done some research on apple trees. Now, twenty years later, the thing was still too wispy to cast a shadow worth mentioning, but it was thirty feet tall, its branches tangling with the forsythia that had seemed so distant when he planted it.

And it certainly knew how to pump out the apples, which, having fallen, got caught in the lawnmower and made the yard a paradise for bees and slugs. No doubt he should have picked them before they fell, and given them away—but that would have required a ladder, and an effort, and someone to give them to. So every morning before work he plucked the windfalls from the dewy grass and heaved them one by one over the little cape, waiting to hear the crash as they hit the woods behind; and every evening as he did the dishes (his chore, since Becky did the cooking) he watched the damn woodchuck enjoy its fruity meal. The beige fur of its belly, exposed as it stood eating, looked as soft as a cat's.

The Person Part

"Honey?" he said, poking his head back in the kitchen door. She was still at the breakfast table. "I'm going out to buy us a heavy-duty woodchuck trap. Need anything at the hardware store? They're having a special on kalashnikovs."

"Don't forget—I need the car this afternoon. I'm showing that house over in Lakeview."

Right. Her car was in the shop. "No problem," he said. "I'll just be here slaughtering woodchucks, anyway."

And then the car wouldn't start. The so-called good car. It wouldn't do anything. He turned the key, and all it did was click-click-click-click. He peered under the hood. He might as well have been gazing into the guts of a broken computer, or the brain of a kid with Down syndrome. He knew nothing about cars. His father's idea of car maintenance had been to buy a new Buick every three years, which made the Buick dealer so loyal that he would send a mechanic to the house anytime there was the slightest trouble. Winters wasn't exactly on that kind of maintenance plan: he had had the Subaru for ten years now. He jiggled something, tightened the cap to something else. He didn't even know where the dipstick was.

It occurred to him what Becky would say, and he almost laughed. Name some damn fool crazy suffering inexplicable sonofabitch thing — a suicide bomber attacking a school, or a tsunami taking out two hundred thousand unsuspecting Asians, or even just an ordinary woman having a miscarriage — and she'd sigh, and say, "Everything happens for a reason." A reason like what? he used to ask. And she would answer. To teach the nation that it needs better security. To remind the survivors how precious life is. Or or or — she was still working on the miscarriage one.

What the hell would be the reason for disabling his car? To remind him how incompetent he was? He closed the hood and tried the ignition again. Click-click-click-click and then, suddenly, the engine groaned and turned once, twice, sputtered, and coughed into life. He gave it some gas. Oh, the power. Life was good again.

But he knew that he had only dodged a bullet; he'd have to get it to a mechanic right away. He didn't bother going back in the house to tell Becky; he was afraid the car would die on him and never start again. She didn't need to know. With any luck, he'd get the car fixed, buy that trap, and be home before noon.

Of course, on Sunday the dealership was closed. Winters

had heard that only suckers take their cars to a dealership for service—but he did it anyway. He didn't know one mechanic from another, so why should he choose old Rusty Toolbelt over the clean, cushy environs of the Subaru service shop, with the big TV, the complimentary coffee, and the stack of recent magazines? But today he was hostage to the calendar, to his sense that something could go wrong at any minute and leave him stranded in all his automotive ignorance in the middle of traffic. What if the engine quit at this traffic light? He kept it revving unnaturally high. The morning sun slanted blindingly through the windshield, and he pulled down the visor.

The doctor had said that the miscarriage was just a freak of nature, nothing was wrong, sometimes these things were just mysterious. They should try again. So they tried again. And again. They had sex in every season, at every hour of the clock, in every position, on every diet, in every room of the house (and also in the MacKinnons' laundry room, during that Christmas party)—and nothing took. Click click click click. They laughed, and tried some more. But every time they tried, Winters felt the spectral presence of this other person in the room, this person they were trying to create. Nothing took, and eventually they just stopped trying. When he suggested that they consider adoption, Becky said no, quickly, in the quiet voice that meant her mind was made up. Adoption wasn't natural.

That was twenty years ago. Becky joined a Bible group for young professionals, and within a year she was number one in home sales for the whole county. Winters didn't know what the hell to say about the Bible group; that kind of stuff was just beyond him. Did people really believe that something written by some sandy scribe in the year 100 should somehow matter in their lives? He kept his mouth shut. But he was always supportive of Becky's work. Even now: he had to make sure the car was ready for her afternoon call.

He always imagined that the person was a girl. He didn't know why. Maybe because he wouldn't have wanted to wrestle with a boy like the boy he had been, intense and painfully sensitive to any imagined slight from his own father, wounded by any suggestion that he could have done better, should have done more. He couldn't quite imagine how to love a son, but a daughter—who couldn't love a daughter?

Here on the left was a service station. At least, he hoped it was a service station, not just one of those multiplex gas-pump extravaganzas with the full spread of Lil' Debbie cakes and no one around who knew a cam shaft from a camisole. The red triangle of the Citgo sign beamed an image of something safe and corporate and not quite English. The more he looked at it, the more nonsensical it seemed. Citgo, citgo, sit-go. It sounded more like commands for a dog than the shop of a mechanic.

It was certainly dirty enough to qualify as an honest-to-God service station. The lot was littered with old Jeeps and Volvos that looked like they hadn't budged in fifteen years. Every inch of concrete was stained with a layer of oil; what if somebody dropped a match? Winters drove up close to the once-white box of a building that brooded over all this detritus. He didn't dare stop and turn off the engine until he was absolutely sure that someone here could help. There were three service bays yawning open, and next to them a little office with glass walls on the two sides that faced the world. The glass was plastered with signs of all kinds. OPEN. Pay Before You Pump. No Checks Accepted. My Other Car Is a Motorboat. And the most beautiful sign of all: Mechanic On Duty.

The Grammar Part

The mechanic, if that's what this kid was, was busy with a car in one of the bays, and too young to trust with anything. Unless it was Sunday and nobody else was open and your wife had to get to Lakeview by one o'clock. He was wearing a standard-issue blue Citgo jacket with "Bill" in friendly script on the chest, and a pair of big baggy denim shorts that hung below his knees, leaving his calves bare down to his grimy sneakers. Wasn't it too cold for that? Shocks of dirty blond hair arrowed out from under his Red Sox cap.

Winters pulled the Subaru to one side of the building, and left it running while he went to inquire. When Bill (if that was really his name) saw him from the corner of his eye, he shouted, "With you in a minute! Soon as I finish this inspection!" Winters stepped into the little office to wait.

Inside there was another kid, even younger, sitting at the counter, watching a portable black-and-white TV. He might have been fourteen, with just the beginning of some scraggly dark facial hair that didn't yet cover his acne. He too was wearing a baseball cap, the standard blue jacket, and the oversized shorts—but he really needed the extra room in those culottes: this kid was a good forty pounds overweight. His jacket said "Butch." Who names a child Butch? Could this be Bill's younger brother? Surely he wasn't old enough to hold down a job on his own.

"Help you?" he said.

Winters pointed vaguely at the window, in the direction of the sign. "I, uh, need a mechanic?" He didn't mean it to sound like a question.

The kid looked toward the service bay. "He'll be right with you. He's almost done that inspection."

Almost done *with* that inspection, Winters thought. When did people decide they could just start leaving out prepositions? When Becky went to spend the night at her mother's place in St. Albans, she said, "I'm going to sleep over Mom's house." And he said, "Really? That doesn't sound very comfortable." He didn't need to answer Butch, who had already gone back to watching the TV.

He should know better by now than to question Becky's grammar; it just ticked her off. There was a time, years ago, when she had rolled her eyes in amusement and said, "I'm just a farm girl, OK? I don't know nothin' 'bout no propositions, Mister Grammar Man!" For a while she even called him GM, lovingly. Now, when he corrected her, she just pressed her lips more tightly together. OK, so no one likes having her mistakes catalogued — but you'd think she would have learned to get certain things right by now. Sometimes Winters thought she peppered her speech with solecisms just to get under his skin.

The problem was, it wasn't just Becky. Mistakes were everywhere. Looking around the little office of the service station, he immediately started finding language problems. "Quality" Used Tires. What the hell did those quotation marks mean? Were the tires quality, or not? And *what* quality, anyway? "Prior to service, it is imperative that the customer should leave their keys in the car." "Prior to"? What was wrong with a good old-fashioned "before"? "It is imperative that" was just a fancy way of saying "should," which was already in the sentence. And the customer should leave *their* keys? A customer isn't a *they*. The whole sentence was a disaster.

Winters' grammar-vision was an occupational hazard. As the PR guy for a small insurance company, he was the only English major in the building, and every official communiqué had to cross his desk for a grammar-check. He might not know what to do about a woodchuck that was tearing through the gardens of his neighborhood, or how to deal with a car that wouldn't start; but he took pleasure in using the right words, achieving a certain clarity in life. It made him crazy that the so-called leader of the so-called free world was such a butcher of language. He couldn't help feeling there was a moral element in marshaling language precisely: it showed that you cared enough to get things right.

Bill stepped into the office. "I'm about done here," he said to Winters. "Just gotta run the paperwork." He went to a computer behind the counter and started punching keys. Butch didn't budge from his high stool in front of the TV.

The Gollum Part

Just then they heard the ding! of something bumping over the line out by the gas pumps, and the clatter of metal on concrete. Seconds later, another guy stepped into the office. It would be more accurate, Winters thought, to say that the guy slinked into the office. He was long rather than tall, because he stooped so much that his wiry body seemed to be sliding in several directions at once, like Gollum. His long stringy brown hair extended below his black knit cap and hung limply over the collar of his denim jacket, and his face was lined with years, or cares, or both; it was hard to tell how old he was. He was the kind of guy who would live in the Pine Street Apartments.

"Hey!" he said to Winters. "Can I get some air?"

Winters was tempted to tell the guy that he was welcome to all the air he wanted, but he refrained. Bill looked up from the computer. "Yeah, just a minute," he said. He looked back down. "Damn computer is slower than a tax refund."

"I know how to solve that one," said Gollum. "Don't pay no taxes and you don't wait for no refund."

Winters winced, but didn't say anything.

"Right?" said Gollum, turning to Winters with a snaggle-tooth grin. "Am I right, or am I right?"

Fortunately, he didn't seem to need a response. He slinked around the little office, took a packet of spark plugs from a shelf, examined it briefly, put it back down. He spoke to Winters again. "Oh, I shoulda said. I don't have no two bucks for the air. But how's if I pay with jokes?"

Winters shrugged. Did he look like someone who worked in a service station?

Butch and Bill seemed to be able to tell that the man hadn't addressed them; they didn't look up. It didn't matter to Gollum.

"So," he said, putting on his straightest face, "Why did the blonde write 'TGIF' on her shoes?"

Becky especially loathed blonde jokes. But she wasn't here. Winters decided to humor the guy. "Why?"

"Toes Go In First!"

Gollum cackled. "But seriously," he added, trying to get the attention of Butch and Bill. "Why did the blondes freeze at the drive-in?"

Butch looked up from the TV and said, "Why?"

Gollum could hardly restrain himself. "Because they went to see 'Closed for the Winter'!" He elbowed Winters, who hadn't realized that the man was standing so close to him. "Get it?"

Winters smiled.

"You laugh," Gollum said — although no one had — "but I'm serious. You gotta feel badly for those young women."

"Feel bad," Winters said, and then wished he hadn't.

"Excuse me?" Gollum backed off a little.

"Feel *bad*," Winters said again. "If you say 'I feel badly' you mean you're not good at feeling."

Gollum looked at him for a second. "No, I don't," he said. "Don't tell me what I mean. I know what I mean."

"Well, then you should *say* it," said Winters.

"I *did* say it," the man said. "You were just listening funny." He looked over at Butch. "Hey," he said, "you know why cannibals don't eat blonde comedians?"

Butch shook his head. "Why?"

"Because they taste funny!" Gollum cracked up. Then he looked at Winters. "Did I get that one right, Mister Wizard? Did I mean 'funnily'? No, and I'll tell you why: because that would ruin the joke!"

Finally, Bill looked up from the computer. "OK. Now. What's up?"

Gollum said, "I need some air for my bike!"

Bill nodded, and turned to Winters, who said, "I, uh, don't know what the problem is, but my car wouldn't start at first this morning, and then it barely turned over and kicked in, so I drove here and left it running . . ." He nodded in its direction, out on the lot.

"How was it running yesterday?"

"It was fine yesterday. I mean, I didn't notice anything. But when I tried to start it this morning, it just went 'click-click-click-click.' My wife needs the car this afternoon. Not that *she* ever thinks about any preventive maintenance. I'm supposed to take care of the cars."

"Ain't *that* always the way," said Gollum. "Can't live with 'em, can't live without 'em, can't make 'em take care of cars." Winters couldn't tell if the man was making fun of him or not.

Bill turned to Butch. "You get off your butt and help this gentleman get some air." Butch scowled, and eased off his stool. Gollum led him outside. Bill looked at Winters and said, "Let's see what we can do." He ducked into the service bay, took a machine the size of a cigar box off a shelf, walked out to the Subaru, and popped the hood. Winters could only follow.

Bill looked up at him and said, "Chances are? It wasn't really running fine yesterday. Chances are it was goin' south already, but just so gradual that you didn't notice." Winters didn't say anything about that truncated adverb; he didn't need to antagonize the one person who might be able to help him. Bill attached a couple of cables to the battery and connected them to the little machine, which he rested on, on—some other engine part. Numbers started flashing on an LED monitor. "OK," he said. "We just let this baby run a few minutes, see what we got." He headed back into the office.

Winters didn't want to follow the guy around like a puppy—but he wasn't doing any good standing out here on the oily concrete, staring at numbers on a display that meant absolutely nothing to him. Over at the air pump, Butch had already given Gollum's battered old bike a shot of air in both tires, and they had disappeared. It was lonely out here.

He stepped back into the office just in time to hear Gollum say, "Shine a flashlight in her ear!" And then crack up again. He was apparently still paying off the full two dollars' worth of air. At this rate, he'd be there all day. Butch had gone back to his stool and TV; Bill was messing with the computer again.

Just then a young woman walked in. An actual blonde. She looked like she was probably a student at the university, up on the hill—tight jeans, a red tee-shirt, an off-white windbreaker that wasn't zipped up. All conversation ceased.

The Blonde Part

She looked at the four men in the crowded little office — Bill hunched over the computer, Butch in front of the TV, Winters in clean blue jeans and a button-down shirt, and Gollum standing next to him, grimy, unshaven, still chuckling at his most recent jape — and she said, "Can somebody tell me how to get to this furniture sale on Route 7? I keep seeing signs for it, you know, it's a special close-out? But they don't tell you how to get there."

Gollum spoke first. "What kind of furniture you need? Like, a dining-room set? A bedroom set? A chair? I can sell you a good chair."

She looked at him for just a moment, and then addressed Winters. "This place I'm looking for is some kind of factory outlet. It's one of those end-of-season sales, you know? But their signage is terrible."

Signage? Winters saw the would-be word in his mind with a squiggly red line under it. No wonder this girl was lost. But she was cute, and she had obviously chosen to speak to him because he seemed the most respectable person in the room, the one most likely to help. Unfortunately, he had no idea where this furniture store would be. Before he could speak, Gollum broke in.

"He don't know nothin', girlie. He thinks you need to be a walkin' dictionary to tell a fuckin' joke. He can't even reckonize a dead battery when he hears one. He's so full of shit his eyes are brown."

Winters was speechless. His eyes were blue. How did he know it was the battery?

Gollum went on. "So: a chair? A waterbed? What do you need?"

"I just need some directions," she said—again, addressing herself to Winters. "I just want to find this store."

"Listen to me," said Gollum, slinking his neck in Winters' direction. "This guy's a cigar-store Indian. Why do you think he's here on a Sunday morning? His wife can't stand him. His car goes click-click-click-click. At least he's *got* a car. Not that he knows shit about it." He leaned in closer to the young woman, who leaned back a little but held her ground. "Just between you and I, honey," he said, "Be careful with this guy. Use the wrong word, and he'll have your sweet ass on a platter."

That was when Winters decked him.

The Ending Part

Bill helped Gollum sit up. "You all right, man?" Butch watched from his stool. The young woman had backed away as far as the doorway to the office. She must have wanted to dispense with the directions and just try her luck on the road. But who could walk away from a scene like this?

Winters watched, too, as if from another body, from another planet, through a telescope. He hadn't hit anyone since second grade, when he and Laird Schick used to have fist fights in the back of the school bus for the amusement of the older kids. He wasn't sure who that was, the person who hit this guy. His hand was stinging.

Gollum moved his jaw up, down, sideways. Suddenly, he seemed like a frail old man. Had Winters just clocked someone's grandpa? But he didn't seem to be seriously hurt. Bill got him a little paper cup of water from the cooler in the corner. The woman continued backing out the door, and then just turned and walked to her car. She started it up and cleared out.

Finally, Gollum spoke. "Nice one, guy." He was looking at Winters. "You scared her off." He rubbed his jaw.

"Hey," he said. "Who's the dead blonde in the closet?"

When nobody answered, he said, "The winner of the 1999 Hide-and-Seek contest!"

He cracked up. Then he rose to his feet, slinked out to his bike, got on it, and rode off without another word, waving as he went.

Bill shrugged, and went out to check on Winters' car. Butch turned back to his TV. Winters stood there in the office, looking out the window towards the road. He wanted the girl to come back. He wanted to explain. He wanted to give her perfect directions to that store. He would give her a ride himself, and they would talk. She would tell him how her parents never understood her, how her sister got all the attention. She would describe her boyfriend, and ask him why guys were so screwed up. And he would explain. He would explain it all.

Bill came back in, and told him he needed a new battery. He said OK. He probably paid way too much for it. But the car started right up.

He had a little trouble gripping the steering wheel with his right hand. He didn't go to the hardware store. He wanted to catch up with the girl, make sure she found that furniture place. But he drove right home. When he got out of the car, he went to the foot of the apple tree, where the grass was strewn with apples. He picked one up. It was cold and slick in his fingers, still wet with dew. He imagined Becky at the window, watching. She was going to be pissed about the trap.

He heaved the apple over the house. It made his hand hurt like hell. He picked up another one.

ALEX IN DODOLAND

So here she was, in a hot, scratchy, suffocating dodo costume, virtually blind because the eye holes were cut for
someone taller, a crick in her neck from the effort of holding up the heavy plastic beak, and tired of hauling around
her huge and ridiculous football-shaped body, flapping her
nonfunctional wings at visitors. That was part of her job:
Be sure to flap your wings. All afternoon Humpty Dumpty
had been hitting on her, literally, bumping his three-pil-
lowed girth into her tufted backside whenever he thought
their supervisor wasn't looking. The little crypto-fascist.
He wasn't even supposed to be in her part of the park; he
was supposed to be sitting on a rustic stone wall over by
the croquet ground. But he was terrified of the Queen of
Hearts, and he'd rather be over here harassing the Dodo,
anyway. He said the visitors would rather see Humpty in
action than just sitting on a stupid wall. He was probably
right about that—the visitors seemed delighted by his antics,
no matter how inauthentic—but couldn't he find something
better to do? Every time he bumped her big old awkward
bird butt, she couldn't help teetering over onto her top-heavy
beak, because her damn wings were too stubby to break her
fall. And then she couldn't get back up on her preposterous

three-taloned feet unless two of the non-costumed workers came and pulled her up. She lay there flapping her useless wings and squawking while Humpty mugged for the laughing visitors, who seemed to think it was all part of the show. No wonder she became extinct.

She needed to pee. Badly. Whatever genius designed this costume apparently didn't think about the excretory needs of its wearer: in order to attend to such business, she had to take off the whole damn thing, which took at least five minutes (oh, for a pair of opposable thumbs!), and then another five to get it back on. As it was, she had to rely on the kindness of a relative stranger, the Queen of Hearts, who, it turned out, really wasn't so terrifying. She was an older woman, a local whose English was pretty limited, but all she had to say in public was "Off with their heads!" and if she said it with a bit of a Frenchy accent then she just sounded like a real mad monarch should sound. On the very first day, she took pity on the poor girl in the changing room after work, struggling with those funky little wings to remove the detachable top half of her costume. "Off with your head!" she said, and lifted it clear. Their one break from work, in the middle of the afternoon, wasn't long enough for this whole operation, so the Dodo had learned to drink nothing with her lunch, or during the break, either. As a result she got crushing dehydration headaches, because it was midsummer in Mauritius and she perspired like a horse inside the damn costume. Maybe the dodo died out because of terminal headaches. Or maybe because its bladder exploded. What a way to go.

This wasn't exactly what Alex had in mind when she first signed up for the Dodo Expedition. It was just after graduation, and she was hanging around campus with a work-study job that should have expired when she picked up her diploma, only Professor Niemand cut a little red tape for her, because he knew that she really didn't have anywhere else to go. Not yet, anyway. She was planning to go to graduate school, maybe in archeology. Or maybe paleontology. But they were so hard to spell. Maybe just plain old geology. She hadn't quite got it together to apply to grad schools during her senior year, what with the thesis and all, and — well, you know. She needed a year off from school, anyway.

Professor Niemand, who was a world-renowned archeo-paleo-geologist or something like that, had known about her situation because, well, he and she had had, this, sort of like, *thing*, for a while. Sort of. Only his wife wasn't thrilled to walk into his office one day (she had her own key) and discover him, um, excavating, on the couch that he kept in the corner for naps. So he wasn't allowed to see Alex anymore, and to tell the truth she was pretty upset, even though he had funny teeth and a really hairy back, like some kind of prehistoric woolly mammal. He was basically a nice man, and a famous something-or-other. The wife insisted that he cut all connections, so Alex had to let go of the cushy job checking IDs at the geology lab, as if anybody really wanted to go look at a bunch of bauxite anyway.

And that was when she saw the poster, in the back hallway of the Earth Sciences building, next to the vending machines where she was getting herself some of that crappy coffee that spritzes into the little plastic cup and calls itself cappuccino. "Parlez-Vous Francais?" the poster said, in block letters imposed over a photoshopped picture of a pristine beach framed by two palm trees, looking out to a perfect blue sea. Well, she parled a little Francais — but thank Dieu, the rest of the poster was in English. It was all about The Great Dodo Expedition, the first comprehensive attempt to reconstruct and understand that famously extinct creature. The fine print explained that the dodo had existed only on the beautiful island of Mauritius, off the southeast coast of Africa, where the official language was English but the locals still spoke a French creole. The last living dodo was seen in 1661, but the island was still rich with its remains. The task of the expedition was to unearth its secret. Why did it become extinct? Did its history contain a lesson for the rest of us? How did it get such a silly name? OK, that last question wasn't on the poster—but Alex was curious.

This was perfect. She would get out of her little college town. She would learn how to spell paleontology. She would tell her mother to cool it with the "What are you going to do with your life?" questions, because she'd be supporting herself with this job, at least for now. She would meet a hot cabana boy named Jacques or Pierre. Or Luc, yeah, Luc. Her tongue made that little round shape as she silently mouthed his name. How could she not do this? She sent a curt, triumphant e-mail to Professor Niemand (she could never really think of him as Rolf), announcing her decision. He quickly wrote back to ask if this was really the wise thing to do. Like he knew what was best for her. She decided to stop checking e-mail, and jumped down the rabbit hole.

So here she was, suffocating in this ridiculous costume while that little right-wing egghead played hump-the-big-dead-bird with her behind. Alex suffered this indignity with as much dying-species stoicism as she could muster. It wasn't hard to simulate the dodo's legendary clumsiness, but she also wanted to recreate its mental and emotional qualities. She had done some acting in college, and she was always good at plumbing her character's motivation. How would you feel, she asked herself, if you were on your way to extinction? And the answer came back: long-suffering, imperturbable, accustomed to turning the other cheek.

"*Be* the dodo," she exhorted herself, with all the inscrutable calm of Bill Murray. Let the absurd little nursery-rhyme man make a nuisance and a fool of himself. So she turned the other cheek, and Humpty, apparently delighted by the big tufty target, hurled his rotundity at it with glee. Down she went again, with a muffled squawk.

Well, she thought, as she lay on her plastic belly and flapped her stumpy wings, when the customers complain about this travesty of history, science, and literature, at least Rijsdijk will fire Humpty's reactionary ass.

But in fact, after this brief flurry of action, she noticed that the customers weren't complaining at all. They were applauding! They had come to Dodoland because it was the only show in town, fearful of a dreary history lesson, hoping for a little cotton candy and if they were lucky maybe a spin on the tilt-a-whirl, and instead they got to watch a giant egg buggering a giant bird. They roared with joy. She heard a Frenchman shout, "Allez, 'Umptee!"

So 'Umptee didn't lose his job. In fact, when Rijsdijk spoke with them after work, he suggested that they engage in further "horseplay," since it was clearly popular with the customers. Humpty, divested of his pillows and his plastic egghead, was a skinny little Italian whose biggest hero in the world was Dick Cheney. Vaffanculo was a Law 'n' Order kind of guy, as long as boys could still be boys. In the employees' lunchroom Alex had heard him fulminating in his pidgin English about the war on terrorism. She had tried, in her imagination, to transform him into a Luc, but he had insisted on being skinny and non-French and in favor of regime change. He was sure they would still find weapons of mass destruction in some fiendish Dr. No-like bunker. He beamed a narrow smile at Alex, who was sitting at the other end of the couch in Rijsdijk's office, her snarly blonde curls trailing over a black Dodo Expedition t-shirt. Ever the good student, she nodded brightly at her boss.

Rijsdijk was the founding father of Dodoland. He was thirtysomething, blond and lanky, one of those ridiculously good-looking northern Europeans who spoke better idiomatic English than most Americans, with a little extra aspiration on the h's. "Since your hhhijinks obviously struck a chord with our audience, let's continue the festivities, eh? Whoever is most convincing—most able to, shall we say, destabilize the other?" He paused, with a knowing smile. "That person will get a raise."

Vaffanculo, whose English was a little more, shall we say, Italian, grinned and said, "Eez good, boss." He turned an appreciative gaze on Alex, as if he were dressing her in a dodo costume with his eyes.

Alex couldn't believe it. She hadn't prepared for anything like this. This was war. Nature red in tooth and claw. Sanctioned by the boss. She nodded brightly some more.

* * *

She had expected, upon arriving in Mauritius, to be doing something slightly more than waving cartoon appendages at visitors to a theme park called Dodoland. In fact, she *was* doing more: like all the other characters, she was a digger as well. Every morning at seven, hung over as French sailors on shore leave, they reported to the dodo dig, the actual reason they had signed on for this extravaganza. The thing was, digging dodo bones didn't pay. At least, it didn't pay the handful of dreamers who had responded to that ridiculous advertisement without being bankrolled by a department of archeo-paleo-geo-whatsit. Dodoland was their salvation. Or at least their lunch ticket, until they could save enough money for airfare back to the world. It was the brainchild of Rijsdijk, a Dutchman with an unpronounceable name and a genius for promotion. He was a thoroughly postmodern scientist, absolutely dedicated to the resurrection of the late lamented dodo and at the same time convinced that its famous failure was just the thing to finance that endeavor. Take a beautiful south-sea paradise, add a bit of legendary quasi-science, and hey presto, you've got eco-tourism. After all, it was working for the Darwinians who were exploiting the shit out of the Galapagos, and all they had to work with was a bunch of oversized turtles. Which were still *alive*, and dull as sponges. The whole advantage of the dodo, according to Rijsdijk, was that it was a goner, a memento mori, an unsettling presentiment of all things earthly. It was a murder mystery. It didn't pop up inconveniently to bore anyone with its scientific actuality. Toss in some tatty fairground rides and a few gratuitous characters from Lewis Carroll to please the kiddies, and you could start printing money. Carroll himself had once done essentially the same thing: he had written a dithering dodo into Alice's adventures back in 1865 just because a contemporary discovery had catapulted the poor dead bird into the headlines. All's fair in love and commerce.

But the gates to Dodoland never opened before noon, so every morning there was time for the diggers to dig. It was a perfect closed system. They all lived in a dorm just outside the park, in cheesy cinderblock rooms with the barest of amenities. Next door was the Hotel Mauritius, where cruise ships plying the waters between Capetown and Calcutta deposited unwitting tourists almost every day of the summer. Rijsdijk had cut a deal with the cruise line, guaranteeing a captive audience for his park. Then he had enlisted a crew of hopeful Mauritians and recent college graduates to dig, with the contractual understanding that every afternoon they would morph into smiling cartoon characters.

Across the street from the gates, down a hill of scree towards the interior of the island, was the actual focal point of The Great Dodo Expedition: the Mare aux Songes. When Alex had first done a little online research about the whole undertaking, she had loved this evocative name. The Sea of Dreams. How could you not want to go there, holding hands with Luc while you unearthed the secrets of life and death?

As it turned out, *songe* was a local creole term for some kind of tropical root vegetable, and the *mare* was not so much a sea as an unnavigable bog. But it was a bog that was chock-full of dodo bones. Mauritius was the only place on earth where they had ever been found, and the Mare aux Songes was ground zero. Apparently the dodos used to hold their conventions here. Or maybe they had been herded down here by the Dutch settlers who first discovered them in the sixteenth century, offered them a last cigarette, and then executed them *en masse* with blunderbusses. Or maybe they had just been mortified by their own ungainliness, and had toddled down here to expire in this swampy declivity, embarrassed to death. Nobody knew for sure. But the Great Dodo Expedition was intent on finding out.

Another reason for digging at this ungodly hour was that the mosquitoes were slightly less lethal at seven. Alex was almost always the first to arrive, because she tended to get a little less blitzed than the other diggers the night before. The English-speaking diggers, anyway. She didn't know where Vaffanculo hung out. Maybe he actually went to The Bandersnatch, the one bar in Cap Malheureux. Alex had checked it out on her first night, and decided it was the best hypothesis yet for the extinction of the dodo: you'd die, too, if the only place you could get a beer smelled like Clorox and sported a poster of Mister T above the bar. Instead, the English-speaking diggers usually congregated at the dorm room of Tweedledum and Tweedledee, the happeningest guys on the dig. Alex never learned their real names; everyone just called them Dum and Dee. They weren't twins, or even countrymen; Dum was Welsh and Dee was Scottish, or some such not-quite-English origin. Like all the other diggers, they had arrived on their own, looking for the light that never was on land or sea. But they had coagulated right away, and gathered around them a bunch of lonely buggers who were perfectly happy to drink their hooch and play cribbage and talk talk talk every night until the booze was gone. Some nights there was a bong, too, provided by Zimmer, a tall dude from St. Louis who wore a caterpillar suit during the day and sat on a giant plastic mushroom pretending to smoke from a hookah. So the room of Dum and Dee was very distinctly a testosterone zone. Sometimes they tried to get the Queen of Hearts to join them, but she just laughed and headed back into town, where she had to put dinner on the table for three little Cap Malheureuvians. Try saying that three times fast. The diggers didn't even try; they called all the Mauritians Martians, and then cracked up at their own cleverness.

Alex really didn't mind being the only chick in the room. Her father had cleared out when she was six, following which her mother entertained a series of friendly but slightly sketchy male friends who came by at all hours, and her three rowdy brothers kept the house loud and stupid, just the way she liked it. In the high school bathroom, she never really understood what the other girls were talking about. Dum, Dee, and company were nice guys, so laid-back they were falling down, and that was just about her speed right now. If there was more e-mail from Professor Niemand waiting on her laptop, well, it was a tree falling in an uninhabited forest.

So every morning, only slightly hung over, she was the first person at the dig. It was the coolest time of the day, and she liked sitting there on a fallen tree while she had her first head-clearing cigarette. Summer was supposed to be the rainy season, but so far every morning had dawned clear. She watched the light rise across the bog, and she thought. Basically, she thought about survival. How could you not, in a place like this? It was the ultimate cemetery: this was where a whole species bit the dust. Alex had always been a Darwinian, more or less, even before she learned about natural selection and all that stuff in high school bio. It just made sense to her. After all, the whole world was a competition—Arabs and Jews, Yankees and Red Sox, jocks and goths, professors' wives and girls who weren't quite diligent enough to make Phi Beta Kappa. And now there was little egg man and big dumb bird, vying for one narrow ecological niche in Rijsdijk's lanky Dutch heart. History hadn't been kind to either of them. But somebody had to win.

"Musing among the ruins?"

She looked up. The sun, which had sneakily risen while she was contemplating mortality, was streaming over the broad shoulders of the person speaking, utterly blinding her.

"You look different when you're not in costume," he said in a plummy voice.

She squinted. "Yeah, well, I'm never really at my best in papier-mâché and feathers."

"Ah, but you were splendid yesterday. When you showed such sang-froid after that attack from Humpty."

He said it with about three h's. Hhhumpty. She had never actually spent any time with Rijsdijk one-on-one; even the initial interview had been a group meeting with the other new diggers. She knew he was a big-deal scientist with degrees from every important university in western Europe, and he was also some kind of maverick: not every geo-ethno-rhino-laryngologist (or whatever) gets written up in *Newsweek* for his controversial theory on psycho-evolution. It was something about the latest dodo discoveries, and how they showed that the human race was on the fast track to extinction. She had mentioned all this to her mentor, hoping to score points for something besides having a cute butt. Professor Niemand had laughed. He said the theory was absurd, and Rijsdijk himself was obviously just a publicity hound, a fossil-scoffer with a messianic complex.

Right now, though, Rijsdijk was practically the sun-king.

"So," Alex said, clearing her throat, "what do you think we'll find here?" She pointed her cigarette towards the mephitic swampscape of trash-trees and stumps that lay before them, steaming in the early light.

"Oh, I don't *think*," he said. "I *know*. This is the last great graveyard of the dodo. We will find not just bones, no" — he paused for effect — "we will find entire skeletons. We will find what they were doing when it happened. The extinction. We will find the evidence of *why* it happened. This place is like Pompeii, you know? Except that Pompeii was two thousand years ago, and that was only one little town. *This*," he said with a flourish of well-muscled forearm, "was just three hundred years ago — practically yesterday, in geological time — and a whole species disappeared. I know why. We will find the proof."

Alex was about to ask him to explain when she saw the skinny legs of Vaffanculo making their way down the path from the parking lot up by the road.

Rijsdijk followed her eyes. "Ah, Mister Hhhumpty! Ready for some digging?" He turned to the gleaming set of shovels that waited in the back of his pick-up. "There's no time like the present!"

Vaffanculo smiled.

That afternoon he was worse than ever, buffeting her whenever he got a chance, knocking her from pillar to post. And she let him. She knew her part. If she fought back, it would just encourage him, like a bully on a playground. She was going to be bigger than this. That was how she would win.

Besides, she was starting to get better at managing the costume. After being knocked down, she found that with a complicated twist of one leg she could plant a talon behind her and pull herself back upright without assistance. Even better, if she heard him coming—and he always gave himself away with a high-pitched "snee-snee-snee" of excited laughter just before making contact—she could brace herself and take one of his stupid belly shots without even falling down. The first time this happened, it took him so by surprise that he bounced backwards on his own butt with a heavy thud. The crowd cheered. Someone yelled, "Go, Dodo!" Alex allowed herself a stoic little smile.

That evening, instead of going over to Dee and Dum's room, she pulled out her laptop, which she hadn't even unpacked since arriving three weeks before. She had made a vow to remain incommunicado, and she was keeping it. Her cell phone was turned off. When she passed the newsstand in front of The Bandersnatch, she looked the other way. Above all, she was resisting the temptation to send pleading, self-pitying, don't-you-want-me-back e-mails to Professor Niemand. She didn't need that creep. BE HERE NOW, she told herself every day. You big dummy, she usually added.

Getting online wasn't a problem. For all its isolation, Mauritius was proud of its status as the first nation in the world with coast-to-coast wireless. Of course, it helped that the whole nation was just thirty miles from coast to coast, but still. Alex noticed that she had dozens of new e-mails, and took care not to read the senders' names. Probably just a bunch of spam, anyway. Her penis was already big enough, thank you very much. She went straight to the web. She just wanted to know more about Rijsdijk's ideas.

What she found was fascinating. She wasn't too clear on all the technical terms, but she had learned enough evolutionary biology to get the gist. Essentially, he seemed to be saying that Darwin was wrong. Evolution wasn't a matter of random mutation after all; it was driven by psychological needs. Certain monkeys didn't just happen to inherit a gene that gave them a physical advantage over other monkeys; they *needed* to find a certain kind of shelter or a certain kind of food, and their need drove them to find it. And the other monkeys, the ones that didn't make it? They just didn't have the same drive. Oh, it was couched in much more scientific language, citing all sorts of studies—but that was it, really: need and desire. It even applied to plants, which needed to develop in their own ways. Who are we, Rijsdijk asked, to decide that plants don't have a kind of desire? We just don't understand their inner lives. If you've ever seen one of those time-lapse photos of a leaf turning towards the sun, it's hard not to see some kind of *volition* there. *Unless*, Rijsdijk wrote (he liked italics), *unless* you had been trained, like most mechanistic modern scientists, to deny the whole idea of *soul* in nature. He was proud, he said, to reject the soulless hypothesis. If you opened your mind to the deep *resonances* of the world, you would find that there was soul *everywhere*.

And the dodo? The dodo was Rijsdijk's great test case. What he seemed to be saying was that the dodo just gave up. It was managing fine, foozling along on its paradisical island without any predators to speak of, until the first humans landed. Suddenly, the dodo wasn't king of the hill anymore. The early settlers (who *happened* to be Dutch, Rijsdijk noted with shame) found that this big awkward bird couldn't fly, and that it was pathetically slow of foot. To hunt it they didn't need guns; they just walked up to it and clubbed it to death. And then they discovered that its meat didn't even taste good. At first, they called it *walghvogel*, or "loathsome bird." But then another name took hold: *dodaars*. "Fat ass."

Well, what would you do, if you had just lost your paradise and been branded a loathsome fat-ass to boot? According to Rijsdijk, the dodo simply lost its *drive*, its reason for being. It withdrew to the Mare aux Songes and it gave up the ghost.

And this, he said, could happen to humans, too. *Was* happening to humans. How else would you explain obesity and drug abuse and self-destructive apathy in one part of the species, while the rest of the race was busy starving or dying in natural disasters? Humans, he said, have become the *fat asses* of the modern world, sheltering ourselves in bogs of our own making, deluding ourselves that we're actually doing fine. *Unless*, he said, *unless* we find a new sense of purpose, some new desire that drives us to adapt, we are *doomed* to go the way of the dodo.

Alex let out a deep breath. It made so much sense. Oh, she could imagine that Professor Niemand would laugh at it, call it "soft-headed" and non-scientific—but what did Niemand know? He hadn't published anything in years. What was *his* need? He was tenured, with an office so big you hardly even noticed the couch in the corner. Where was *his* drive? If he had wanted to stand up to his wife, he could have. The man was *whipped*. And his ass was really pretty fat, if you wanted to be honest about it. Not to mention that hairy *neanderthal* back. She fell asleep with the computer still open in her lap, thinking of plants that want better lives. And imagining Rijsdijk's lanky expeditionary buttocks.

The next day in the park, the strangest thing happened: Humpty didn't bother her. He didn't even venture into her territory, apparently choosing to remain on his appointed wall like a good egg. What was his deal? Couldn't he take a little setback? Alex had to admit, she kind of missed him. The constant danger of a sudden rear assault from the egg-man had made the time go quickly. Now that she was just standing near the gate and waving feebly at idiot visitors with her wonky little arms, the hours dragged by as if she was already extinct, living out a posthumous eternity. What was up with Humpty? Was he still planning an attack? Was he just being perverse, now that Rijsdijk actually wanted them to tussle?

This was what Rijsdijk seemed to be wondering, too, when she ran into him outside the changing rooms that afternoon.

"Alex!"

How did he know her name? Well, he had the personnel files, duh. The Queen of Hearts, who was also just leaving, seemed to give them a funny look, but then she kept on moving. She had her little Martians to look after in town.

Rijsdijk said, "I notice that you and Hhhumpty did not, shall we say, *compete* this afternoon." He was looking especially sharp today, in his khaki shorts and khaki shirt, sleeves rolled up over his golden-haired forearms. With a pith helmet, he'd look ready for a descent of the Nile. But that would cover up his lustrous yellow hair.

"Um, no. He didn't come near me."

"Well, of course not."

"What do you mean?"

"You embarrassed him."

"I embarrassed *him*?" It was hard to think of Vaffanculo as capable of shame.

"Yes. You made him fall."

She bridled. "Well, if he didn't throw himself at me all afternoon, maybe he wouldn't fall."

Rijsdijk smiled, with an ostentation of oversized teeth. "But he *must* throw himself at you. This is his job. This is his definition in life. Like a salmon that swims upstream." He said "sal-mon" complete with the "l."

She absorbed this idea. "Well, maybe so—but that doesn't mean I just have to collapse at his feet."

"Ah, but it does. You are the dodo. The dodo falls. What are the customers to think? They think, 'Why does the dodo not fall?' You are the dodo. The dodo falls."

"So what am I supposed to do if he just stays over on his stupid wall? Fall down all by myself? I'm sorry, but I am *not* that lame."

Rijsdijk smiled again. "Sometimes," he said, "a person has to take some initiative." He looked at her meaningfully with his china-blue eyes. "Maybe he's nervous. Maybe he's playing hard to get."

"You don't mean you think he has, like, a crush on me?"

"I think this is possible. Think about it. I'll be at The Snatch." And he walked off.

Wait. *What* was possible? Alex was perplexillated. Was Vaffanculo actually interested in her? Did Rijsdijk just suggest that she meet him at the bar? Could she really be attracting all this masculine attention? It was true, she did have a cute butt, but she had never been Miss Popularity in school. Partly it was just that she always hung out with the guys: she was everybody's pal, and therefore not a candidate to be anybody's girlfriend. Until Niemand came along, and everything changed. For a while. But Vaffanculo? No way. She was saving herself for Luc.

She went back into the changing room, to make sure her hair looked OK.

* * *

One thing you had to say in favor of The Snatch: it was so dark in there, no one could really see that your hair was a mess, or that Mister T had become a little beige over the years. There were a couple of coffee-can ceiling lights down at one end of the bar, creating one bright patch on the scuffed hardwood floor and making everything else even darker. Still, as soon as Alex walked in she saw the gleam of Rijsdijk's hair, over in a corner booth. Barry White was groaning on the jukebox.

Rijsdijk looked up, and smiled. She made her way across the room, stumbling against a table or a chair in the dark. When she got to his booth, she found that someone was sitting across from him. The Queen of Hearts. Was that a look of embarrassment on her face?

Alex couldn't help asking, "Where are your children?"

The Queen of Hearts said, "I have no children. I tell men about children, they leave me alone." She looked at Rijsdijk with a smile. "But not *all* men." She put her hand out on the table, and he took it in his.

Alex didn't know what to do. Sit down with them? Leave them to their coochy-coo? Before she could decide, Rijsdijk nodded toward the bar with a grin. There was a stir of activity over there, and suddenly the music changed. Her hips recognized the rubbery guitar riff before her brain could place the words. "Well, you can tell by the way I use my walk I'm a woman's man . . ." And there at the bright end of the bar, emerging from the shadows in a blinding white suit, was Vaffanculo. Dancing. A gold necklace dangled at his open shirt, glinting in front of his hairless chest, and he pointed at the ceiling as he shook his cheekless booty. "Ha, ha, ha, ha, stayin' alive, stayin' alive." It was even more ridiculous than the routines they did in the park.

But the worst thing—yes, even worse than a skinny neo-con egg-man doing a full Travolta—was the look on Vaffanculo's face. Alex could see, now that her eyes had adjusted, that he was smiling straight at her. This whole spectacle was for her benefit. Vaffanculo seemed to think he was her beamish boy.

He gestured for her to join him in the spotlight. Alex did what her instinct told her to do: she waved, as if she took his invitation as a mere greeting, and she pointed to her watch, as if she had an important appointment to keep, and then she beat feet out of there. Too strange, too fast, too much sal-mon.

Back at her room, she took from her mini-fridge the pint of Cherry Garcia that she had been surprised to find at the general store, and that she had been saving for a rainy day. Ten spoonfuls later, she pulled out her laptop and went to mail, went directly to mail, did not pass Go, did not collect two hundred dollars. Discovered all the usual crap, which she didn't bother deleting. Found the one sender's name she was hoping for. Took another spoonful. Opened the message, already a week old. Read.

> *Dear Alexandra,*
>
> *How are you? It seems so strange to write to you so far away, after so much time. I know it has only been three weeks, but it seems like forever. Well, we all know that time is a psychological phenomenon . . . Still, it seems like yesterday that you were here, in the office . . .*
>
> *But I can't think about that anymore. Mimi says she will forgive me. Somehow. I'm sure she will watch me more closely now. Maybe that's what I really wanted, anyway.*
>
> *I have no claim on you, I know. Still, I wonder what you're doing in that strange place halfway around the world. I just miss you, is all.*
>
> *How's the Dodo Expedition going? I wonder, what's the point? I mean, all discoveries can be useful, so if you find some fossils, more power to you. But really, why should we care so much about the poor dumb dodo? Do you remember what we read in archeo-paleontology? Ninety-nine point nine per cent of all species that ever lived have become extinct. Why not the dodo? Why not, for that matter, the human?*
>
> *Good luck, my dear —*
> *Rolf*

She stared at the screen until the pixels imprinted themselves on her retinas. Then she blinked, hit the off button, and finished her pint.

And then, stoked on a sugar high, she headed back out,

onto the mean streets of Cap Malheureux. The night was still young. She didn't know where she was going. She just needed to walk.

It was raining now, steadily, softly, purposefully. Maybe the season had finally arrived. Even though the temperature was still in the eighties, there was a breeze off the ocean; it was almost refreshing. Alex let it rain on her, washing over her head and shoulders.

She turned a corner somewhere in town, and ran smack into Dum. Or was it Dee? Whatever. He smiled. "Alex! What's a nice girl like you doing in a place like this?"

She shrugged. "Oh, you know." Maybe it *was* Dee. He had sort of a nice smile. He nodded sympathetically, as if indeed he did know. Or maybe it was just that she might as well have been competing in a wet t-shirt contest. She had never liked bras.

He kept smiling. "You know what you need?"

"Please tell me."

"You need a pick-me-up." Was that a Welsh accent, or a Scottish one? She had never been sure which was which. She felt a hand on her shoulder.

In the rain, somehow, the hand felt more urgent, like it had more fingers than the usual friendly hand. Alex shook her head. Luc! she thought. *Luuuuuc!* She swatted at the hand, which Dum (or Dee) withdrew immediately.

"Alex?" he said. "You OK?"

"Yeah," she said. "Yeah. I've just . . . just got to . . . just . . ." And she walked away down the sidewalk, into the rain.

"Alex?"

She kept walking. After a while, she noticed that she wasn't in town anymore. She had wandered into a little residential district, where modest wood-frame houses stood side by side with tar-paper shacks. A real Martian neighborhood. She found herself standing under a canopy of trees, gazing into an illuminated window.

Inside, there was a little group of people, what do you call that, a *family*, that's it, sitting around a table. Mother and father and two little kids. Mother served food. Father talked. Kids took food and ate, and sometimes they talked, too. Alex stood there and stared. It was like domestic pornography. Oh yeah, baby, give me some more of that stew. Talk clean to me. Offer me some biscuits like you mean it. Alex couldn't stop looking. Maybe it was just the rain, but fat tears seemed to be streaming down her face.

The next morning, she slept in. It was still raining, perfect weather for staying in bed. Who needed to slog around in a muddy swamp on a day like this? She dreamt that she was a giant bird incapable of flight. Nothing would lift her from the goddamn ground. She wore the earth like a straitjacket.

At noon, she reported for duty at the park. She still needed that paycheck. In the changing room, the Queen of Hearts gave her a welcoming smile, and said, "'Allo, Dodo! Ready for another day?"

Alex shrugged and said, "What's the point? The Dodo is still going down."

The Queen of Hearts paused. "Well? Everysing is going down. So? Off with zeir heads!" She smiled a happy little genocidal smile.

Alex climbed into her costume, then toddled out and took her place just inside the gate. What the hell, she thought.

Thanks to the weather, there was just a handful of customers in the park, faces hardly visible beneath their umbrellas, like so many toadstools sprung up overnight in the rain. The Dodo waved politely, but her mind was elsewhere. She was waiting for something.

After a while, she heard it: "snee-snee-snee." She turned, and got up on her tiptoes to see through the little eye-holes in her chest. There he was, distending his ridiculous belly to bump her anew. She reared up above him, gathered all the weight of her heavy beak, and brought it down on top of his stupid round head, striking him a mighty crushing blow. All Humpty could do was sit down so heavily that he seemed to have had a great fall indeed. One practically expected yolk to puddle around him.

Let's see what all the King's horses can do for you *now*, you little nazi. Anyone for an omelet?

From under a clutch of umbrellas, the audience huzzahed. Humpty pulled off the top of his head. Underneath, Vaffanculo was grinning like the Cheshire Cat. Turning to face the crowd, the Dodo struck a body-builder's pose with her wings down in front of her.

Then she faced Humpty again. He put his top back on, stood, and wiped some mud from his weird little pants. Then he lowered his head and charged. Bring it on, eggman, the Dodo thought. Bring it on.

THE FEATHERS OF THE JUB-JUB

Once there was a woman whose brother was dying. Sickness had been eating him cell by cell for three months, and nothing could be done. The doctors held out no hope. And so she hoped.

Every day she made deals with herself. If, she said at the office, if I get this story edited before I go to the hospital, the doctor will be smiling. If I get the recycling out to the curb on time, his white cell count will stay above ten thousand. If I walk around the block clockwise on my way from the parking lot, it won't happen tonight. If I pray every day . . .

But she couldn't complete this sentence, because she wasn't a believer. She wanted to be. She used to be; as a child and a teenager she had been remarkable for devotion. But then, when she was seventeen, her father died in a car accident, while he was at a conference in a distant city. Her father, the principle of life, the great professor, the one who loved her above all things: she was his only daughter.

And then something worse. After the accident, it became clear that her father had been in that distant city because he was having an affair with a woman much younger than his wife, a former student, hardly older than his daughter. This woman had the nerve to come to the funeral. She wasn't even pretty: a wispy redhead with an overbite, pale skin blotchy from crying. No one spoke to her. They should have screamed, the daughter thought, they should have hurled things and spat. But they were reasonable and civilized; her mother merely looked away. The daughter glared. Her brother didn't even come to the service.

What kind of God would kill her father so brutally, and then heap upon him such indignity? What kind of God would allow her father to make such a fool of himself? And now kill her brother, the baby of the family? Only one answer: none.

So she could not pray. She believed in keeping honest accounts. When her mother telephoned from across town, asking for her company at church, she said no. She stood in the doorway of her white kitchen with the phone hunched to her ear, and she gazed at the snowy courtyard of her apartment building. Her mother was talking about the young minister and how it would do her good. In the courtyard, enormous black birds were patrolling the snow. What were they called? They were too big for crows. But ravens sounded too dramatic, ravens seemed too nevermore. Into the phone she made vague humming sounds of understanding and assent, and then said she was too busy just now.

"On a Sunday morning you're too busy?"

Especially on a Sunday morning. "I'm working on a story, Mom, OK?"

There was a silence on the line, and Lucy let it sit. The birds kept pecking at the snow. How did they find enough to eat in the winter? Her mother wanted her to be married, to have children—but didn't say this, exactly. What she said was "I just want you to be happy, dear."

"I *am* happy, Mom."

"You call working on a Sunday morning happy? That's not what *I* call happy."

"I'm as happy as I know how to be right now, Mom. There's no such thing as happily ever after, you know." She didn't say anything about her brother; she knew it was eating her mother alive.

Grackles? Maybe.

She told her mother that the dryer had just buzzed: she had to get the laundry out, in order to avoid wrinkles.

Wasn't she happy? She wasn't sure anymore. When you focus too long on a word, it starts looking like nonsense. Cuticle. Insensate. Chimichanga. Happy happy bo-bappy banana-bana fo-fappy . . .

In fact, Lucy was going to the hospital. Every weekend morning, every evening after work, clockwise from the parking lot. It wasn't pleasant: the rubbish workers were on strike, and trash was piled up everywhere. Her mother would have hated it—but her mother never went, because she wasn't welcome. After the death of her husband, after the revelation of the affair with Wispy Redhead, her son had cut all ties with her. He was outraged at his father's betrayal of them all. He said their mother had no self-respect, and as long as she clung to the image of The Great Man, the one in the photographs she kept on her parlor wall, he allowed her no place in his life. He took a job in another part of town and married a woman who never even tried to get to know them. Lucy heard about his illness one day on the street, when she ran into an old high school friend who said, "I was so sorry to hear about your brother." Now she went to the hospital every day, and she bargained with a nonexistent God.

She had never been close to her little brother. Growing up, they had often fought, and then as young adults they had discovered that the road to peace was mutual neglect. After their father's death, he walled her out with everyone else. One time, when she was on his side of town for a story she was writing, she persuaded him to meet her for a cup of coffee. She meant well—but within fifteen minutes she found herself telling him to grow up.

"Oh," he said, "and your relationship with Winston is the epitome of adult behavior?"

This was unfair. She had been seeing Winston for years, on-again off-again, through stormy break-ups and teary reconciliations. He was the brilliant, hard-driving, egotistical editor of the newspaper—which meant he was her boss. It wasn't ideal. But who expected the ideal? Twice now, Winston had asked her to marry him, and she had found a way to put him off. He said they loved each other, didn't they? She said yes—so why did they need to get married? He had already been married once; wasn't that enough? She had never wanted children. She wanted to keep her own apartment. She liked things the way they were. So what (she said to her brother) if Winston was twenty years older than she? Who said couples have to be the exact same age? Her brother just nodded in that infuriating way of his, and took a sip of coffee.

The hospital visits were not easy. That first time, after hearing from the old high school friend, she had made her way through the piles of garbage on the sidewalks, imagining a tearful reunion in his hospital room, a smile of surprise and sudden gratitude—and instead, he had greeted her with a wary look. His hair was gone, the long wavy brown hair that had been his glory; his skin had a yellow tint. Blue circles under his eyes. He looked like a deathbed hologram of their father. He cast his gaze beyond her, towards the hallway.

"You don't have Mom out there waiting, do you?"

She winced, then held up a paper sack. "I brought bagels and lox," she said. "The ones you always liked, from Lehrmann's."

He gazed at the bag. "If I ate one of those, I'd puke it up in no time." He laughed a brittle laugh. "You should see some of the shows I put on with the hospital food. You'd never believe such bland, beige stuff could produce so many colors." He nodded toward the white plastic covering over his sunken chest. "Like my bib? I get to wear it all the time now."

She didn't know what to say.

He went on. "You're not going to expect me to be all brave, are you?" He looked out the window: a dusky view of more hospital rooms across the way, a ventilation duct sending smoky clouds into the iron dark of a late February afternoon. "I want to be out there," he said. Then he looked at the other bed in the little double room. "I don't want to be like that guy." The other bed was empty.

She left after fifteen minutes, and tossed the unopened bag into an overflowing bin. And yet she went back the next day after work. She intended to stay longer. She thought she might read aloud to him — though she had no idea what kind of books he liked. Or maybe they could do crossword puzzles together. Maybe she could just sit quietly by his bed and edit some copy. But no. There was the television, which he refused to turn off, up on the wall across from his bed, too loud, too ridiculous. He nodded at the books she brought, and put them aside immediately, hardly checking the titles. Maybe he thought that if he refused to soften, she would just give up.

If so, he didn't know his sister. She was the one who always got to the school bus stop first, no matter how much snow had fallen; she was the one who fed and walked Scout, even when the old mutt could hardly walk anymore. Her brother was the one who made lists, endless lists of adventures never accomplished—a hundred things to do by age fifteen; ten girls to date; seven mountains to climb, one on each continent. She was the one who took things in her teeth and didn't let them go. Again, she didn't stay long. But she was going to keep visiting. If she went to the hospital every day, clockwise from the parking lot, nothing bad could happen.

Now it happened that this brother had a daughter. Lucy hardly knew the girl. But the next evening, when she arrived at her brother's room after dinner, she discovered that his wife was there, sitting by the bed. The television was blaring a game show that seemed to be on every night; whenever you turned on the TV, there it was, smarmy host and embarrassing contestants. The wife smiled a tight smile. She was fashion-model thin, with big dangly earrings that made her head look too small. No one looked happy; even the smiling game-show host clearly didn't want to be there. But there they were. Lucy asked about her niece, and was told that the girl was down the hall in the "activities room," where there was better light for reading. Lucy wondered: how could you leave your daughter alone at such a time, in a big city hospital? Stella couldn't be more than, what, six or seven?

On the TV, beautiful girls carried shiny metallic brief-cases like shields. The host said, "If you choose the wrong case, you could lose everything. But if you choose the right case, you're still in the game." The contestant squirmed, her family shouted, the audience roared. "Or," the host said, tilting his goatee at the camera, "you can quit now and keep everything you've made."

Lucy said, "I'll go say hello to Stella."

The activities room wasn't bad: large cushy chairs around the walls, except for the side that consisted of a kitchenette; a corner with a chest of toys and some bright posters of animals; another corner with a TV, blissfully dark; and several formica-topped tables in the center, where a man was reading a newspaper while three women sat drinking from paper cups, talking quietly. In the Kids' Korner, half-swallowed by a beanbag chair, sat a little blonde girl with her head in a book, lips moving silently. Lucy felt like she was looking at a picture of herself from twenty years before.

"Stella!"

The little girl raised her face with a lost-in-the-ozone look.

"It's your Aunt Lucy!"

A tentative smile.

"What are you reading?"

Stella showed her the book's cover.

"Oh, do you like fairy tales?"

The little girl shrugged.

"I used to *love* fairy tales," Lucy said. "Let's see." She pulled up a matching beanbag chair. "Oh, yeah," she said, turning the pages. "What's the deal with Goldilocks, anyway?" Stella looked puzzled. "I mean, have you ever tried the kind of soup bears eat?" Stella shook her head. "Well, I don't care what temperature it is, it's gross. It's made out of weasels and cabbage. And goat boogers." Stella's eyes widened, and Lucy went on. "And would you want to sleep in a bear's bed?" Stella shrugged again. "You know where bears do their business? Right under the bed, that's where. Completely skeevy." She wrinkled her nose, and Stella smiled. Lucy sat with her for twenty minutes, and then left the hospital without returning to her brother's room. She didn't think his wife would miss her.

Meanwhile, her work was slipping. She was the best reporter they had, the one Winston relied on for the biggest stories. Out on the beat, she knew how to ask the hard questions without antagonizing, without letting anyone off the hook. She knew how to write a killer lead, and drop in a devastating quote at just the right moment. Winston called her the Genie of the Newsroom, the one he would summon when he needed a little magic.

Lately, though, she had been off her game. She fell asleep at a City Council meeting, and came back with half a sheet of garbled notes. She used some uncorroborated evidence in a profile, and it resulted in a defamation suit that was looking bad. One morning at a staff meeting Winston turned to her.

"Luce," he said, "We've got to do a bigger story on the garbage strike."

"So? That's City. That's Smithson."

"Yeah, but this one needs you."

"But I'm doing the school board fight. And eleventy-seven other things. You know how I work. I can't wipe Smithson's ass for him."

"I don't want you to wipe his ass. Nice mouth, by the way. I want you to do this one on your own. I'll put someone else on the school board."

He was right, actually: the garbage strike needed her. The workers were overdue for higher pay, better benefits, more humane conditions. The workers had shitty jobs, who could deny it? The mayor said she understood, but the taxpayers weren't ready for another hike. The city could not be held hostage.

Except that it could. They were into the third week of the strike, and the streets were a god-awful mess. Pizza boxes, dirty diapers, carcasses of half-eaten roasts—it was amazing to see the stuff that crowded the pavement. One rainy morning Lucy walked past a sodden pile of something that, upon closer investigation, turned out to be a bra. A DD, from the looks of it. The sidewalks were nearly unnavigable. Pedestrians had started walking in the busy streets instead, and now the taxi drivers were striking, too, because the streets were too full of people and trash for driving. In the cafés, people said the subway would be paralyzed next: how could it manage all the extra traffic? As they said this, they looked fearfully at the waiter and the barman. What if café workers followed suit?

She knew it was an important story. It involved the whole warp and woof of the city. If the strike failed, the rubbish removers were screwed, and their families suffered; if it went on, and the streets got filthier, suburbanites and tourists would simply stop coming to town, and the economy would go in the toilet. And then there would be even less to pay the workers. The environment could be seriously compromised by toxins; the drinking water was already dicey. If she wrote a vivid expose of these conditions, if she put together one of those poignant profiles of a worker's suffering family, she could make a difference.

And yet she couldn't bring herself to get to work on it. Every day, she walked through the garbage to the office, where she sat at the computer reading medical web sites. Every evening, she walked through the garbage to the hospital, where she sat with her silent brother watching TV, or, if his wife was there with him, she went to the activities room to sit with her niece. Every time her mother called, she said fine, and heard all the unasked questions. Why wasn't she married yet? What was wrong with Winston?

Nothing was wrong with Winston. Winston was a prince. Except that he was a little old for a prince. His two grown children were almost as old as she was.

One day at the office, she looked up from her computer to see him standing in her doorway. He was a big man with a high forehead and well-trimmed silver hair.

"How's the garbage story?"

"Trashy," she said.

"I noticed. Got a draft you want me to look over?"

"Not yet. There are a lot of moving parts, you know?"

"Yeah. I just haven't seen them moving, is all."

"OK, then. That's why I've got to get back to work." She looked back at her computer screen. He kept standing there.

"Seems like the rubbish guys aren't the only ones on strike."

"What do you mean? Look at me work. Work, work, work."

"I mean, we haven't slept together in three weeks."

She looked back up at him. "Oh, is that what this is about?"

"I don't know what it's about," he said. "You tell me." When she remained silent, he added, "When you're ready." And he walked off.

That evening at the hospital, the wife was in the room. She hardly looked up from her magazine when Lucy arrived. Her brother looked thinner and paler than ever. He barely nodded hello. The game-show host teased a young woman who couldn't make up her mind. Lucy stood by the bed a few minutes, and then headed down the hall to the activities room.

Someone was making coffee in the kitchenette; an older couple sat at one of the tables, talking in low tones. Stella sat in a beanbag chair, long spidery legs protruding from the book in her lap.

"Hi, Stell! How ya doin'?"

The little girl shrugged.

"Reading, huh?"

Stella nodded.

"Hey, what if I tell you a story? Your grandfather used to tell me these great stories when I was your age."

"Before he became a scumbag?"

Lucy looked at her niece. "Yes. Before. So—can I tell you a story?"

Stella nodded again. Lucy sank into the other beanbag chair. Good thing she wore slacks to work. Once you settled into one of these chairs, it was hard to get up again.

She began.

Once there was a king who was very sick. In fact, the whole kingdom was suffering: no one wanted to do anything. The castle was a mess, and the farmers weren't getting the harvest in. Fruits and vegetables lay rotting in the fields. The king's doctors told him, Your Majesty, if you want to be cured, we'll need a feather from the Jub-Jub bird. And this was a difficult remedy, because everyone knew that the Jub-Jub ate people for dinner.

The king told everyone at court, and no one dared take the challenge. But in the castle there was a serving girl who was loyal and brave, and she said, I'll go.

The king didn't want to send a mere strip of a girl— but what choice did he have? He promised that if she succeeded, he would marry her, and she would be queen. So they gave the girl directions: at the top of a certain mountain there were some holes, and in one of them lived the Jub-Jub bird.

The girl—"what should we call her?"

"Natasha!"

"Natasha?"

"Natasha!"

Natasha set out, and was overtaken by darkness on the road. She stopped at an inn, and the innkeeper said to her, Maybe you could bring me one of those feathers, too? Since they do so much good and all?

Oh, I'll definitely bring you one, said the girl.

And if you talk to the Jub-Jub, said the innkeeper, ask if he knows anything about my daughter, who disappeared when she was a baby.

I'll ask him, she said.

The next morning Natasha continued her journey. She came to a river, and the ferryman whose boat carried her across said, Could you bring me a feather, too? I hear they bring good luck.

Sure, of course I'll bring you one, said the girl.

Oh, and maybe you could ask him how come I've been stuck here so many years, unable to get off this boat?

I'll ask him, she said.

She got off the boat, and continued on her way. At an empty fountain she sat down to eat a little bread, and two well-dressed gentlemen stopped to chat with her.

Why don't you bring us a feather, too? they said.

Why not? she answered.

And then you should also ask the Jub-Jub about this fountain. It used to pour forth gold and silver, and now it's all dried up.

I'll be sure to ask, she said.

She continued on, and darkness fell again. She came upon a monastery —

"A what?"

"A place where priests live."

"Oh."

She came upon a monastery, and knocked. The friars came and let her in, and she told them her story.

The Prior — that's the main priest — said, Do you know all the conditions?

They told me there were some holes at the top of the mountain, and at the bottom of one of them there's a door. I knock, and there's the Jub-Jub.

Ah, my daughter, said the Prior, if you don't know all the conditions, you'll surely be eaten alive. You think you can fool with the Jub-Jub? I'll tell you all about it — as long as you do us a favor.

OK, said Natasha.

When you reach the top of the mountain, count seven holes. The seventh is the one you want. At the bottom you'll find it so dark you can't see anything — but take this candle and these matches. And be sure to go down exactly at noon, because that's when the Jub-Jub isn't there. Instead, you'll find his wife —

"The Jub-Jub has a wife?"

"Who's telling this story?"

You'll find his wife, and she's a good woman who will tell you everything you need to know. But be careful! If the Jub-Jub happens to see you first, he'll eat you in one mouthful! Now, here's what you can do for us. For a long time we friars lived here in peace, but for the past ten years all we've done is fight. Someone wants this, someone else wants that, we're always shouting, always at odds. Ask the Jub-Jub why. Oh, and bring us a feather, too.

The next morning Natasha climbed the mountain and counted seven holes. At eleven o'clock she was ready, but she waited until exactly noon to descend into the seventh hole. It was pitch black down there, but she lit her candle and found the door. As soon as she knocked, a beautiful young woman opened.

Who are you? said the young woman. What are you doing here? You don't know who my husband is! If he sees you, he'll eat you in an instant!

The little girl—"what was her name again?"

"Natasha!"

Natasha replied, I came for some of his feathers. Since I've made it this far, I'm not stopping now. If he eats me, well, so be it.

How many feathers do you need?

Five, said Natasha. And she told the young woman her story—about the king, the innkeeper, the ferryman, the two gentlemen at the fountain, the friars, and all their questions.

You seem like a good girl, said the young woman, and all those people were good to you, too. I can help you. But he mustn't see you, or he'll eat you. I'll hide you under the bed, and I'll get the feathers for you.

The Jub-Jub's wife gave her cakes and tea, and they spent hours talking. Now it was getting late, and they heard the Jub-Jub coming home. Quick, said the wife, under the bed! And she greeted her husband at the door. As he stepped in, he said:

> *Eenie, meenie, mastie, meastie,*
> *I smell the blood of a human beastie!*

What are you talking about, said his wife. That's just

the stew for supper. You must be starved. Here, sit down and eat.

The Jub-Jub ate and ate, and drank and drank, and finally he was so full that he wanted nothing but to go to bed. He fell asleep in seconds, and started snoring a great raucous snore.

Under the bed, Natasha was all ears. The wife leaned down and whispered, Be ready! I'm going to get us some feathers! She plucked a feather from her husband's chest and passed it quickly under the bed.

Ow! cried the Jub-Jub. What are you doing?

Oh, I was dreaming, I'm sorry.

What were you dreaming?

I was dreaming about the monastery: for ten years, the friars were all so mean to each other that they could hardly live together anymore.

That's no dream, said the Jub-Jub; that's true. The friars have all been so mean because ten years ago the Devil moved in with them, dressed as a priest.

What should they do to get rid of him?

They have to start doing good deeds. That way, they'll know which one is the Devil. And the Jub-Jub rolled over and fell back asleep.

About a quarter-hour later, the wife plucked a feather from his backside and passed it quickly under the bed.

Yow! What the hell?

Ah, I was dreaming again.

Again! About what?

About that fountain down there. I dreamed that it used to spout gold and silver!

That's not a dream either, said her husband. The fountain did spout gold and silver; it's just blocked up. If they dig down into it, they'll find a snake has wound itself around the source and squeezed it shut. If they crush the snake's head before it can react, the fountain will spout gold and silver again. And saying this, he fell back asleep.

Another quarter of an hour. She plucked another feather and slipped it quickly under the bed to Natasha.

Hey! he cried. Are you trying to skin me alive?

Oh, she yawned, I was dreaming again.

What was it this time?

The ferryman, down on the river, was complaining that he can never leave his boat.

All your dreams tonight are true. The ferryman just needs to know one trick: when someone takes a ride, if the ferryman jumps ashore first, his passenger will be stuck on the boat, and the boatman can walk away free.

The wife plucked another feather.

Have you lost your mind?

Oh, sorry, I was still dreaming. This time it was the inn-keeper, who was saying that for many years he has longed for his missing daughter.

Ah, that's a dream about your father.

What?

Yes, you're the missing daughter. Now, no more feathers!

The wife said nothing. When her husband had fallen asleep again, she passed the fourth feather under the bed, and lay awake for hours.

In the morning, the Jub-Jub got up and had his break-fast, said goodbye to his wife, and went off to work.

"Jub-Jubs go to work?"

"He, um, had a village to terrorize, OK?"

As soon as he left, the wife got Natasha out from under the bed, dusted her off, and said, I'm going with you. And the two of them set out together.

They stopped at the monastery, and gave a feather to the Prior. Natasha told him, The Jub-Jub says that one of you is the Devil, and if you start doing good deeds he'll leave. The friars started doing good deeds, and sure enough, the Devil departed.

The two stopped at the fountain, and gave a feather to the two gentlemen. Natasha explained about the snake, the gentlemen did what was necessary, and sure enough, the fountain started spouting silver and gold.

The two arrived at the river and got on the ferry. Natasha said to the ferryman, Here's your feather!

I thank you. And what did he say about me getting off this boat?

Um, I'll tell you in a minute.

As soon as they got off the ferry, she told him the trick.

They arrived at the inn, and now Natasha knew she had a problem.

"She only has one feather left!" Stella had grabbed Lucy's forearm.

"So? What should she do?"

Stella hesitated for just a moment. "She promised to give it to the innkeeper."

Lucy nodded, and went on.

They arrived at the inn, and Natasha cried, Innkeeper, here I am with your feather! And your daughter! So they were reunited.

In the meantime, the Jub-Jub had returned home and discovered that his wife was missing. He tore out of his hole in hot pursuit. Everywhere he stopped to ask, the people quaked and pointed, That way. He arrived at the river and got on the ferry. Just before they reached the other side, the ferryman said, That will be two ducats. As the Jub-Jub looked for his money, the ferryman jumped to the land, and the Jub-Jub was stuck on the ferry forever-more. The end.

Stella was still holding her forearm. Visiting hours were almost over. There was no one else left in the room.

"So," Lucy said, "What do you think?"

Stella looked out a dark window, as if the answer were out there, where the garbage was piling up higher in the street.

"She didn't want to marry that old dude anyway," she said. "Tell me another story."

Everybody Row

Varney was having Chocolate Blastems for breakfast again, and Meredith was giving him grief about it.

"Did you get your free toy this morning? What is it today, a ray gun? So you can pulverize those nasty marshmallow aliens?"

She was standing by the kitchen counter, already dressed for work, next to her coffee and grapefruit. He was still in his pajamas—the blue and white striped ones she got him for Christmas. She loved it that he actually wore them, instead of the droopy boxers and tee-shirt he used to wear.

He looked up. With his hair sleep-tousled, he looked like a prematurely gray ten-year-old.

"Hey, don't underestimate the marshmallow guys. They may seem all soft and squishy, but they are BENT ON WORLD DOMINATION." He plucked a marshmallow bit from his bowl and held it up to her. "Look at that face," he said. "Butter wouldn't melt in his mouth. But this guy would strangle you in your sleep." He set the bit of cereal on the formica table top and pounded it with the flat of his spoon, scattering drops of milk. "Not on my watch, Marshmallow Man! Not! On! My! Watch!"

He picked up the flattened piece of sucrose, which (in a high-pitched Victim voice) was screaming, "No! No! I'll talk! I'll talk!" He said, "Too late for you, Mister Fluff," and popped it in his mouth, cutting off a last desperate gurgle. "Let this be a warning to your kind." And he went back to reading the cereal box.

Meredith sponged up the milk. "All right, then. Another alien invasion thwarted."

"Damn straight," he said, without looking up.

She took a sip of coffee, black. The watery light of early spring washed the yellow walls. She shouldn't be having coffee at all, but who was going to stop her?

"So, were you planning to get dressed anytime today? Maybe shower, shave, comb your hair?"

Varney studied his reflection in the toaster, and winced. "God, I look awful, don't I?" Then he flashed the toaster a toothy smile. "But I feel great!"

She knew what was coming, and she couldn't stop it.

"I must be a vagina!"

He cracked up, and she smiled in spite of herself. Then she slipped her uneaten half-grapefruit into a plastic bag and put it in the refrigerator. "Well," she said, "some of us have to go to work."

He glanced at the clock in the microwave. "Eight o'clock!? Mother of God! Who got me out of bed? Leave me alone, woman!"

She left him alone. She could walk to work; that was one of the advantages of his apartment. The only advantage she could think of, in fact. The ceilings were low, and the carpet was worn, and it always smelled of onions and popcorn. Her air fresheners hadn't made any difference. The college boys across the hall were ridiculously loud at night, and it creeped her out a little when she passed one of them on the stairs; she was only a few years older than they were. When she saw some of the skanky girls they brought home, she thought, There but for the grace of God. Still, it was a good thing she could walk to work. He needed the car to make his rounds. Her mother always said walk everywhere you can; it keeps the glutes firm. Not that her mother, who favored loud muumuus, was the best model of glutitude. But you had to get out and appreciate the world.

"Don't forget to feed Nobody," she said. "And don't let him out!"

Varney didn't feel like making his rounds. What was the point? At the Stop and Rob they would just tell him no thanks, they still weren't stocking his brand; at Merchandise Mart they would say they hadn't sold the last shipment yet, come back next week. Two phone calls should be enough to settle this, and he wouldn't have to get dressed, comb his hair, brush his teeth, and take the risk of using the car with his suspended license. But no, Steve insisted that you had to have Face Time with the customer, even if you weren't likely to make a sale. You had to have A Foot In The Door once a week, no matter what; you wanted them to Remember You. You weren't selling a mere product, you were selling the company, you were Selling Yourself. People will buy, Steve said, even if they don't need the product. They'll buy just to get your ugly mug out of their face, ha ha. Maybe this worked for Steve, back when he was still a salesman, in the nineteenth century.

Varney just wanted to stay in the kitchen, in his pajamas, and have another cup of coffee. God, he loved coffee. The doctor said it wasn't good for his arrhythmic heart; he didn't need more stimulants. So he stopped going to the doctor.

There was the newspaper, open to the crossword puzzle Meredith had started. African mammal, three letters. She had written "Awi." What the hell kind of word was "awi"? But what else would work? Riu? Ivo? It could be anything!

If he just stayed home, maybe Layla would call. Or maybe she came by sometimes, during the day, when he was out making his rounds. Maybe she got discouraged because no one was home, and that was why she didn't phone. If he just stayed here, in the kitchen, she would stop by, just to say hello, and he would offer her a cup of coffee like it was the most normal thing in the world, and she could help him with the crossword puzzle. The way he used to help her with her homework when she was a kid.

Wasn't she still a kid? How could she be nineteen? Same way he could be forty, apparently. The March of Time.

Amu? Freaking African mammals. He turned to the sports section.

Ah, the brackets for the tournament. First, there was UC. OK, they didn't stand a chance in hell. But what if McMaster got hot, sometimes he did. So he hadn't been shooting well lately, still, it could happen. He was due. Varney penned in UC to win in the first round, and then—what the hell, Duke was overrated. He put UC down for the second round, too. And then, well, the pen just had its way with him as it filled in the next lines. Down goes Kansas! Down goes Clemson! Down goes Pitt! McMaster would be unstoppable. It would be the story of the tournament. And Varney would have called it. So there they were, in the championship game, ready to face off against North Carolina. And once they got to that point, how could you bet against them? You'd have to be a Communist. UC all the way. Team of Destiny. He could already see them cutting down the nets.

In the storefront reflections, Meredith looked OK. She looked fine. Why wouldn't she look fine? She was a pretty girl. Not beautiful, nobody said beautiful, not since her father; but pretty. "Easy to look at," that's what Varney always said. No, he added, he didn't mean "easy." She punched him in the arm with her little playful punch. God knows, he said, she wasn't easy for *him*; he never knew a girl who took so long to give it up. She punched him some more. She did *not* "give it up," like sex was something you traded for goods and services. She loved him! She didn't like it when he talked about their bed life that way — except that she did kind of like it. You weren't supposed to treat sex like an ordinary pleasure, like food or a movie; it was more than that, and you shouldn't even talk about it at all, really — except that it was *fun* to talk about it, a little. Because they loved each other. She even sort of liked it that he was so experienced. If he had been with so many women and he still liked her — loved her — then this must be the real thing.

Yes, she looked OK. Thank goodness she didn't show yet. But she wanted to see how that would look, too. Varney was so down about his work, she didn't want to tell him yet. They couldn't afford a lot of new outfits. But they would figure it out, he would be fine with it. Look how he loved playing with his nephew! He was great. He was younger looking than any of the men at her office; he still played basketball in the park. Just the other day he said he schooled those college guys from across the hall. She would tell him soon. He just needed to make a few sales, to feel a little more positive about himself. He was so good at talking to people, he was a natural for that job. He was just going through a rough patch, it happened to everybody. That which does not kill you, she said. Makes me longer, he said. She punched him in the arm.

Her mother kept talking about marriage. Like she doubted it was going to happen. She would never *say* she doubted it; she didn't say things like that. But when they talked on the phone, every day, she kept mentioning little wedding ideas from the bridal magazine that she never canceled after Meredith's sister Paula got married. She still kept her copy of Paula's wedding album out on the coffee table. Meredith imagined her leafing through it as they talked.

Her father would have said, "Hey, elope if you want. Just make sure the guy marries you. Why should he buy the cow if he can have the milk for free?" Her father could be an a-hole sometimes. Paula said she'd never forgive him for walking out on Mom. But since he was gone, five years ago next month, Meredith tried not to think of him that way. What good did it do?

She fixed her hair in front of the corner store, metallic flashes of light splashing around her. The hot fudge sundae on the big plastic sign looked so good. But it was only 8:20! And she wouldn't be able to keep it down, anyway. She unlocked the door at Coldwell Banker, first to arrive. She put the coffee on.

The night before had been a little touchy for both of them.

"Varney?"

"Yeah."

"It's OK, sweetie."

"No it's not. This never happens to me. Not OK."

"It's OK."

"You don't mean that."

"Yes I do. You think it's never happened to me before?"

"Oh, great, tell me about your past lovers. That'll help."

"I'm just saying. It happens."

"Like with who?"

"Who?"

"Yeah, who did it happen with?"

"You want me to tell you?"

"Yeah."

"Bruce."

"Bruce?"

"Bruce."

"The scrawny guy from your office?"

"He's not scrawny."

"I could break that guy in two."

"He's slender."

"Slender? That's a Diet Pepsi word. You slept with *Bruce*?"

"Yeah—but like I said, nothing happened."

"So do you wonder if maybe *you're* the problem?"

"Oh, that's nice."

"I mean, there *is* a common denominator."

They were quiet for a minute. They could hear the bass from across the hall. Reggae again.

"Hey, mon," he said. "Shouldn't you have had your period by now?"

She could have pretended to be asleep. But she said, "I did. It was a light one. I just didn't mention it."

She couldn't sleep until she heard him snoring. It took a while.

* * *

The cat jumped up on the kitchen table—strictly forbidden when Meredith was around—brushed against Varney's arm, sniffed at the bowl of Blastems, and knocked over the cereal box with its tail.

"Hey, guy! How's it hangin'? Easy with the tail, man!" He hated cats, but this was part of the bargain when she moved in, proof that he was serious: you can even bring your cat. It promptly decided to ignore her and cling to Varney. It curled around his ankles, jumped in his lap while he watched TV, slept in the crook of his arm.

Who names a cat Nobody? Who thought a cat was a good pet, in the first place? It just wants food and warmth, and occasionally it allows you to think that it enjoys being stroked. His family always had a dog or two, sometimes as actual pets, sometimes just hanging around the yard because his father threw them food. Varney could see him in the kitchen, winking at the kids with a Don't Tell Your Mother look as he took some fresh ground beef from the fridge and headed for the yard. What his father had really wanted was a hunting dog. He almost never got to go hunting; he worked most Saturdays, because they paid time and a half at the factory. When he took a vacation, it was always to visit her parents, with all four kids in the car. He croaked at the factory, right near the end of a shift, lifting another box from the belt.

Varney got up and knelt next to the table, so the cat could climb on his shoulder. The claws digging through his pajamas hurt a little — but you had to give the damn cat credit: it knew what it wanted. He took its bowl from the floor, pulled an already opened can of cat food from the fridge, removed the plastic lid, and spooned the stuff out, wrinkling his nose at the stink. And she complained about the way his apartment smelled? He was supposed to put the bowl on the floor, but the cat was already down off his shoulder and onto the kitchen counter, eating and purring. What difference did it make where the cat ate?

He didn't feel like shaving. He didn't have much of a beard after one day, anyway. At the bathroom mirror he raked his hair with his fingers: it wasn't really receding that much. His father never lost a single hair. But then there was his brother Charlie: last time they got together — two years ago, at their mother's funeral — Charlie was practically bald. Varney teased him about it, said he had a nice full head of hair until he got married; and Charlie just laughed and said something about baldies having all the testosterone. When did *he* get so damn mature?

He turned on the TV. Regis and Kelly, sparring, teasing, smiling entirely too much for this time of the morning. He wondered if Regis could be hitting that. She was way too perky for Varney's taste — but still, the perky ones could be wild. That was one of the great things about sex: the way it could surprise you. Anyone would have thought that Meredith would be a priss-pot, she was so proper and shy. But that was part of her appeal — that downcast glance. The first time they kissed, they were just walking along Vine Street, talking, flirting, and he stopped her right there, in front of the Photo Garden, and gave her one of his best. She looked up at him as if she'd just been thrown into the deep end, and she said, "Really?" He said, "Really. More than really." She blushed, and laughed, and he could see her resisting the pleasure she felt — and he knew he had her.

He couldn't keep watching this nonsense. Instead of the usual khakis and dress shirt, he pulled on a tee-shirt, sweatshirt, jeans, and sneakers. He dug the basketball out of the closet. The cat was yowling at the door. He let it out as he left.

She really didn't feel so good. During her morning break, she sat on the toilet as long as she could. It was better to be in the little bathroom, with the light turned off and the walls close at hand.

Everything happens for a reason. He hated it when she said that—so she stopped saying it. But no one could keep her from saying it to herself. She believed it, too. Think of the first time, with Royce: she wasn't married then, either. But it had turned out for the best. If it hadn't happened, she would still be with Royce. And if she hadn't taken care of it, she would have a two-year-old now. What a disaster that would have been. But she wasn't ready then, that was why she had taken care of it. And if she hadn't, she never would have met Varney. Now she was ready.

But she really didn't feel good. She should have eaten something. Paula said you had to keep eating, no matter what. Paula should know: one healthy baby already and another one on the way. Meredith knew it wasn't a competition. She fingered her phone like a rosary.

It was a fine March morning, chilly but bright, sunlight glinting on the ice that crusted around the edges of puddles on the sidewalk. You never knew with March: you could have a brilliant sharp-edged day like this, like the HD TV he lingered in front of at Radio Shack, and then the next day there could be a shit-storm of snow and slop that spattered you on the slippery sidewalk because you couldn't drive, thanks to your latest DUI. Just because you were a few miles over the limit on that stretch between downtown and Norwood. Seriously, who drives 55 on the highway? But he should have known, there was always a trooper in that stretch. He had just been trying to get home to Meredith before she wondered why he was late. No reason to worry her about the suspended license and all. She worried enough already.

He dribbled the ball on the sidewalk, left hand then right, the back-and-forth drill Coach McKibben gave them in high school. The steady thump of nylon on cement created a tempo for his heart, his breath, the song he was half-singing to himself, "Misery's the River of the World." Tom Waits at his finest. "Call no man happy 'til he dies, there's no milk at the bottom of the pail." Meredith hated this one; she said it was depressing. But how could you not love Tom Waits? The man was golden. "Everybody row, everybody row, everybody row." That cheered him up every time.

In the park there were a few people walking dogs, carrying little plastic bags full of turds, and an old guy doing some kind of jujitsu moves by the bandstand. Varney used to come to this park with Layla and her latest toys—pogo sticks on which they bounced, laughing, like drunken kangaroos; hula hoops that made them imitate Shakira, her favorite; jars full of soapy liquid that they blew into gleaming bubbles and sent drifting off into the sunlight.

He was the only one on the court at this hour; the college guys were either in class or still in bed. He probably should have gone to college—but after high school he couldn't imagine sitting through one more class, taking one more note, pretending one more time that whatever the teacher said was important. Working out of his car had seemed like the ultimate freedom: no factory, no office, nobody on your case. You just drove around all day, and talked to people, and when you made your quota you went home. Or you went to a bar, and talked to people some more.

He liked shooting by himself, starting with little bunnies, then mid-range jumpers, then working his way out beyond the three-point line, launching shot after shot, his palms darkening from handling the ball on the grimy court. Now he was McMaster—no, *now* he was McMaster—no, *now* he was McMaster . . . they'd start falling soon, he just needed to find his rhythm.

"Meredith? Are you OK?"

It was Lisa, the office manager, outside the bathroom door.

She was not OK. But she *so* didn't want anyone's help right now, especially not Lisa's—all that kindness and clucking, all that bloody *talking*. If she wanted a mother, she could call her own. She just wanted to be left alone. She splashed some cold water on her face, dried it on her sleeve, and opened the door.

"I'm fine, I'm fine—it's, just, you know, that time."

"Oh, honey, I know, let me tell you. Or I used to know." Lisa must have been about fifty. It was hard to tell, in between thirty-five and fifty-five. "I used to get these blinding headaches, every month, right on schedule. Listen, sweetie, why don't you take a walk, get some fresh air. Do you a world of good." When Meredith protested, Lisa said, "Go on, shoo. I'll watch the desk. No one will even know you're gone."

He finally started hitting. Four in a row, five, six. If McMaster got going like this, there was no telling what UC could do in the tournament.

Layla was probably still in town somewhere; he couldn't imagine her actually moving away. Her mother would know how to find her—but he was *not* going to give her the satisfaction of lording it over him because their daughter had cut him off. No way. Besides, that dude she was with now would break his face if he got within fifty feet of their house. Varney remembered the last time, when he was a little drunk. He tucked the ball under his arm and rubbed his jaw.

Was it too early to go to the Woodside? He could just go in for a cup of coffee; he didn't have to start drinking. Not that he needed more coffee; his chest was already feeling kind of tight, just from shooting around a little.

As he was leaving the court, three young guys showed up, in cut-off shorts and expensive sneakers. They stripped off their shirts, the way some young idiots always do as soon as the temperature gets above forty degrees. One of them, a tall, buff kid with long red hair and lots of freckles on his shoulders, said, "Hey, man, wanna play? Two on two?"

"No, sorry, I gotta go."

"Oh, come on, man. Just a little game to eleven. Look, we didn't even bring a ball." The kid spread his hands. "Josh and I'll be skins. You get Billy. He's a rebounding machine." Billy flexed for the cameras. The freckled guy added, "We saw you shooting, man. You can fill it." He went to the top of the key and gestured for the ball. "Hit or miss," he said.

What was Varney supposed to do, walk off like a five-year-old taking his ball home? "OK," he said. "One game." He threw Freckles the ball.

The kid caught it, and in the same motion, without even taking aim, he coiled and lofted a perfect jump shot: swish. Josh returned the ball to his partner, who held it at his hip and waited for Varney to come guard him. "Make it take it," he said. "Clear everything."

Meredith went into the corner store. She sat on a revolving stool at the counter; to her right, through a big plate glass window, she had a view of the busy street corner. There was no one else in the store at this hour, and only one person on duty—a girl with her hair swept up in a white kerchief, wearing a green apron and a faded tee-shirt that said "Built to Spill." When Meredith asked for the hot fudge sundae, she felt the heat rise in her face. She couldn't remember the last time she ordered something like this. Varney liked her slim; he ran his hands down her sides and said, "You put the 'oo' in smooth." She loved that. But she was supposed to eat. She was about to gain a lot of weight, anyway; how could this make a difference?

The girl in the apron nodded and turned to start combining ingredients on the counter behind her. Outside, an ambulance went flashing by. On the back of the girl's shirt was a list of dates and cities all over the country: Tucson, Austin, Atlanta, Miami. Places Meredith had never been. She could see this girl standing in a big dark room, with her hair down over her shoulders, holding a bottle of beer by her hip, intent on the stage as the music was about to begin. The lights from the catwalk gleamed in her eyes.

When the girl turned back to set a newly made sundae on the counter, there were tears streaming down Meredith's face.

The girl said, "Ma'am? Can I help you?"

Meredith shook her head. Then she took a big spoonful of ice cream. It was so cold and sweet, it almost hurt the roof of her mouth and the back of her throat.

By the time she turned onto their street, she could tell: she was totally going to hurl. She made it to the open garbage can at the corner, and then she totally hurled. Well, now she didn't have to worry about those empty calories. When she looked up, she was surprised to see the car out in front of their building.

Well, damn. Did he not go to work at all? He was probably still in his pajamas, sprawled on the couch and watching TV. He'd better not be drinking.

Maybe, she thought, as she made her way up the front steps, maybe this was for the best. Maybe this was finally the time to talk. She took a handkerchief from her purse, wiped her mouth, tried to swallow the aftertaste.

Just as she went to open the downstairs door, she heard a familiar meow.

"Nobody!"

The cat was rubbing his back against the wall outside the door.

"How did you get out?" She swept him up in her arms. Oh, now she was really going to give Varney a piece of her mind. She was feeling stronger with every step up the stairs.

But the apartment was empty. The car keys were on the counter, next to Varney's phone. No note. She dropped the cat, picked up the keys, and stomped out the door.

She would start with the Woodside. If he was just sitting there at the bar, spending her hard-earned money . . .

But she never got as far as the Woodside. When she drove past the park, she saw a little clutch of people gathered around something, under a basketball hoop. She turned in at the service entrance and drove right up to the court. She never doubted who it was. She ran to the group.

A tall guy with red hair saw her and said, "He just keeled over. We better call somebody. You got a phone?"

She went straight to her knees next to Varney.

He looked up with a weak smile. "No sweat, Mer. I must have hit my head on the rim."

"Sweetie, where does it hurt?"

He clutched his chest grandly, and proclaimed in his General Custer voice, "I'm too young to die!"

She smiled. Then she said, "Somebody needs a shave."

"Who?" He looked around at the little group of guys, and saw something else. "Hey, you brought the car?"

She nodded.

"Let's go for a ride."

"Where?"

"I don't care. You drive."

He didn't care. She drove.

And if there was a reason, it was hiding where the reason always hides, findable only by the one who knows precisely how to look.

We Rode with Ronald

"We'll never get away with it." Mark pushed his glasses up his nose. "The Dean doesn't mess around with these things. Leila and I met with him when we transferred. He's got Harvard's reputation to protect, you know? The last thing he needs is a bunch of undergraduates getting arrested for larceny."

We were gathered around the dining room table, a giant cable spool that Jermaine, Simon, and Mo had liberated from a construction site near campus. It was low to the ground, so we all sat on the floor for dinner; there wouldn't have been enough chairs for all seven of us, anyway. Now it was long after dinner, and we were all lying back from the table, tufts of the carpet making hectic imprints in our forearms. From the stereo in Mo's ground-floor room, the Talking Heads were howling.

Jermaine sat up. "But we're not going to get arrested! I've got it all laid out. It's going to be a snap." Jermaine had prepared "the operation," as he called it, drawing it all out on continuous sheets of computer paper.

"Anyway," Simon added, "We don't *want* to get away with it, Mark. That's the beauty of the whole plan. Think about it. What do we want?"

Mo said, "We want everything to be beautiful, and nothing to hurt."

Mark rolled his eyes. Simon laughed, and said, "Seriously. Amanda, what do we want?"

Amanda was tall even when sitting. She said softly, "We want to call attention to the unnecessary suffering of animals."

"Right. And publicity equals attention. So: if McDonald's answers us, we win. If we're caught in the act, we win. If we get in trouble with Harvard, we win. How can we lose?"

Mo said, "By sitting around with our thumbs up our asses?"

"That's easy for you to say," said Mark. He took the hand of Leila, who was sitting beside him. They were the only couple in the house. "You aren't applying to grad schools. Your father isn't going to cut off financial support if you do something stupid."

Mo laughed. "Well, that's for sure. My father doesn't have anything financial to cut off." Mo's father, back in Steubenville, was a mechanic, and, according to Mo, a most unsightly man.

Simon looked at me. "Curly? Are you in?"

"I think so," I said. "Yeah."

"Leila?"

She was wearing a long blue skirt. With her knees drawn up in front of her and her dark hair hanging around her eyes, it was hard to make out her expression.

Mark said, "It doesn't matter if you call attention to the problem. It's not going to change anything. People are going to go on eating what they like, and McDonald's is going to go on selling them burgers."

"Same as it ever was," said Mo.

"Yes," Mark said. "Like it or not. We should give our time to something more important."

Simon scratched his reddish beard. "Do you know the story about the tidal wave that washed thousands of fish on shore? Afterwards, a man went down to see the damage. He found a woman among all the stranded fish, picking them up one at a time and throwing them back in the sea. The man said, 'What you're doing doesn't matter. You'll never save them all.' The woman held up one fish, still wriggling in her hand. 'To this one,' she said, 'it matters.'"

"Pretty story," said Mark.

Leila disengaged from his hand in order to sweep the hair out of her eyes, and then she said, "I'm in."

"All right!" shouted Mo. "Eat the rich!"

When Mo said "Eat the rich!" he meant "Screw those country-club bastards." Of course, several of us *were* country-club bastards. When Simon said it, he meant "All this worldly striving is meaningless anyway; we might as well flare out against the emptiest images of nothingness." When Jermaine chimed in, he meant "Isn't my plan cool?" He spread it out now on the table.

Mark cleared his throat. "How in the world," he said, "are we going to lift that thing? Even before that, how are we going to detach it from its base?"

Mo said, "A chainsaw can work wonders—right, Jermaine?"

Jermaine said, "Absolutely. It's made of polystyrene. It may look solid, but the right blade will take care of it in no time. Of course, we'll do this at some inconspicuous hour"—he looked at his watch—"say, 2 a.m. This is a standard layout for Mickey D's. I've looked at a bunch of them. They're all so much alike, it's almost too easy. See," he said, pointing to one of the sheets, "we post look-outs here and here. If there's a security guard, he'll be in back, where the safe is. But we aren't interested in the safe." He paused for effect. "We're after the big guy himself."

It was too ridiculous, really. Who ever heard of a security guard at McDonald's? But we were all hushed in the moment. You had to hand it to Jermaine; he had dramatic flair. Even Mo seemed a little bit in awe.

"As for lifting him—well, that's why we need every one of you on board. It's hard to say how heavy he is, but if there are seven of us, ready to heave him into the back of The Beast, I'm sure we can be out of there in less than sixty seconds." The Beast was Mo's pick-up, which had hauled a lot of junk in its time. It had probably never carried an eight-foot tall statue of Ronald McDonald—but there's a first time for everything.

It was rare, at Harvard, for undergraduates to live off-campus. Everything about campus life was based on a housing system that enabled students to live in miniature colleges of three to four hundred, each with its own dining hall, library, squash courts, intramural teams, and even some classes oriented specifically to that group. Seen in a positive light, those undergraduate houses were cunning little worlds that made the big bad university more livable. But to us, they were just random agglomerations of tools who got put together by some clueless administrator and who then decided to be proud about where they happened to fall. We thought our classmates were just as irrational in their allegiance to Kirkland or Dunster as all the idiot Red Sox and Yankee fans, living and dying each autumn with the guys who happened to wear the right city name on their chests. We were different. We were Omega House.

We had found each other the previous spring, when we all answered an ad in The Harvard Crimson. "Intentional community seeks undergraduate residents. Apply in person." It was an experiment started by somebody at the Div School in the seventies, and it was still hanging on in the Reagan era because no one had decided yet what else to do with that beat-up old half of a duplex on Trowbridge Street, just three blocks from The Yard. It was dark, and shabbily furnished, and the wind whistled through the badly insulated joints at the windows and doors—but it was perfect for a bunch of campus castaways. Except for Mark and Leila, none of us had ever met before. We were just committed to this idea.

Or else we were all just desperate. Mark and Leila were transfers from Johns Hopkins who had arrived too late for the housing lottery. Jermaine was looking for space near the Science Center, and far from his former girlfriend. Amanda wanted her own kitchen. Simon said he had *too* good a time on campus; he said college was just "high school with beds." He was planning to become an Episcopal priest, and he wanted something bigger, something more.

Mo wasn't even enrolled just then. At the end of his first year at Harvard he had been "rusticated" (as the administrators called a one-semester suspension) for three Fs and a D. But he hadn't told all the Mos back in Steubenville. His actual name was Ben Morrissey—but every member of the family was known as Mo. His father was Mean Mo; his mother, Florence, was Flo Mo; his brother was Joe, so that was obvious—but Mo called him Bro Mo. And Mo, our Mo, was always called Slow. Not mentally; he just didn't like moving too fast. And indeed, he was taking his time getting it together after that suspension. The deal was that you could apply for readmission after one semester away; he was now starting his fourth. The rules didn't say you had to go home. What is "home," anyway? When we said "home," we meant Omega.

The name of our intramural hoops team was The Illegal

Aliens. Jermaine got us mismatched t-shirts with spooky ET heads on the front. Since there were just five guys in the house, and most of the time Jermaine couldn't make it, we usually played four on five, with Mo and Simon and me dashing around the perimeter of our zone defense while Mark, our 6-foot-1-inch "enforcer," anchored the middle. The on-campus teams always wondered who the hell we were, and they always killed us. But it was a moral victory for us every time.

And me? I had been in a fog all the previous year, so busy being a Good Student that when it came time to find roommates I had no clue. I had a big paper due that week, and missed the housing lottery. I was homeless. I saw that ad in The Crimson and I jumped.

We were all seniors, except for Mo, who couldn't be categorized in such an earthbound way. Sometimes, sitting around the table late at night, we worried out loud about The Future, which was coming all too soon. One of our favorite daydreams featured Omega Tech, the college we'd start on our own someday. Jermaine would teach math and computers, Leila would teach art and music; Simon would cover religion, while Mark took care of government and philosophy. Amanda would be our expert on third-world countries and nutrition; I would teach English and French. Mo said he was all over Sex Ed.

And even as we pipe-dreamed about all this, we were busy making plans, sending out applications for graduate schools. Come May, one way or another, we'd be splitting for good.

Still, motley as we were, we tried to make it work. We agreed that we would share all our evening meals, taking turns with the cooking, even though Amanda could cook circles around any of us. She had to put up with some real disasters. My specialty was hot dogs cooked in beer; somehow tofu pups didn't translate to that medium. When it was Mo's turn we each got a toasted English muffin with a fried egg swimming in Texas Pete's Hot Sauce. He laid a steaming platter on the table and said, "Egg MoMuffin, hold the sausage!" Then, with a little flick of the Groucho cigar, he looked straight at Leila and said, "Please?"

Every evening, no matter how bad the meal, we sat down together around that big low table on the floor, and we held hands for a moment of silence, since nobody wanted to impose a religious grace on everyone else—and sometimes that moment just went on and on. You could feel all the tensions of the day rising in fumes above us, as if some spirit was being invoked and propitiated; some smoke of everydayness was being coaxed forth and released, and we all felt lighter. I did, anyway.

Now of course there wasn't a McDonald's in Harvard Square; McDonald's doesn't cater to the intelligentsia. But that wasn't going to stop us. We just had to take The Beast out on the highway, somewhere in the 'burbs, and conduct our action there. And that's what we did. Jermaine and Mo and I did the recon. At one point we almost got sidetracked by Frank's Steakhouse out on Route 1 in Saugus. It had a huge plastic cow out on its hillside lawn, lit up by spotlights to be visible from every direction. As we approached it, Mo said, "Let's take the cow instead! Talk about an image of the oppression of animals!"

Jermaine said, "No—it's too local, too limited. We want the icon of Happy Meals around the world. Besides," he added, "what kind of impression would it make if we published pictures of a cow as our hostage? Are we *with* animals, or *against* them? No, we need the image of The Man, the clown that tries to put a happy face on our barbarism."

Mo sighed and said, "Could we kidnap the cow *too*? We wouldn't have to publish anything about it." But when Jermaine didn't answer, he didn't press the issue.

And then we stopped at another McDonald's, for another Big Mac. That's right: we had a burger and fries at every joint we cased. The fact is, we loved the stuff — and we never got to eat anything like it at Omega, where Amanda ruled the kitchen. Not that Amanda was dictatorial in the least; you never met a milder-mannered arbiter of taste. But she was so dedicated to the cause, so humble in her devotion to eating the right way and respecting all God's creatures, that you just couldn't imagine unwrapping a cheeseburger in that kitchen. She was an African Studies major; Mo called her Amandla!, complete with the exclamation point, and she just smiled. She could tell you how indigenous diets had been ruined by western customs, and how the forests were being leveled in favor of grazing land just so American chain restaurants could go on producing cheap burgers. As a household, under Amanda's quiet but iron-willed direction, we were strictly veggie. Among the chores we all shared, posted on the fridge with our names on tabs that could be inserted in different slots every week, there was the baking of bread, along with the making of granola and yogurt. The house often had that great yeasty smell, and it was cool that you could mix a little yogurt culture in an old container with some powdered milk and warm water, put it in a tub of warm water, cover it with a towel, leave it in a warm dark place overnight, and have a fresh batch of tasty yogurt for breakfast. Magic! Like getting something from almost nothing!

Still, there are times when you just have to have a

burger, you know? Once a week or so, after I got back from the library, Mo and Simon and I would head out in The Beast, saying we were just going for a ride — and we'd end up at an all-night McDonald's, intent on the ingestion of animal carcasses in special sauce.

We didn't think this was hypocritical. We were not, strictly speaking, opposed to the eating of meat; we were opposed to the obscene profits McDonald's was making on our habit. And we were opposed to the damn clown. The whole idea that this giant doofus in huge red shoes was supposed to make us want burgers more than we already did was just too insulting. We wanted to eat our badly fried meat in surly peace like everybody else. If we chose to chew on cow byproducts while simmering in the juices of our own bad faith, that was our right. We did not want anybody telling us to be happy about it. We had to take him down.

It was a nasty night in January, one of those deep-freeze nights when your nostril hairs tighten and your breath congeals in front of you. It wasn't just for the faux-terrorist look that we were all wearing ski masks; we were fighting frostbite. We didn't look much like terrorists, anyway, because Jermaine didn't mention that the ski masks ought to be black. Leila's was fuchsia. Simon's was red, with a big reindeer across the forehead; Mo's was green, with little Frosties repeated again and again. Side by side as they headed for The Beast, those two looked more like Christmas elves than desperadoes. Only Jermaine had a proper black mask, with white highlights around the eyes; he looked like a Victorian hangman. "You guys!" he said, as we bustled out of the duplex, bitching about the cold.

"What a bunch of amateurs!" But you could tell he was totally jazzed about the whole thing, getting us to count off as we piled into The Beast.

Most of us had chosen an alias for the operation. Mo was Psycho Killer. Fa fa fa *fa* fa fa fa fa *fa* fa. Simon was Billy Pilgrim. Mark was Bananaman, theoretically because he loved bananas, though it led, of course, to all sorts of rude innuendo. Leila was B612, after the asteroid in *The Little Prince*. Jermaine balked at that one, saying B612 wasn't a proper alias; and she said, "Do I get to choose a name or not?" Amanda was Annie Cockledoux—so christened by Mo, after his favorite queen of the roller derby. It was so absurd for the gentle, demure Amanda that she accepted it with her usual laughing grace. Jermaine was Tom Swift, Boy Genius. I was Blue. Just Blue.

We had already worked out the list of demands that we were planning to tape to the door of the Natick McDonald's, as well as Xeroxed copies that would get posted all over the Square.

To: The McDonald's Corporation
From: The Food Liberation Army
Re: Operation Free Ronald
We, the Food Liberation Army, have liberated Ronald McDonald from his place as sentinel in front of this establishment. The operation was peaceful; he has not been harmed. We are holding him at an undisclosed location. We will not free him until the following questions have been answered:
1. What is the source of your meat?
2. How are the animals treated?
3. What are they fed?

4. In other words, what the hell are we eating?

5. What is your favorite color?

We will expect a response in the form of an advertise-ment in The Boston Globe. We will be watching. Respond by January 30, OR THE CLOWN GETS IT.

With love and squalor, The FLA

In the accompanying picture, Ronald wore a black blind-fold and a gag; an anonymous hand held a remarkably re-al-looking gun to his head. Jermaine had created this com-posite photograph on a computer. He wasn't happy about the last question on the list; it was Mo's idea. But Simon said, "That's perfect! Asking a corporation what its favorite color is! It'll blow their minds!" So Jermaine let it go.

As it turned out, the chainsaw wasn't such a great idea. First, there was the noise issue. Even out by the mall in Natick, it's damn quiet at two in the morning. When Mo fired up the Black and Decker (which he had lifted from Mean Mo, God knows why he thought he'd need such a thing at college), it sounded like a jet about to take off. We all looked around, expecting bedroom lights to go on—but that was the beauty of commercial zoning: there weren't any bedrooms within half a mile. Mo himself didn't even seem to hear it.

But he hadn't counted on Amanda. Somehow, suddenly, she was standing in his way. He backed down the saw.

"Amandla! What's the deal?"

"Mo," she said, "I don't think we should do this. With a saw, I mean. It's just so—violent. Is that the image we want?"

Mo said, "But think about what they do to cows and chickens! You were telling us about those crates yourself!

The way they live in their own shit, never seeing the sun! Never getting to have sex!" Mo was not a fan of artificial insemination.

"Yes," she said, "That's all true—but if we respond in a violent way, we're no better than they are." She looked at Simon.

He said, "She's right, Mo."

Jermaine looked crestfallen. "But the plan!"

Mark said, "Um, guys?"

We all looked at him. He was studying the clown. "It's not bolted down," he said.

At first, having that thing in the house was a little creepy. Mo set it up in the living room, in a corner where it would be visible from the kitchen/dining area, and of course it promptly started getting abused. Someone hung a bra over Ronald's upraised waving hand, then a jockstrap; someone stretched a Yale sweatshirt over his torso; someone pulled a black ski mask over his face. You'd think that would help, covering up that maniacal smile—but you could still see him grinning right through it; he looked like an executioner on uppers. Mo started calling him Ronny, then Ron-boy, then Ronbo, and then, inevitably, Ro Mo. As in "Yo, Ro Mo, how's it hangin'?" Mo waited politely for an answer, then said, "Awright, my man, high five!" And he clapped a hand to that big red hand. The bra and the jockstrap dangled in unison.

Meanwhile, the ransom note went out to McDonald's headquarters in Oak Brook, Illinois, and also to a bunch of local media outlets—the Globe, WBZN, WCAS, channels 4, 5, and 7. We didn't really expect any coverage: who was going to care if a bunch of merry pranksters lifted an overgrown toy? But two days later Jermaine came home at lunchtime with a copy of The Crimson and a satisfied smile. He spread the paper on the kitchen counter.

"We're in business, friends." He pointed to the picture of Ronbo, right there on page 1 above the fold, with the gun cocked at his temple. Mo whooped over his PB & J, and punched the air. "Take *that*, McDank's!"

"Now," said Jermaine, "we wait."

It didn't take long. Not that Mickey D's national office responded promptly. Or at all. But two days later The Crimson ran the picture again, along with an open letter from the Dean of Students. It seems that someone at the Natick McDonald's saw our photo, figured it was under-graduate hijinks, and called the Dean. They wanted their clown back, no questions asked. The Dean's letter said all would be forgiven—but added that this was unacceptable behavior for educated men and women.

"No questions asked?" said Jermaine. "No questions asked?" Jermaine wanted questions. Like How did you pull this off? Who masterminded this scheme? Who made that cool photo?

"Unacceptable behavior?" said Mo, a bottle of Rolling Rock in one hand. "You think *that* was unacceptable? *We'll* show you unacceptable. Right, guys?"

Mark worked a fork through his tofu scramble. "I don't know, Mo. The Dean sounds pretty serious. And he does have a point. I mean, it *was* theft, after all. I mean, if we don't give it back."

"Give it back? Man, you are a wuss with a capital P."

"A capital P?" I asked.

"Yeah, for pussy. We can't just give it back! That would mess up everything!"

Mark said, "Most people don't care where their food comes from, Mo."

"Fine," said Mo, sulfur in his voice. "But we are not *mostpeople*. We are Omega Tech!" He looked at Leila. She took her plate to the sink, to wash it.

He looked at Amanda. She said, "Well, it *would* be good to get some answers to our questions." Amanda was doing a research paper on the excessive use of corn as feed for animals that used to eat grass.

"Damn straight," said Mo. "Simon? Are you with us?"

"I'm with the group," said Simon. "Property is theft."

"Right on," said Mo. He got up and strode over to Ronald, who was peering at us through his mask. "Don't worry, big guy. We've got your back."

He turned to Jermaine. "Now what?"

"Phase II," Jermaine said. You could just tell he was using a Roman numeral. "The pinky finger."

"OK," said Mo. "Wait. What?"

Mo didn't like it; he had this thing about dismemberment. Amanda didn't like the violence, or the polystyrene dust left by the chainsaw on our living room floor. That stuff is hard to cut neatly. But Jermaine persuaded her that it was just symbolic violence, and we couldn't take Ro Mo out on the porch without the risk of blowing our cover. Mark refused to have anything to do with it, which made things rough for Simon: what was the group doing? But when Mark walked off to his afternoon class, Leila stayed, even though she didn't say anything. Jermaine, Mo, and Simon composed the next letter.

To: The McDonald's Corporation
Cc: The Dean of Harvard College
Re: Operation Pinky
This ain't no party, this ain't no disco, this ain't no foolin' around. Answer our questions, or you will be responsible for further actions.
Yours in solidarity with cows and chickens everywhere,
The FLA
P.S. Yes, we are giving you the finger.

Mo said, "What does that mean, 'further actions'?"

"It means," said Jermaine, "that we'll do what we have to do."

For a couple of days, Omega felt like a bunker. As if it wasn't already dark enough in there, we had pulled all the blinds; you never knew when a neighbor or a postal carrier might peer in. And the tension in the air made it feel even darker. Mark started leaving the house early in the morning and coming back late, after dinner. Every meal was an unhappy meal. Nobody had the nerve to ask Leila what was up; what went on behind their bedroom door had always been their own business. Everyone was just on edge — everyone except Jermaine. Jermaine was lovin' it.

McDonald's, of course, did not reply. The Dean, however, did — and he was not amused. Two days later there was another letter from him in The Crimson. Theft, he said, was one thing; malicious destruction of property was another. He said a serious discussion of food sourcing and distribution could take place only after the return of Ronald, along with restitution for any damages. Otherwise, the College would turn the matter over to the civil authorities.

Mo said, "Oh, now this is for real. They hate the PR they get when they have to call in the cavalry."

Jermaine said, "All right, then. Phase III."

"Phase III?" Mo asked.

I know, it's amazing that none of us had asked for the phases in advance. But we were just riding this thing, step by bumpy step. That was part of the fun.

Until it stopped being fun. Mark was AWOL. Leila was incommunicado. Amanda spent all her time baking things that nobody ate. Simon seemed ready to rally one night and then itching to confabulate the next. Maybe we were all just waiting for Phase III. We looked at Jermaine.

"Execution," he said.

Mo raced over to Ronald and covered each non-existent ear with a hand. "Don't listen, Ro Mo!"

Jermaine was standing in the doorway between the kitchen and the living room. "We have to call their bluff," he said. "If we return him, the Dean wins." Mo winced. "And McDonald's wins, too," he said, turning to Amanda. "If we really want anybody to pay attention to our questions, we have to carry through on our threat. We can't capitulate! Harvard is a corporation too, you know."

There was silence for about thirty seconds. A car washed by on Trowbridge Street.

"Not in my living room," said Amanda.

* * *

The idea was another photograph—only more grisly this time. Jermaine said he could take care of some special effects on his computer—but it was still going to require "certain steps" to look realistic. He asked Amanda if we had any ketchup. He said we didn't have to participate, if we didn't want to—he was looking at Mo—but he'd welcome help. He'd work on it the next morning, which was Saturday. He looked around the room. Nobody said anything. "All right then," he said. "I'm going to bed."

The next morning, when Jermaine walked into the living room, we were all sitting there—including Mark, next to Leila. The blinds were up, and the room was awash in winter light. In the corner, where Ronald had been standing, there was just a well-swept space.

Jermaine looked at us all. He started to speak; his shoulders sagged; he started to speak again; then he managed a tired smile.

Mo broke the silence. "Who wants an Egg MoMuffin?"

Every one of us did. Leila told him to hold his own damn sausage.

This was a long time ago. We never got in trouble. At the end of the year we scattered, and someone at the Divinity School finally decided that the Omega experiment had run its course. They sold that old house to a developer. Last I knew, it had been razed and replaced by a luxury condo. But if you go to the Natick McDonald's, look closely at the left hand of their clown.

I haven't been in touch with all those people for years; I don't even know where they are. But I remember being with them that night in the bed of The Beast, as Mo got us lost among the one-way streets of suburban Boston. We were trying to hold down a tarpaulin from which two big red shoes protruded, and we were freezing to death, grinning at each other through our masks, in the dark, happier than we would ever be again.

Fomite

About Fomite

A fomite is a medium capable of transmitting infectious organisms from one individual to another.

"The activity of art is based on the capacity of people to be infected by the feelings of others." Tolstoy, *What Is Art?*

Writing a review on Amazon, Good Reads, Shelfari, Library Thing or other social media sites for readers will help the progress of independent publishing. To submit a review, go to the book page on any of the sites and follow the links for reviews. Books from independent presses rely on reader-to-reader communications.

For more information or to order any of our books, visit:
http://www.fomitepress.com/

More Titles from Fomite...

Novels
Joshua Amses — *During This, Our Nadir*
Joshua Amses — *Ghatsr*
Joshua Amses — *Raven or Crow*
Joshua Amses — *The Moment Before an Injury*
Jaysinh Birjepatel — *Nothing Beside Remains*
Jaysinh Birjepatel — *The Good Muslim of Jackson Heights*
David Brizer — *Victor Rand*
Paula Closson Buck — *Summer on the Cold War Planet*
Dan Chodorkoff — *Loisaida*
David Adams Cleveland — *Time's Betrayal*
Jaimee Wriston Colbert — *Vanishing Acts*
Roger Coleman — *Skywreck Afternoons*
Marc Estrin — *Hyde*
Marc Estrin — *Kafka's Roach*
Marc Estrin — *Speckled Vanities*
Zdravka Evtimova — *In the Town of Joy and Peace*
Zdravka Evtimova — *Sinfonia Bulgarica*
Daniel Forbes — *Derail This Train Wreck*
Peter Fortunato — *Carnevale*
Greg Guma — *Dons of Time*
Richard Hawley — *The Three Lives of Jonathan Force*
Lamar Herrin — *Father Figure*
Michael Horner — *Damage Control*
Ron Jacobs — *All the Sinners Saints*
Ron Jacobs — *Short Order Frame Up*
Ron Jacobs — *The Co-conspirator's Tale*
Scott Archer Jones — *And Throw Away the Skins*

Fomite

Scott Archer Jones — *A Rising Tide of People Swept Away*
Julie Justicz — *Degrees of Difficulty*
Maggie Kast — *A Free Unsullied Land*
Darrell Kastin — *Shadowboxing with Bukowski*
Coleen Kearon — *#triggerwarning*
Coleen Kearon — *Feminist on Fire*
Jan English Leary — *Thicker Than Blood*
Diane Lefer — *Confessions of a Carnivore*
Rob Lenihan — *Born Speaking Lies*
Douglas W. Milliken — *Our Shadows' Voice*
Colin Mitchell — *Roadman*
Ilan Mochari — *Zinsky the Obscure*
Peter Nash — *Parsimony*
Peter Nash — *The Perfection of Things*
George Ovitt — *Stillpoint*
George Ovitt — *Tribunal*
Gregory Papadoyiannis — *The Baby Jazz*
Pelham — *The Walking Poor*
Andy Potok — *My Father's Keeper*
Frederick Ramey — *Comes a Time*
Joseph Rathgeber — *Mixedbloods*
Kathryn Roberts — *Companion Plants*
Robert Rosenberg — *Isles of the Blind*
Fred Russell — *Rafi's World*
Ron Savage — *Voyeur in Tangier*
David Schein — *The Adoption*
Lynn Sloan — *Principles of Navigation*
L.E. Smith — *The Consequence of Gesture*
L.E. Smith — *Travers' Inferno*
L.E. Smith — *Untimely RIPped*
Bob Sommer — *A Great Fullness*
Tom Walker — *A Day in the Life*
Susan V. Weiss —*My God, What Have We Done?*
Peter M. Wheelwright — *As It Is On Earth*
Suzie Wizowaty — *The Return of Jason Green*

Poetry
Anna Blackmer — *Hexagrams*
Antonello Borra — *Alfabestiario*
Antonello Borra — *AlphaBetaBestiaro*
Antonello Borra — *Fabbrica delle idee/The Factory of Ideas*
L. Brown — *Loopholes*
Sue D. Burton — *Little Steel*
Christine Butterworth-McDermott — *Evelyn As*
David Cavanagh— *Cycling in Plato's Cave*
James Connolly — *Picking Up the Bodies*

Fomite

Greg Delanty — *Loosestrife*
Mason Drukman — *Drawing on Life*
J. C. Ellefson — *Foreign Tales of Exemplum and Woe*
Tina Escaja/Mark Eisner — *Caida Libre/Free Fall*
Anna Faktorovich — *Improvisational Arguments*
Barry Goldensohn — *Snake in the Spine, Wolf in the Heart*
Barry Goldensohn — *The Hundred Yard Dash Man*
Barry Goldensohn — *The Listener Aspires to the Condition of Music*
R. L. Green — *When You Remember Deir Yassin*
Gail Holst-Warhaft — *Lucky Country*
Raymond Luczak — *A Babble of Objects*
Kate Magill — *Roadworthy Creature, Roadworthy Craft*
Tony Magistrale — *Entanglements*
Gary Mesick — *General Discharge*
Andreas Nolte — *Mascha: The Poems of Mascha Kaléko*
Sherry Olson — *Four-Way Stop*
Brett Ortler — *Lessons of the Dead*
Aristea Papalexandrou/Philip Ramp — *Μας προσπερνά/It's Overtaking Us*
Janice Miller Potter — *Meanwell*
Janice Miller Potter — *Thoreau's Umbrella*
Philip Ramp — *The Melancholy of a Life as the Joy of Living It Slowly Chills*
Joseph D. Reich — *A Case Study of Werewolves*
Joseph D. Reich — *Connecting the Dots to Shangrila*
Joseph D. Reich — *The Derivation of Cowboys and Indians*
Joseph D. Reich — *The Hole That Runs Through Utopia*
Joseph D. Reich — *The Housing Market*
Kenneth Rosen and Richard Wilson — *Gomorrah*
Fred Rosenblum — *Vietnumb*
David Schein — *My Murder and Other Local News*
Harold Schweizer — *Miriam's Book*
Scott T. Starbuck — *Carbonfish Blues*
Scott T. Starbuck — *Hawk on Wire*
Scott T. Starbuck — *Industrial Oz*
Seth Steinzor — *Among the Lost*
Seth Steinzor — *To Join the Lost*
Susan Thomas — *In the Sadness Museum*
Susan Thomas — *The Empty Notebook Interrogates Itself*
Paolo Valesio/Todd Portnowitz — *La Mezzanotte di Spoleto/Midnight in Spoleto*
Sharon Webster — *Everyone Lives Here*
Tony Whedon — *The Tres Riches Heures*
Tony Whedon — *The Falkland Quartet*
Claire Zoghb — *Dispatches from Everest*

Stories
Jay Boyer — *Flight*
L. M Brown — *Treading the Uneven Road*

Fomite

Michael Cocchiarale — *Here Is Ware*
Michael Cocchiarale — *Still Time*
Neil Connelly — *In the Wake of Our Vows*
Catherine Zobal Dent — *Unfinished Stories of Girls*
Zdravka Evtimova —*Carts and Other Stories*
John Michael Flynn — *Off to the Next Wherever*
Derek Furr — *Semitones*
Derek Furr — *Suite for Three Voices*
Elizabeth Genovise — *Where There Are Two or More*
Andrei Guriuanu — *Body of Work*
Zeke Jarvis — *In A Family Way*
Arya Jenkins — *Blue Songs in an Open Key*
Jan English Leary — *Skating on the Vertical*
Larry Lefkowitz — *Enigmatic Tales*
Marjorie Maddox — *What She Was Saying*
William Marquess — *Boom-shacka-lacka*
Gary Miller — *Museum of the Americas*
Jennifer Anne Moses — *Visiting Hours*
Martin Ott — *Interrogations*
Christopher Peterson — *Amoebic Simulacra*
Jack Pulaski — *Love's Labours*
Charles Rafferty — *Saturday Night at Magellan's*
Ron Savage — *What We Do For Love*
Fred Skolnik— *Americans and Other Stories*
Lynn Sloan — *This Far Is Not Far Enough*
L.E. Smith — *Views Cost Extra*
Caitlin Hamilton Summie — *To Lay To Rest Our Ghosts*
Susan Thomas — *Among Angelic Orders*
Tom Walker — *Signed Confessions*
Silas Dent Zobal — *The Inconvenience of the Wings*

Odd Birds
Micheal Breiner — *the way none of this happened*
J. C. Ellefson — *Under the Influence: Shouting Out to Walt*
David Ross Gunn — *Cautionary Chronicles*
Andrei Guriuanu and Teknari — *The Darkest City*
Gail Holst-Warhaft — *The Fall of Athens*
Roger Lebovitz — *A Guide to the Western Slopes and the Outlying Area*
Roger Lebovitz — *Twenty-two Instructions for Near Survival*
dug Nap— *Artsy Fartsy*
Delia Bell Robinson — *A Shirtwaist Story*
Peter Schumann — *All*
Peter Schumann — *Belligerent & Not So Belligerent Slogans from the
        Possibilitarian Arsenal*
Peter Schumann — *Bread & Sentences*
Peter Schumann — *Charlotte Salomon*

Fomite

Peter Schumann — *Diagonal Man, Volumes One and Two*
Peter Schumann — *Faust 3*
Peter Schumann — *Planet Kasper, Volumes One and Two*
Peter Schumann — *We*

Plays
Stephen Goldberg — *Screwed and Other Plays*
Michele Markarian — *Unborn Children of America*

Essays
William Benton — *Eye Contact: Writing on Art*
Robert Sommer — *Losing Francis: Essays on the Wars at Home*